Under Witch Moon

MARIA E. SCHNEIDER

Bear Mountain Books

A Bear Mountain Books Production
www.BearMountainBooks.com

Under Witch Moon
Maria E. Schneider
Copyright October 2010 © Maria E. Schneider

Printing History:
POD printing June 2011, Sept. 2011
Second POD printing June 2012, 2022
E-format October 2010

Cover Art: Deb Wentz

This is a work of fiction. Names, characters, places and incidents are either the product of the author's imagination or are used fictitiously, and any resemblance to any person, living or dead is entirely coincidental.

ISBN-13: 978-0615485010 (Bear Mountain Books)
ISBN-10: 0615485014

Acknowledgments

To Grammy and Mom for their love of gardening and respect for spiders. To my other Grandma for her love of herbs and for teaching me. Turns out, I needed all three of you to be a complete person. To Dad for his love of the earth and the heritage that is always a part of me.

A special thank you to Cinderspark, a fairy who flew by with encouragement and suggestions when I needed them. Even though LeAnn didn't do the editing on this particular book, her wisdom still shows in places--thankfully. And to Irene; I owe you one.

To Deb Wentz for patience and fabulous artwork. To the folks at Baen's bar, especially Paula Goodlett, who plucked the first chapter of this story out of the slush because she saw a worthwhile glimmer. To Meredith, because you believed, and you had good suggestions as well.

To my husband--who keeps the magic alive.

ACKNOWLEDGMENTS

Under Witch Moon

Chapter 1

Being a witch isn't easy. It's smelly, grueling work. I'm not talking about magic. Magic is a power that comes from natural forces. I'm talking about witchery, the chemical reactions for spells. Mind you, I dabble in magic; most witches do, but the bulk of my work involves a lot of formulas. It's a chore like any, much like caulking a house--messy, stinky and the results don't last forever.

Yes, spells wear out. They sometimes glue themselves to the wrong thing or dry too fast or don't dry at all. When I'm finished, I need a bath and in some cases, just as paint needs turpentine, I need special solutions to rid myself of the chemicals that have made themselves at home on my person.

At present, I was working on a spell for protection. It was an easy spell and thankfully cleaner than most. Salt, a purifier and element that worked well against rogue spirits, was the main ingredient. While it was wonderfully effective, it was unfortunately, quick to break down. The main job of a witch in this case was to make sure the salt didn't degrade too quickly. Rich patrons paid me to mix it in gold or silver.

I preferred silver myself. It provided additional protection against evil spirits, including vampires and shifters. Gold was better for other types of spells, plus it was coveted by all, which meant that patrons expected me to include a spell of illusion so that the protection object didn't get stolen--*but* those same clients wanted the object to be beautiful, so it was therefore coveted by anyone who happened to see it anyway.

Being a witch was indeed an onerous task. If people accepted us, they wanted the impossible. If they didn't, they wanted to burn us at the stake.

Never mind all that. The important thing when working with metals, as I was now, was to make certain of its purity. I didn't care if a customer told me he dug it out of a mountain with his bare hands under a full moon. Santa Fe, along with most of New Mexico, was chock full of old Aztec gold and silver, and let me tell you, those people could imbue nasty spirits like no other.

I had to burn my entire house to the ground once when working with contaminated gold. I still looked over my shoulder on moonless nights, because I wasn't certain I contained the evil spirit back in that lump of gold.

My new house had a special room made from concrete walls covered in adobe brick, covered in stucco. Mud had the wonderful ability to soak up any number of bad things. Stucco had only one important feature--chicken wire. When coated with the right ingredients, the wire provided a nearly complete mesh of protection against many a magical ill. I only wished I had been able to dip the mesh into silver such as I was using now, fresh from the U.S. minting office.

The mint did a great job of removing impurities, along with any bad spirits. Of course, in doing so they nearly removed silver's strong ties to mother earth. Part of my job was to make sure the silver linked again with the purity of earth. I melted it, salted it and strung it ever so carefully into magical fibers. The magic came from mother earth; it was part of the silver. And in truth, any witch worth her pay added a certain magic of her own, a heartbeat tied to mother earth, an aura if you will--the magical quality of life.

The process of mixing, steaming, melting and salting took several days and exquisite timing. Moreover, when those things were done, I had to weave the silver thread into a careful pattern inside my chosen fabric. Given the trouble the woman was in, Dolores Garcia should have sprung for a fifty-strand liquid silver necklace instead. Such a necklace contained far more silver and wearing it would be an obvious message to a courting werewolf that she was not interested.

I finished my client's shirt on the night of a full moon, making sure the silver threads were placed correctly. As with any project, it felt good to finish, but I was tired. I planned to deliver the shirt the next day, but as I left my workroom, the phone rang.

"Adriel!" a voice sobbed my name and then choked to silence.

"Dolores?" I asked, although it could be no other.

"You must help me! Tonight. It's a full moon. It's…I can't control it, I saw him! I must have the shirt, finished or not, I can wait no longer!"

"Tonight?" Dismay colored my voice.

"It's a full moon! He's watching me, he's…" Her voice trembled with emotion.

"Oh for--"

"Please," she begged, naming a price that I could not afford to refuse.

"Fine." I sighed and then rolled my eyes as she dictated directions to a "safe" location. She insisted the exchange take place in the middle of the desert down in an arroyo so that we didn't stand out in the moonlight. In my mind, it would have been far less suspicious had she come over for a cup of coffee--or even met me at a donut shop.

Whatever. I had an image to uphold, and if the customer wanted me to traipse about the dusty desert after midnight, I just added it to the charge. If she didn't show up after keeping me up most of the night, I'd not only curse her, I'd sell the shirt to someone else, her silver or not.

I got traipsing. With the full moon, I managed to reach the location without too much trouble despite the fact that the spot Dolores had chosen was a mile from any paved road. To her credit, she was on time. From the looks of her though, I was a lot more agile in the dark.

She wasn't any older than me; somewhere in her twenties. She should have been able to easily avoid the prickly cactus, creosote and rocky terrain, but as she approached, she was limping rather noticeably.

She slid down into the arroyo and without ceremony, thrust out a tote bag weighted nicely with money. "Do you have it?" she whispered.

"You won't be able to wear this shirt every single day," I warned, prepared to sell her a kerchief as an additional security measure. "A werewolf is a dangerous--"

"Shhh," she shushed, despite the desert location.

"This shirt will be effective, but I would advise you to purchase some additional protection," I said, exchanging the plain wrapped package for the bag of money.

She grabbed the brown paper bundle from me and held it to her heaving chest like a long-lost teddy-bear. "At last!"

I frowned. I was accustomed to people being grateful, especially in the case of fending off evil, but her elation was almost giddy. "It will keep the werewolf away. Once you start wearing it, he will know that you know what he is. It will make it clear you are not interested."

She spun around in a circle, full Spanish skirts swirling around her legs. In addition to the dress, the idiot had actually worn sandals. Had she worn jeans and hiking boots like I had, maybe she wouldn't be limping.

"He will be mine now," she declared lustily. "I can date him and control him without fear."

"What?" I forgot she wanted to keep our meeting a secret. "Are you crazy? You do not want to try controlling a werewolf!"

"We're all animals! He just happens to be two animals, his were-person and his...person-person."

"That would be were-*wolf*," I emphasized. "Not were-person. The whole point is that he is an *animal* at times, with animal instincts and animal reactions."

She flicked long hair over her shoulder. It should have been as luminous black as mine from the usual mix of Spanish and Native American blood in the area, but she had bleached a gray streak across her forehead. Eagerly she gushed, "He's a person and very intelligent. I'm sure that I will be safe now."

"Nonsense." I shuddered at the thought of dealing with a werewolf in beast form.

She drew herself up tightly, thrusting out rather over-sized breasts. "Are you saying the protection I'm buying won't work?"

"Oh, the protection works. But you do realize that the werewolf will sense it, and it will automatically make you an enemy, especially to the wolf."

"He's human! He'll know that I need to be protected from the wolf. He'll be…attracted to the danger!"

"No. Shifters are not attracted to danger. They run from it or they fight it."

She smacked away my hand as I reached for the goods. I had decided not to sell it to her.

"His human part will be wildly attracted to me!"

"Fool!" I declared. "His human part--"

She turned away in a swirl of skirts and ran.

Who in their right mind wore a skirt out in the desert? Some women had no sense.

Apparently I was one of them, but for different reasons. When Dolores had approached me about protection from a werewolf, I had hoped to keep her away from the threat, not bring her to it. While I worked on the spell, I kept my ear to the ground. Dolores had been keeping her distance from all men. Since I couldn't know who in her community was the actual werewolf, it only stood to reason that if she were interacting with none of them, she was indeed concerned for her safety.

"Drat your silly hide." I hurtled after her up the side of the arroyo. Catching her should be easy. She gimped along, tripping in the dark. Her legs would be good and scratched and the skirt full of rips before she made it home.

I lunged at her, but missed. She was too stupid to stay where the path was clear. Worse, her limp made her run and weave like a drunk.

I dashed forward again, making a flying tackle at her legs. The skirt, with its billowing mass, misled me. I ended up on the ground with a large armful of material. "Stop, you fool! Werewolves are dangerous!"

She yanked hard, showing desperation that should have been saved for the werewolf. "No!" The skirt was already half shredded from her run through the desert. It gave way with a low rumble of protest. "He'll be mine!"

I was left in the dirt holding a fistful of brightly colored material while she made it to her truck and peeled away into the darkness.

Thankfully, in my pocket was the kerchief I had also made her-- intending to tell her to wear it on her person at all times. The silver in the kerchief was from the same batch as the shirt. If I worked quickly, I could use the silver to make a witching fork, track the shirt, and steal it back. Maybe without the false sense of security, she'd give up her wildly stupid plans.

I sighed. It was obvious I could not enlighten her. Mind you, I had nothing against werewolves. I had no problem befriending their human side, but werewolves were werewolves. The animal instincts were there, and so was the animal power. While wolves have been known to fight on the side of humans, it was usually against a common enemy. They were still individuals with goals and instincts all their own.

I grumbled my way to my feet and pushed back the dark strands that had loosened from my ponytail. I had time. The moon would still be nearly full for the next couple of nights. No one would date a werewolf this close to a full moon. It would be even stupider than believing a mere shirt of silver and salt could save someone who jumped into the teeth of a wolf.

I took myself home to begin work on a witching fork. Since the silver was from the same batch as the shirt, my witching fork would act like a tuning fork. Only instead of music, the closer I got to the shirt, the better I would be able to hear the song of the mother lode.

My body demanded at least a few hours of sleep before concentrating on the difficult task of wrapping silver threads along a willow-branch fork. Every silver strand had to be exactly the same length and weight on each side of the fork. I didn't want false readings in the middle of the night while breaking into private property.

* * *

It took until dusk the next day before I was ready with Dolores' address in hand. A quick check with Lynx, my friend who lurked in the shadows of Santa Fe's streets, assured me that Dolores' parents were in town enjoying dinner. Lynx didn't come out of the shadows, but I could hear him chuckle. "I keep them busy for you," he whispered. "I pick up my pay tomorrow night."

"Make sure I have at least two extra hours," I whispered back into the darkness.

He didn't answer, but I knew he would be happy to make sure they were delayed while I visited the Garcia's hacienda on the outskirts of Santa Fe.

The trip, even after I stashed my dusty blue Civic on an unrelated side road and hiked up the short driveway to the house, took me under an hour.

The stucco estate was to my liking, mimicking the pueblos from the ancient past, with adobe walls forming a stepped design from the first to the second floor. The stepladder formation was a very good thing because the witching fork was pointing straight up.

I approached the walled-in garden with trepidation. At only five-five and maybe a half, I couldn't reach the top of the wall, not even on my tiptoes. I hated climbing. It was strenuous work, and I wasn't the most graceful of creatures. Thankfully I wasn't fat or the nearly six-foot barricade would have won.

The top was rounded, which kept me from piercing various body parts, but it was damned hard to balance on the thing once I straddled it. I wouldn't die if I fell, but as I shimmied toward the window ledge, I cursed the wall for not being high enough to allow me to easily reach the window.

I was sure of my destination. The fork was singing louder, a subtle vibration along my fingertips.

I clutched at the side of the house and groped upwards toward the open window. There wasn't going to be an easier entry. I put one foot in front of the other, took a deep breath and jumped.

Don't get me started about witches, broomsticks and being able to fly. I didn't know how to fly yet, and no witch in her right mind would use a broomstick these days. Why bother when there were more comfortable objects to levitate? If I ever learned to fly, I was going with a nice Arabian rug. Whoever spelled those magic carpets understood comfort.

I caught the sill with only one hand, flailing desperately. My next mistake was to try to climb with my hiking boots. Planting my feet on the wall pushed me away from the window. My hand scraped painfully across a metal rim before losing what skin was left to the stucco.

"Aeii!" I couldn't contain a stifled scream. My left foot landed on the wall, but the right kept sliding. A large chunk of adobe broke off under my boot and took me with it. One leg went left, the other right. I sat astride the wall like a drunk on a broomstick. One leg was painfully tangled in a rose bush.

"Why couldn't they have planted nice, safe, lilac bushes against the house?" Stifling a groan, I got up and used the side of the house to keep from falling again. If I kept sliding down and knocking chunks of the wall away, the Garcia's were going to end up with no wall. I would end up with no legs.

I jumped again, this time muttering the ingredients used in levitation spells. I didn't *have* any of the ingredients with me because the only one I was sure about was lodestone, but the list gave me confidence.

More stucco knocked free as I clutched the sill and dug my boots into the wall. The metal cut into my hands, but I kept climbing until I had a leg over.

It was then that I smelled him. Had he been in his human form, I might not have caught the strong scent, but wolves have a unique muskiness. A small light, maybe from a night light in the attached bathroom, gave off just enough of a glow to throw shadows.

"Aztec curses!" I swore in disbelief. "She wouldn't! The moon is practically full…"

One leg over the sill, I dared not move until I had my bearings. There was no sound of breathing other than my own, but if the man had turned werewolf, there had been an emergency or danger at the very least.

By the moonlight and the night light, I saw him. He was in the corner, half-changed to his coyote form. Most werewolves in the area were coyotes; at least the native ones. I hadn't known if I would be dealing with a local or not, but the color of his fur was definitely the dirty-blond of a coyote.

"It would be easier for you to escape as the wolf," I said softly, showing him that I was all about cooperation. I edged to one side of the window to give him plenty of room.

He let out a panting groan from the effort and pain of changing. His growl was a feral moan, but still a threat.

"You'll need to hurry," I advised. If I could talk him into leaving, I stood a better chance of coming out of the experience alive. His face was furry, but not much more than an overgrown, bushy beard. Ears were still poking through, but rapidly disappearing.

Because he was mostly human, I could see why the situation with Dolores had turned into such a problem. He was young. Very young. Eighteen if she was lucky. The barely grown man probably hadn't known how to deal with a flirtatious woman dabbling where she didn't belong. Perhaps he thought he could live in both worlds. Perhaps he was simply too young to understand she had been after him because he was a unique trophy prize.

"I would never have sold her the shirt had I realized she sought to control you with it. You have my apologies."

He was miserably human, shivering uncontrollably in the corner.

"You need to leave," I urged again. "Quickly." I moved away from the window without touching anything.

He bolted, buck naked, for freedom. I wasn't going to stop him. More stress might cause him to revert back to full wolf form, and that stupid I was not. Instead, I looked for the shirt.

It wasn't on Dolores, since she was completely naked. The problem with fabric protection was that it could be taken off and she had, after all, invited the werewolf into her bedroom. Had she somehow thought she could have sex with a werewolf partially clothed?

The scene in front of me was unpleasant, but for a panicked wolf, surprisingly lacking in blood. He had killed her, but crushed her throat rather than ripped it to shreds. There were more than a few deep scratches, as if the coyote had been trying to scramble away rather than do serious damage. From what was left of the shirt, it looked as though Dolores might have tried to wrap him in it.

The wolf had not been amused by the protection spell. I had seen at least two burns, one on his arm and another across his chest.

When it had finally rid itself of the touch of the garment, the coyote had soiled it with urine, destroying any of the spell that hadn't burned itself up when it came in contact with his skin. The silver that was left would have to be purified. Depending on the wolf's abilities...well, it was probably best buried.

I scanned the room one last time. There were two fancy shopping bags on a chair in front of the dressing table. The plastic one was the easy choice.

I held my nose as I bagged the shirt. I would have sighed, but didn't want to breathe deeply. Being a witch was a messy job. Being a witch wasn't easy. I had a bad feeling that retrieving the spelled shirt wasn't going to be enough to keep myself out of further trouble.

Chapter 2

It would have been kinder had I been able to find a way to make sure Dolores's parents weren't the ones who found her body. Trouble was, by the time I got out of there with the evidence of my involvement, my cohort in Santa Fe had long since ceased delay tactics.

Dolores made covering my tracks easier because of her insistence on secrecy, but I still had to zip out to the desert location where I had met her to erase all traces of my aura. If another witch were hired to trace me, I was determined that the witch would come up empty.

When I got home, I was ready to collapse, but my luck hadn't changed. Waiting for me at my humble abode was a message, another problem. I left the shirt in the trunk of my car and got out.

Lynx didn't care that I had had only three hours of sleep in the last twenty-four. His job was to deliver a message to me, and I'm sure whoever hired him didn't stipulate that I had to be anything other than present.

"Job for you," he said by way of greeting.

My friend of the underground was probably a shape shifter, but it wasn't the sort of question you inserted in casual conversation, especially if that person was Lynx. The kid regularly hired out as a spy, thief and general no-good odd-jobber. I tried not to use his more unsavory services because he was young, probably no more than thirteen, although he looked ten.

"Can't it wait?" I whined. If Lynx could shapeshift, he was probably a were-rat rather than a lynx as his name implied. There was an outside possibility that he was a half-starved alley cat with patchy fur, quite likely diseased, definitely filthy. I knew the last part was true because not once had he ever evinced signs of having taken a bath. His black hair was so matted I'd never been sure if he was part Indian, black with an afro glued together by sweat, Mexican, or a white kid with a lot of dirt coloring his skin and hair.

"Lady is in hurry to get this job done." He followed me inside when I unlocked the front door. "It's about a love potion."

"I don't do love potions. No matter what it pays, it isn't worth the trouble." Most witches who did love potions only provided spells that caused wild physical attraction, not love. Those spells were the shortest-lived, but the easiest because there was a lot of unwise human nature to count on. Imagine what happened though, when the thing rotted and decayed as all spells eventually do.

Lynx grinned, a sly twist of lips, no teeth. "I know. It's about getting rid of a love potion. My client swears her husband has been given a potion by some scientist that works at the lab."

"Los Alamos?"

The smile again, giving me the answer. The lab always had rumors swirling around it. It was a place of mystery, its shrouded occupants working on everything from blowing up the world to re-inventing it. "I take it the wife was not the first person he saw after drinking the love potion?"

"Even worse." He licked his lips as though he had just finished a juicy steak. "She claims the potion was brewed as a matched set--the woman who did the brewing works at the lab, and she is the recipient."

My eyes narrowed. Matched potions were very difficult, but they worked with the same basic properties of a tuning fork--some important ingredient, usually a plant if the witch was any good, was grown a certain way and then ingested by both people. An amulet with the ingredient was then used to keep the person bespelled; otherwise, the potion would wear off. The problem with the whole mess was that the amulet was much like hypnotism. Passion became rather…mechanical.

"Sounds to me like the husband is having an affair with some lady at work, and the wife is looking for excuses for his despicable behavior," I said.

Lynx's tail twitched, only he didn't have a tail. The motion was actually his hand as he nabbed a box of unopened girl scout cookies off my counter. He munched them as he explained. "My client doesn't think so. The witch at the lab is old and gross--in no way an attraction for her husband."

"Did you expect your client to describe the woman as young and lovely?"

He grinned, showing a lot of cookie. "For your sake, I left out the best parts of the description my client gave me. And it's true, my client could be dealing with a spell or a slut."

"I'm too tired to think about this right now."

"Do you take the case or not?" He rubbed two fingers together. "I get paid either way. I told her I'd go to the best."

Unspoken was the word, "First." After he checked with me, he would move on to others. If the search went on long enough, the client would end up with nothing more than a loser in an apothecary shop who had bought something from one of the previously questioned witches. The potion might or might not contain any helpful ingredients, but there were some who believed a dead husband was a cured husband.

I never would have taken the case without more facts had I not been so tired, but any answer would get him out the door. "Fine. I'll look into it. But I get paid whether a spell was used or not."

He nodded happily. "Of course."

I pointed to the fridge. "There's sandwich makings in there. Stop with the cookies--take the box for later. Make yourself a sandwich."

He had the refrigerator opened before I finished speaking. "You want one?" he asked as he pulled out slices of chicken and bread.

"Lettuce and tomato," I instructed tiredly, taking a seat at the table.

"On yours?"

I sat at the table and ignored his hint that he had no intention of eating any vegetable matter. I wanted sleep, but there was no way I could leave him anywhere in my house without supervision. He was a professional sneak. He wouldn't waste the opportunity.

I ate my sandwich almost as fast as Lynx ate his. He watched his surroundings warily, stopping his progress on the sandwich every few seconds to listen or twist his head to the windows. I wasn't worried because it was normal behavior for him.

"You come back tomorrow with details," I said. "I'll check things out before I name my fee."

"You don't want the info now?"

This was a departure from normal, but I was too exhausted to retain any information. "Tomorrow." I thought of something. "In the meantime, if you don't have them, I'll want names and dates of when this happened or started happening."

"Already have it."

"Okay." I held up my hand to stave off the recitation. "Tomorrow. Nine o'clock."

His eyes widened briefly before checking the clock. "You don't mean this morning."

It was already morning; dawn was only two hours away. I had to get some sleep, daytime on the way or not. "No, day after."

"She won't like that. She wants action right away."

"Tell her to shoot her husband if she's that mad. If he's already sleeping around, one more night won't make that much difference. If he's under a spell, it's going to take me several days to break it correctly anyway."

Lynx tilted his head and watched me. I didn't look good; my hair had crawled out of its ponytail into snarls, and my black jeans and dark blue shirt were decorated with stucco pieces and desert dust. When I was tired, my eyes went bloodshot, and the funny green hazel streaks that were only in my left eye stood out against the whiskey brown.

No doubt Lynx was curious about my appearance and the mood that had me putting off a desperate client, but instead of talking, I dragged my right foot across my knee and unlaced my boot.

"You need me to do more distracting on tonight's clients?" He inspected the table for crumbs.

It was his way of asking if he had somehow screwed the job up. In his world, those who asked direct questions ended up with no business.

"You did fine. No more need for distraction." He'd find out soon enough about the dead girl. I wondered briefly if he would think I did it, but part of his survival was to know the people he worked for. Even though he hadn't been my contact for Dolores originally, he would know something about her werewolf infatuation or could find out.

"Okay. Tomorrow then." He slid out of the chair. With only a whisper of sound, he was out the door, letting it close silently behind him. I hit the lights and went to the window, but it was impossible to see him. Had it been daylight I might have been able to follow him around the side of the house for fifty yards before he disappeared.

When I was certain he was gone, I retrieved the smelly evidence from the trunk of my car. I rinsed it well with the garden hose, because water was the best cleanser in the world--of spells and of other things. I then stashed the fabric in a warded metal can filled with sand and hid it under an innocuous looking rock cairn in my backyard.

I'd deal with real disposal or purification of the silver later.

I went inside, set the locks and went to bed.

Chapter 3

Law officials generally pretended that I didn't exist. They also ignored werewolf sightings, vampires and a whole host of other ills. There were a few officials who didn't. My favorite was "White Feather." Despite the name, he didn't leave smoke signals. I didn't even know if he was Native American, but it was possible. When he wanted to talk to me, he snapped an extra padlock on the monument gate at the center of the Santa Fe plaza. A barely noticeable colored line around the middle of the lock indicated the church where we would meet.

We never met out in the open pews. Our conversations almost always took place in a confessional. I dressed as a pious Catholic, which I was. Catholic anyway. Mostly I was a good Catholic too, but I was a practicing witch, so no one in their right mind would refer to me as pious.

When I met with White Feather, I went as an old lady in long skirts with one of those doilies on my head. Okay, the doily was more properly referred to as a veil. I walked hunched over as if I was the last of a dying breed, and let me tell you there really were only a few old ladies left who wore hats or those, ah, doilies during Mass.

I also wore lace gloves, even in the summer, because at twenty-six, it was impossible to hide my youth with my hands visible. My Indian policeman, and he was an officer of the law I was certain, dressed as a priest. He wore robes and a cowl. Sometimes when I was sitting in church during Mass, I tried to spot White Feather. For all I knew, he was fifty years old and bald. Hard to say, and that was the point.

Since it was summer, I dispensed with the long wool skirt and wore a shorter dress with hefty support hose. Clever lumps were strategically placed inside the hose to make my legs bulbous and full of veins. I added old lady sock-things that were supposed to keep aged feet from swelling. All they did for me was cut off circulation.

I took my cane instead of the usual walker. As always, I stopped to catch my breath--and to make sure no one else was using the church for an assignation. Hopefully if anyone saw me, well, let's hope no one really thought any local priest was so desperate as to be meeting with the disguised me for anything other than prayer.

It was just after midnight. Well-rested after my day of mostly sleeping, I took my place in the confessional, breathing hard and raspy. "Forgive me father for I have sinned…" I mumbled, clacking rosary beads together.

"As long as it wasn't you who had anything to do with murdering a young woman and trying to make it look like an animal had done so." His deep baritone was barely muffled by the screen separating us.

I sucked in a breath so fast that had I really been old, I'd have swallowed my dentures. I knew I'd be asked about Dolores eventually, but it hadn't even been twenty-four hours.

Before I could begin my denial, White Feather started with dry details. "No sign of sexual trauma, but like the others, she was naked, her neck ripped apart, and an arm torn completely away."

My cough got worse, but luckily it only made my character more believable. "Others?" I squeaked. "What others?"

"We're desperate here, Merlin."

Merlin wasn't a terribly original name, nor was it really mine. I only used it with White Feather because I didn't need the law knowing who I was in real life. Adriel Pacheco was the name my great-grandfather used, and the one I went by professionally. I never, ever used my birth name because it could be used to bind my soul or destroy me. Granted, there weren't many witches powerful enough to bind another witch, and none who I actually knew. But even someone with minimal talent could use my real name to mimic my aura, send minor chaotic pranks my way or call images into my dreams.

"I'd be happy to help," I told White Feather agreeably. "But I can't. I wasn't aware of the...bodies." I wondered briefly if someone had torn Dolores apart after I left, but that made no sense. What bodies was he talking about if not hers? Had the werewolf gone crazy afterward?

"Merlin, you can't tell me you don't know about it! It's been in the papers. Three bodies over the last two weeks. The first one we could pass off as a violent offense. Then the second one happened right before the full moon and that got the rumors going. Thank God the last one wasn't torn apart."

I hated to name the last one. "Dolores Garcia?" I asked weakly.

He snorted. "Well? What else can you tell me? I knew her name!"

White Feather was usually more patient, but then, he had never asked me about serial killings before. He generally came to me about the odd witch's vengeance or crimes that occurred in the hodgepodge community of paranormal types. "I can't tell you much else. There was a werewolf involved, but...it wasn't really his fault."

"Name?" he snapped.

"I don't know. Young werewolf, inexperienced. The kid didn't realize she was trying to control him, possibly capture him. He got hurt during the attempt, and she ended up dead."

"You aren't trying to tell me it was self-defense? A werewolf against a young woman?"

It had been though, in a lot of ways. If the kid had kept his head, he probably could have escaped without killing her, but he hadn't the experience to realize what he was dealing with--not the woman or the protection spell. I tried to explain this to White Feather. "Look, she was trying to trap him. She had the means to injure him. It's a...it burns. She may have thought it was harmless fun, like light ropes holding him, but it's not. It would have been very painful, and the kid panicked."

"So I'm looking for a young man with burns? Where? Face, arms? How old do you mean when you say young?"

I wasn't sure the guy deserved to be captured, but I also knew the chances of White Feather finding him were slim. Of course, if the kid had been killing other women that was a whole different story. "I'd guess he was fifteen to eighteen." I tried to remember the burns, but the light hadn't been good. "The burns were probably...around the shoulders...maybe one across his chest, but I'm guessing based on the object used."

White Feather gave another snort of disbelief. "His name?"

At least I didn't have to lie. "No idea."

"I want this kid."

"I can't help you. I don't know who he is, I only know the likely results of the spell that was used."

"You know he was young." The anger gave way to curiosity, a larger danger for me.

Before he could ask how I knew the age of the werewolf, I said, "He had to be young. No experienced werewolf would have been in the room with the protection there. No sane werewolf would have been messing with someone like Dolores."

"No one said the werewolf was sane," he muttered.

"Well, yes. There is that possibility." I crossed myself and pushed to my feet, creaking noisily. My bones really did crack without any false effort on my part. "I'll let you know if I find out more."

"How?"

"Same signal at the plaza, just as you do." The plaza was full of tourists much of the time, making it easy to check for signals without standing out. I had missed the padlock a couple of times when things were busy, but he knew if I didn't appear by quarter after midnight, I wasn't going to show. He had the keys to the various churches, so if the door wasn't open, I knew something had come up, and he was a no-show.

"I'd appreciate help on this one." I started to answer, but he whispered, "It means a lot."

I hesitated when I heard the plea, but I had nothing else to give him. I left first, wondering why this particular case meant so much to him. He was always diligent, but rarely angry.

Maybe if I had paid more attention to current events, I would have known the answer. Luckily that was something easily rectified.

Chapter 4

I was in no mood to deal with a recalcitrant employee, especially a smirking one, but I had already told Lynx we would talk about his new client in the morning. I collared him by the back of his neck the minute he showed up at nine o'clock. Before I got distracted with his business, I asked him about mine. "What do you know about bodies being found that might be related to a werewolf?"

Lynx didn't struggle; he just gave me his cat smile, the one with no teeth. "What bodies?"

"What good does it do me to pay you for rumors in the night if you don't report rumors?"

He shrugged skinny shoulders. "Those aren't rumors. Those were on the news."

I really had to start getting my information from places other than the underground. Apparently death by a werewolf wasn't newsworthy enough for anyone in my circle to talk about.

"Tell me the story. What is it with women being killed by a werewolf?"

"Besides the one you know about?"

I growled. "Talk."

"You want details on all three of them?" he asked. "You got anything to eat?"

I let go of him so that he could sit down. "You can skip Dolores Garcia. I know about her."

"That's what I meant," he said, catching the bag of baby carrots I tossed him. "The other three."

Luckily I had turned back to the cupboard so he couldn't see the expression on my face. White Feather had said three total. Lynx implied there was a fourth body. "Go on," I encouraged him as I opened a can of bean and bacon soup.

"They didn't find the one body yet. It was the first one, and it's out in the mountains. The second one was left ripped up right in town. You can read about it in the papers."

"You know where this first body is at?"

He nodded. "Yeah. You can smell it."

Sure, if you roamed around the mountains like a wild cat, but most people had jobs to go to. "Tell me how to find it," I said with a sigh. After starting the soup heating, I put bread in the toaster.

When I turned back to Lynx, he was staring at his carrot in disgust. "How come you eat stuff like carrots for breakfast? How come you never have potato chips like my other clients? These don't taste nothing like chips."

"You were going to tell me how to find the body, and then you were going to tell me who is doing this."

He shrugged. "I can tell you about the body. I don't know who done it. I don't know if it was the ladies--you know, getting jealous of each other or if it was the werewolf. See," he held up his carrot to keep me from butting in, "there's this group. They are fine ladies lookin' for a little extra excitement. They pay Arturo--and it's okay if you know that name because he wants everyone to know to come to him. Arturo, he makes sure the ladies get the time of their life by providing special dates for them."

Knowing Dolores and her idea of excitement meant that I didn't have to have the kid spell it out for me, but I wanted to be very, very sure of what was going on. "These ladies are looking to sleep with a werewolf?"

He smirked. "Escort. They want a big, bad escort, you know, so they can show off. Arturo, he gets them the escort they want for a fee."

"Escort." I didn't know if he was that innocent...I narrowed my eyes. He might be thirteen, but he was street thirteen. "And after this escorting, do they pay extra for other activities--such as the ones that get them killed?"

"Nah, it's one price. What happens on the date, that's up to the lady."

"Except a few of them have been killed, Lynx. You can't tell me that was up to them!"

The soup was about to boil over. I ignored it, but Lynx must have been hungry because he jumped out of the kitchen chair and hurried over to take it off the stove. He knew where the bowls were.

"The killing I don't know about. Something went wrong. Maybe they were all like your client, trying to buy protection and messed it up."

"That wasn't what happened! If she had stuck to buying protection it would have been fine. Instead, she had some stupid idea she could have more fun if she used the protection against the werewolf."

"Whatever."

"You know for a fact that the werewolf who got Dolores is one of Arturo's escorts?"

He nodded. "Sure. How else them rich ladies gonna get hooked up with a werewolf? No werewolf is gonna go around advertising. But they know these ladies want to know them, and Arturo helps set it all up." He blew on his soup placidly.

"Arturo is a pimp? Doesn't that bother you?"

Lynx didn't answer so I tried another question. "Did Dolores know about the other two bodies?"

"If she reads the papers. I tol' you a lot of people know about the last ones, which were really the second and third."

So Dolores had decided to go ahead with the escort, but buy a protection spell. And I had blissfully kept an unsuspecting eye on her, but ignored the rest of the world.

"The guy who got Dolores--he isn't Arturo, right?"

Lynx talked through a mouthful of bread. "I love this bacon stuff. Nah, Arturo, he ain't even a shifter, I don't think. He just sets up the dates." He looked up at me over the matting of hair that was trying hard to fall into his soup. "These ladies want escorts and they pay well. I bet I could escort them, but I ain't going to give no cut to Arturo."

I grabbed his ear and missed. "Don't go there, Lynx. This isn't a game. You start leaving dead--"

"I don't have to kill them," he yelped, dodging my hand. "You think I'm too young to appreciate a nice woman?"

I blinked. Sometimes I forgot that it had been three years since I stumbled across Lynx, half starved, badly bruised, and rummaging through a trashcan for food. Sympathy would have gotten me killed. Instead, I had swallowed my heartbeat, looked over my shoulder and whispered, "You the guy willing to do the job?"

Lynx had jumped on the chance to earn money and never looked back. He hadn't changed much over the last three years, although I suppose he was an inch or four taller. I still had the occasional, ridiculous urge to make things better for him, but I knew what I was up against. There was no handing him a childhood. It had been too late long before I met him. I tried to blink away the old image, but he hadn't changed that much. He still looked half-starved. "Yes, Lynx, I happen to think you are too young, but that isn't what I'm talking about. I'm talking about women who are dying. Sooner or later the werewolf or his cohorts are going to die because of those deaths. The normals *will* put a stop to it."

When he didn't respond, I added, "Now isn't the best time to experiment even if the catch seems easy, kid." I didn't emphasize the "kid," nor did I leave it off.

He was too busy dreaming of riches to notice; his eyes positively gleamed with enthusiasm. "I thought the normals were all afraid of us. It's nice to know that some of them appreciate our…talents." He licked his lips happily.

"They are afraid," I corrected softly. "That's what makes it fun for them. Don't think it means they are ready to take you in and provide a happy home."

His face froze. I'd pushed too far. Before he bolted, I demanded, "The body. You were going to tell me how to find it."

He did. In a lot more detail than I cared to know.

Chapter 5

Lynx left me with a headache, the name and info on the new client and directions to a dead woman. It was more work than I could handle. Since I couldn't meet with White Feather on such short notice, the dead woman would have to wait.

There was no putting off the client though because I had already stalled for a day. If she got too anxious, Lynx would pass the info on to another witch. There were enough bad vibes in the air without two witches working on eliminating the same rogue love potion. While most witches were secretive, there were a small number who demanded bragging rights for problems solved, and I didn't need a territorial problem.

It wasn't worth the effort to dress in anything particularly witchy so I went in a clean t-shirt and blue jeans, my true and favorite uniform. Since Viona Johnson lived in one of the upscale neighborhoods in Santa Fe, I left off my hiking boots in favor of sneakers.

To get to north Santa Fe, I had to pass the plaza. On impulse I took a detour to the little side alley where my best friend Matilda had a shop. The storefront reflected her main clientele, which, sadly, was groupies. Her image involved a lot of flowing robes, glitter, funny headpieces and strange lights. Matilda excelled at witchery long before I did, at least on the surface, because she was more of a show woman.

I touched the door lightly, knowing it would open soundlessly to what appeared to be an unattended shop. Matilda made more money than I did even though I charged considerably more per spell. She never lacked for clients though, while I had slow spots.

"Hey Mat," I called softly in the direction of the beaded door that led to the back.

Matilda was rarely in the front of the shop. She was an entrance kind of gal.

For me, there was no dramatic pause in the doorway. Instead she squealed, "Adriel!" and dragged her headdress off as she came from the back. "Where have you been?" Bottle-enhanced auburn hair leapt free, highlighting her ever-so-white skin. She had been born and raised here, but she wasn't Hispanic. She was whiter than most beach sand.

I braced myself for her hug, patting her back awkwardly because my arm tangled itself in her flowing blue silk sleeve. Matilda's magic was different than mine, which was precisely why I was here. Unlike my earth magic, hers was lighter, mistier--of water rather than earth, of vapors rather than metals. Did we cross over? Definitely, but we each knew our strengths, and Matilda was all about potions and emotions. She could mix pinches of steam and water into concoctions of smoke that softened anger or caused love to bloom. If the ingredients were just right, watery shadows would show her the future. What she couldn't brew, she bought from other witches and sold, an unusual liaison in our competitive and secretive world.

"How's business?" I asked.

She stepped back and wiped her forehead in mock distress. "Busy, incredibly busy. Tourist season goes longer each year. Used to be mostly spring and summer, but now Santa Fe attracts skiers too!"

I laughed. "And you love it and have a potion for all of them."

"Absolutely."

"Speaking of potions, are you selling a lot of love mixes lately?"

She rolled blue eyes. "Are you kidding? No matter what season, it's the best seller, right alongside the revenge potions. The love potions get a little higher sales around New Year's and Valentine's day." She shrugged. "The revenge ones don't see much variation; they are high sellers all year."

"What about matched set love potions?"

Her eyebrows rose and wiggled. "I don't sell that. Too dangerous." She pointed to a row of colorful bottles on a shelf along one side of the shop. "There are varying degrees of like me or love me or respect me. Anything from "give me a new first impression" to "give me a raise." Plenty of "love me for the night," too but I stay away from anything coercive."

"I know. But have you had any requests lately? Or any to break such a spell?"

"Lately?" She thought about it, tapping her long red nails against the counter. "I actually keep track of those requests because when I get one, I'm likely to get a revenge request from the same person a week or two later. I don't do the seriously dangerous revenge potions either, but I keep track of those requests in case someone ends up in an alley." She made a slicing motion across her neck. "Sometimes the police come a'callin."

She turned towards the back of the shop. "Come on back, and I'll check, but it's been a while."

I followed her flouncing form through the beads. Since it was just me, she saved the colored misting that usually went with her entrances and exits.

The back of the shop was nothing more than an ordinary, comfortable living room with a tweed couch, a sleeping cat and a desk with her computer. Her copper teapot sat next to an Asian teacup. "Tea?" she offered.

"No, I need to get to a client, but I wanted to check with you first on this."

She sat at the desk and started typing. "I don't remember anything recent, and I almost never get real names, but let me run through the dates where I noted anything."

Humming lightly under her breath, she found the file she wanted, opened it and scanned through it. "It's been a few weeks since I've been asked outright for anything stronger than I sell on the shelves..." she trailed her finger down the screen. "No requests for a matched set in the last year--is that far enough back?"

"I think so, but I'm not sure." Since I hadn't talked to the client yet, I didn't have a lot of detail. "I don't imagine most people who come in here know to ask for something like that."

She agreed. "It would take research to know enough to ask about a matched set. Maybe twice since I've opened, I've had another witch come in and request it. The witches in question couldn't do the spell, but wanted to sell it. I offered to have someone get in touch with them, but both times, the ladies refused."

I wasn't surprised. Witches would deal with Matilda because she offered secrecy and a way to sell potions to the public without having to give up normal status. That didn't mean a witch would deal with just any other witch. We guarded our abilities--and our lack of abilities--pretty carefully. "And no one asking about undoing such a spell lately?"

"Nope. I'd have remembered that."

"Okay. Call me if someone comes in looking, will you?"

She nodded. "I can tell you if someone comes in. I may not be able to tell you who it is."

"Of course." Matilda protected her clients, as we all did. She followed me back to the front of the shop. "I owe you lunch."

She laughed. "Dinner now. You already owe me lunch!"

"I'll have you over to Mom's. That counts for both, right?"

"Absolutely!"

I blew her a kiss and hurried back outside, not wanting to be any later than I already was.

Thankfully, rush hour was long-since over and traffic was light heading north of town. It took me less than fifteen minutes to follow the directions Lynx had provided. The adobe home was off Camino La Tierra, and the place was as beautiful as I expected.

Viona, on the other hand, was nothing like I imagined. Knowing she had been a scientist at Los Alamos, I figured she was old and befuddled, having turned to a witch in sheer desperation when science and logic as she understood it, failed her.

I was wrong. Viona was in her late-thirties. Her brown hair was streaked with worn highlights and pulled into a clip. Large brown eyes were not in the least befuddled, but they were quite angry. "I don't suppose this was of national importance to you," she snapped out after I introduced myself.

"I wasn't trying to be cruel by making you wait. I had other clients I couldn't leave hanging. Now that I'm here, tell me about this love affair, and we'll see what can be done."

"*Not* a love affair!" She opened the heavy wooden door wider, and allowed me to follow her into the tiled entryway. "A love affair I could solve without your help."

Like a lot of the newer homes in the area, the sprawling house was southwestern in design, but her interior decorating didn't shout it. Instead of houseplants along the entryway ledges, she had herbs. A skylight and two long windows by the door bathed the entry with light. Rugs led into the natural stone floored living area. Rather than the typical paintings depicting squaws and horses, she had striking black and white photos of old buildings next to full-color shots of skyscrapers.

"Since we'll be doing business, drop the Missus. I go by Vi," she informed me as she led the way to a leather couch. "We have two children. I do plan on telling them what is happening if word gets out, but for now they are at camp. It wouldn't surprise me at all if Sheila made sure the kids got wind of this mess to cause even more problems."

"What could Sheila--do you know her last name?"

"McFay. She lives in White Rock, near the lab."

"Okay, what would she gain from your children knowing that your husband has been having," I changed my words when she glared at me, "is the victim of a spell?"

"As far as Sheila is concerned, the more trouble the better. She wants me to divorce Harold, of course."

"She's in love with your husband?" I ventured cautiously.

Vi gave a very unladylike snort. "Sheila needs his cooperation to gain permission for projects at the lab. Without his signature, she doesn't get funding for her pet projects. I worked there. I understand the politics far too well to believe she only wants my husband to warm her bed."

"I see." To give myself time to think, I sat down.

"My husband does not like Sheila, nor does he believe in her research," Vi continued. "That is how I knew she used some," she waved a hand that was noticeably touting a wedding band, "paranormal means to get him to agree to sign off on one of her projects."

"How long has it been since you worked there?"

She put her hands on her hips and glared at me. "I can see you are going to take some convincing."

"Well, I could probably figure out whether he was bespelled or not without the questions, if I had to."

"Then why not do that?"

"Because information never hurts. You seem to have figured out why she wanted your husband bespelled, but if you don't work there anymore, how can you be so certain it is a spell?"

She started to speak, but then whirled toward the window that framed the Jemez mountains. It took her several deep breaths before she said, "He brought the papers home, the ones for her projects. They required his signature for funding. He was sweating profusely, his hands were shaking, and he threw up three times. I thought he had the flu, but he handed me the papers." She closed her eyes. "He couldn't say a *word* to me."

"He had signed them."

"No. Well, one of them." Her fingers bit into her arms. "I ripped them to shreds in front of his eyes."

I thought about that. "And after that he stopped throwing up?"

She nodded and looked back over at me. After a moment she said, "Maybe you do know something about these things?"

"What did he say after you ripped up the papers?"

She shook her head. "He still couldn't tell me anything. The more questions I asked, the worse he got."

"Was this episode before or after he slept with her?"

Her chin lifted. "I don't know. He doesn't talk about that either."

"How do you know he slept with her then?"

It took her an extra heartbeat to answer. When she did, it was almost a whisper. "He moved out of the bedroom."

I gave her a minute to deal with the pain. I doubt she had told many people, if anyone. "Have you actually asked him if he has slept with her?" I asked gently.

She shook her head, once. "I think he would tell me if I asked. Sheila wouldn't bother to put any kind of coercion against him telling me. It's not her style."

Conflicting coercions were also extremely hard to do. A passion spell tended to get rid of inhibitions, not increase them. If Sheila went after the sex to control him, she wouldn't also try to force him to forget about it or deny it. "He's still sick, not eating?"

A sharp nod. "And rumors at work that he slept with her. I think it would only take once. Now she can use that against him, use it to keep him in line."

"But if she doesn't care if you know--"

"Not because of me." She balled her fists into her white skirt. "Because you don't sleep with co-workers, especially if you sit on committee with them and have say over approval of funds."

"Okay, okay. How long ago did he bring the papers home?"

"Last week. Can it...can this kill him?"

I didn't answer that. Instead I said, "He will have signed the papers by now."

"No! He wouldn't do that!"

"He won't have been able to keep from doing it."

"He'd quit before he would! That's why he brought them home. He knew what it meant."

I shook my head, sorry to have to tell her the truth. "When he signed them, even the first time, it's doubtful he knew what he was doing. These spells have to override a lot of awareness. In his case, he probably signed the first of the papers, was interrupted, and the spell had time to wear off. When he looked at the papers later, he knew something was wrong, but couldn't fix it. He brought them to you. But it's quite likely she was able to make him sign them again."

"No." This time it was a hoarse whisper. "I know she hasn't turned them in! My friends at the lab would have told me. You have got to stop her!"

I tapped my fingers against my knee. "One way or another, she will have gotten his signature by now. It's easier to reassert control if done sooner rather than later." I tapped some more. "You're certain they haven't been turned in?"

She nodded.

"She probably doesn't keep the papers at work because someone else might find them. She will have them in a safe place, somewhere accessible only to her," I said.

Vi sucked in a near sob. "He'll have to quit."

"If we remove him from the picture, she'll likely go after whoever takes his place."

"I don't care! As long as it isn't him!" Tears boiled over her eyelids.

I stood and said as gently as I could manage, "A replacement isn't likely to make your husband feel any better. It's going to take a lot to repair his psyche. The good news is that I think there may be a way to make it all work--if we can get the papers back. For that, I'll need something of Harold's to use as a link."

Vi bit on her fist, shivering and trying hard to gather herself. Quietly, having no other comfort to offer, I outlined my plan.

By the time I left, she had pulled herself together and if nothing else, had a semblance of hope.

As for me, I had picked up any stress she had dropped. That happened when I assigned myself dangerous projects like break-ins. After the last one, you'd think I'd have learned.

Chapter 6

I'd planned a relaxing evening at home. No way was I going to start on Vi's project without some rest.

I was all locked in, snug and well fed, but it wasn't to be.

The vamp didn't knock, he just slammed the door open. I screamed.

The spelled garlic across the top of the doorway started smoking.

Let me be clear: I didn't like vampires, and I didn't do business with them. Fine, I was prejudiced; throw me out of society. But let's face facts here. Vampires suck blood. *Human* blood. Don't give me that crap about synthetics or animals. That was like telling me to eat a soy burger. Vampires might occasionally drink animal blood for all I knew, but I bet it tasted like an unseasoned soy burger.

When the vampire said, "Good evening," I nearly died and saved him the trouble of killing me. It would have helped greatly if he had knocked so that I could have run away. It would have helped if he hadn't shown up *at all*.

"Get out," I squeaked, bolting upwards off the living room couch. One of the garlic pieces exploded; the rest sent waves of choking smoke as they burned, proving beyond a doubt that he was a vamp. "Don't you dare cross that threshold, you aren't welcome here." I invoked the ancient protection spell, although I'd heard withholding an invite didn't work that well.

The vampire smiled, showing a hint of fang. I'd heard that was a compliment. I was insulted and scared out of my mind. "Go…ge..get--out." About the last way I wanted to die was to have some night creature suck out all my blood. It was supposed to feel great. Bull-ony. I'd seen death, and it was never great.

"I mean you no harm," it said, erasing the smile. "This is a business proposition." His face was incredibly handsome. A guy could die with pimples, be a hundred pounds overweight and bald. Make him a vampire and he would sleek down, get hair and his features, over time, would be molded to perfection. Or so I heard. And I had never seen an ugly vampire so I believed that one.

"Go away." My silver jewelry echoed the sentiment, tingling. "I don't do business with vampires." My friend, Matilda, worked with vamps, but she also advertised herself as a witch, owned a shop, the whole nine yards. Just because she was stupid didn't mean I had to be.

He smiled again, no fangs. "Of course you do. Everyone needs customers."

I could feel myself turning blue. Sucking in as much air as my shriveled throat would allow, I said, "Find yourself another witch. You are not welcome here. Next time knock, and I'll tell you that through the door."

He inclined his head. "My apologies. I would have knocked, but with the spell around the doorway it was easier to touch the door only once." He shrugged beautiful shoulders, his perfectly creased black dress shirt didn't dare wrinkle.

"The spell worked?" I gasped, without thinking.

He actually chuckled. "It's a good one. That's why I'm here. You are considered one of the best witches, maybe the best in the area."

"Flattery," I mumbled frantically. That was one of their weapons. I had to--I made the sign of the cross and headed for the crucifix over my fireplace.

"Don't bother. Besides, if you take that down, it makes the chimney more accessible to my kind."

I froze. It never occurred to me when I enacted protection against night-creatures that putting the cross there might keep vampires from coming down the chimney. The old texts advised a crucifix in every room and not always by a door or window. Together they formed a magic diagram.

"The reason I am here, if I may get on with it, is to hire you before the enemy hires you to find one of us."

"I don't work for vampires," I croaked.

"Then that is a problem." He was no longer smiling. "I don't have all night to convince you that it is better to work for me than against me."

"I don't work against you either."   An infinitesimal, almost inconsequential bit of curiosity got past the fear in my brain. "What...what are you talking about?"

Eyes like smooth black tar calculated silently. I didn't want to look at his eyes too long, so I stared across his perfect midnight hair. It was swept into a tucked ponytail at the base of his neck. His skin was a rich olive, flawlessly...preserved.

"It is rumored that there is a witch who wants the power of the vampire without becoming one," he said. "You are a witch. Why wouldn't you help another witch find a vampire unless I pay you to stay out of it?"

My mind couldn't grasp the concept for over a minute. He was patient. Finally I said, "Sorry, buddy. I can't think of a single good reason to help anyone find a vampire." I bit down hard on my lip to keep from stuttering. "I suppose if a vampire was kidnapping children, I could be persuaded to do something about it. Truthfully, I'd probably help if the vampire were rampaging against humans in general." My upper body trembled violently at the thought of having to track a vampire, a violent killer who was already *dead*.

He inclined his head politely. "Vampires do not rampage against live humans. That would be self-destructive."

"I'll say." I backed towards the chimney so that the crucifix was within reach. "But you can't say it hasn't happened before."

The elegant shrug again. "Of course not. But we take care of our own. We're not looking to be annihilated. Any vampire that goes rogue will be a dead vampire."

He didn't smile at his own joke. Neither did I. My mouth already felt as if fangs were growing just because I was within a hundred yards of the guy. "I am not going vampire hunting. I am not for hire for such jobs."

"You are certain?"

"Damn straight."

"I can pay you well to ensure your cooperation."

I didn't like the sound of that. "You mean you can buy my cooperation?" I knew that was not what he meant.

The fangs again. "No, I meant that if you agreed to my business proposition, I would ensure your cooperation, although I would also pay you for the agreement."

"Figures." Taking a deep breath, I straightened my shoulders. "I won't bargain with you, sell my soul to you, be hired by you, paid by you or… stalked by you. I am not for hire where vampires are concerned."

"Not even for the hunt."

"Especially for the hunt," I corrected. I was calm enough now that an evil thought surfaced. "Correct me if I heard wrong, but this hunt, whoever wants a vampire…you said you weren't talking about a hunt to get rid of a vampire?"

"No." He waved an elegant hand, getting too close to the garlic. It flared again, burning away entirely.

"You're telling me that someone out there wants a vampire for the power."

Even before he nodded, my skin crawled. "Heaven help us," I whispered.

"Someone had better."

Swallowing hard, I promised, "It is not I who is looking for such danger." Had he come here thinking I was good enough to mess with a potion that required vampire fluids? Was he insane???

"You are a very talented witch."

"I'm also one attached to staying alive. No offense."

"If a witch were to capture one of ours, death wouldn't be what she would fear." He didn't snarl, but it was close.

"I can imagine." I held up my hands in a peaceful gesture. "But it isn't me. Trust me, I'm not that stupid."

He studied the door frame. "I can see that you are not stupid." Pointing to the door frame he said, "You won't sell this spell either."

"To another witch?" My livelihood was selling spells, and that might include spells against vampires.

"That is partly what I came to pay you for. You must not help."

I shook my head. "I sell spells. I don't necessarily check to make sure that someone--uh-oh," I said softly, thinking of Dolores. She had bought what should have been a protection spell. I hadn't known her intent. "Oh."

"Yes, it's a rather touchy problem. I would advise you not to sell this particular knowledge for a while. Until we take care of the problem."

"You don't know for certain who this witch is?" I dared ask.

"We will find out."

I shook my head. "If she is good enough to be thinking of capturing a vampire, she will already know this spell."

The smile again, without fangs. "Exactly."

Like the myth, he was gone. The door did not close by itself. I was too scared to walk over and shut it. He had visited because he knew I had enough knowledge about vampires to keep them at bay. My hands cramped as I hugged myself.

It was bad enough that he knew I knew a few spells, but it scared me even more that vampires anywhere thought I might have the means to track them. That was not the kind of knowledge I needed, wanted or would want to use. If I were very, very lucky, I had convinced him of that.

Chapter 7

It was late, but I went to the grocery for garlic. I wasn't sleeping another night without more protection in my house. While I was there, regular groceries wouldn't hurt either.

I already had a blessed crucifix and was wearing it, but a spare or six seemed like a really great investment. There wasn't time to design one myself given the circumstances. I woke up my regular supplier of silver and bought the two in his inventory along with some extra silver strands.

Crucifixes didn't come blessed, so I'd have to wait for morning to get Father Dan to do it for me. I also wanted some holy water.

It was almost midnight when I got back home, but the place still felt violated. It couldn't wait until morning. I called Father Dan.

"Can I bring over a couple of gallons of water to be blessed?" I hoped he'd tell me he was awake, no problem, bring it over.

"What? Why in the world do you need so much holy water?" he sputtered. "Are you running baptisms out of your yard?"

Father Dan knew me too well to swallow a "visit the poor" excuse. "I, uh…" Luckily, inspiration dawned. "The werewolves," I whispered into the phone.

"The--oh for--Give me patience, Lord! You're the tenth person to call me about that."

"It wouldn't hurt to have it, right?" Every time I talked to the man, I was overwhelmed by guilt. It wasn't that witches couldn't be God's workwomen, it was that the priest didn't necessarily believe in the things I tried to protect against. "And I have another cross that needs blessing," I added, so long as I was already upsetting him.

"After Mass. You wait until after Mass on Sunday."

"Are you sure you can't do it tonight?"

"Yes!"

"How about a blessing for me and my house? Over the phone?" It was weak as far as spells, but unless I wanted to drive over, pound on his door and wake him again, it was the best I could do.

"Fine, fine, a prayer, but then you hang up and let me get some sleep!"

"Okay," I promised.

Begrudgingly, he muttered prayers. I added my own voice to the, "Amen," and then said, "Thanks, Father Dan. I'll bring my new cross to Mass."

He was still muttering when he hung up.

I dragged out my toolbox and pried off the trim around the front and back doors. To my relief, the silver around the front door had not melted. I wasn't quite sure why the garlic had nearly burned off; that problem required more study. The entire house still reeked from the smoke. "Has to be garlic," I grumbled. "Couldn't it be other herbs?"

That gave me an idea. "Chile…" New Mexico chile was more caustic than just about anything. It was readily available in dried forms too. "Powdered?"

Of course, if the chile burned, the cayenne would be released into the air. I'd choke myself out of my own house if I did the spell wrong. "I could use it in the chimney where the fumes would go up."

I went into my lab and worked up a formula. The literature gave me some stats on why garlic worked against vampires. There was no earthly reason that chile wouldn't help. In fact, after studying the problem I was pretty sure chile was a better anti-vampire tool. Caustic peppers weren't all that common in medieval Europe when the first spells were developed. That and there was still the whole threat of dying from inhaling cayenne if things went wrong.

I happened to have a *rista* that hadn't been lacquered for use as a decoration. I ground some of the red chile into a fine powder.

It was three in the morning before I finished my task, but I had finished some nice ropes made from dried chile and garlic wrapped in linen. I strung the stuff under the door frames and tapped the trim back on. The chile might smoke, it might do nothing, but it most likely would enhance the garlic.

Hoping the vamp had no reason to come back any time soon, I lined the porch with some of the new silver I had purchased. The vamp had to touch the silver to be burned, but I was hoping the vamp would *feel* it under the boards and stay away.

I was exhausted, and I still hadn't done my bedroom. A couple of extra garlic bulbs hardly seemed enough protection. I had to sleep in there. "How much silver has to be in a stake?"

I got on the internet and then backed the research up with some old texts in my lab. It turned out the answer was none. The stake had to go through the vampire's heart. "Does it have to be ash? How about oak? And how 'bout I tip it with silver?" Double protection. "What about a silver dagger?"

I read long enough to figure out that ash had some properties where vampires were concerned that oak did not. With a big yawn, I shut my books. A stake was going to involve more than carving up a spare chunk of wood.

I took the rest of the thin silver thread and worked it around my bed. It would have to do if a vamp found a way past the other protections. I muttered some more protection spells and put bundles of chile powder at the foot and top of my bed. I think I even finished the spells before I fell asleep.

Chapter 8

In the morning, late as it came for me, I had to face facts. I couldn't just sit on the information Lynx had given me. There were two choices. I could go out in the mountains and find the body Lynx described, or I could get the information to White Feather.

My aura had been all over the Dolores thing. Even though I had taken care of that as much as possible, I didn't think it was a good idea to go putting myself near another body. I didn't need anyone telling the authorities that the same aura appeared near two murdered women.

Unfortunately, if I met with White Feather, he'd have questions. I didn't have many answers. Checking on the body myself might answer some of them, but White Feather could get that information as easily as I could if he followed the directions to the body.

I drew a map and made sure my aura was nowhere on it. Instead of wasting time with a long description, I added the words "forensic team required" to the bottom. The man wasn't an idiot; the message and map were clue enough. Unless he had forty other informants in the paranormal world, he would know it was from me, but he couldn't prove it.

As soon as I finished the map, guilt made me go directly to the post office where his box was located. White Feather was usually grateful for any information I sent in, but in this case he was likely to be angry. He already thought I was playing some sort of game on the Dolores thing.

The morning was gone, which left me a short afternoon to get spells ready for Vi's project. If I got the ingredients now, tonight was as good a time as any to practice.

I ran through my list of chemicals for the levitation spell. "Capsule of helium, wire for current…"

Two stops later, I had everything in hand. Instead of going home to eat, I went to the burrito drive through.

Once home, I made sure the slim, coated windows around the top of my workroom were closed tightly before setting out my supplies to begin the spell. Even though the shelves lining the room looked disorganized, most of the leather bound books, herbs and liquids were alphabetized. The polished pieces of wood, odd sculpted metal, stones and pottery were also organized, but I was probably the only one who could possibly understand the method.

I set out the few items I needed on the long work table. Since flying didn't require furniture, I moved a stool and chair out of the way and stood next to one of the bookcases. If the spell worked, I had a clear flying aisle all the way to the sink.

The most effective way to levitate was to use magnets underneath something, such as a broom or carpet. My sneakers were an easy choice because there was room in the soles for the paraphernalia I needed in the spell.

The next challenge was activating the spell. With a protection spell, it was all a chemical interaction. In the case of flying, I had to construct the spell so that it could be started and stopped when I wanted. I had considered using Faraday's Principle of Induction--motion of the magnet, such as me running, to cause an electric current that would activate the spell, but I didn't want to take off every time I ran.

This very problem was how witches ended up with a reputation for strange incantations. We sometimes had to use Words of Power, and if we used any old English word we could end up accidentally triggering a spell in the middle of a conversation. Don't think spoken commands weren't powerful either. My father could crack an order that stopped my childhood legs in their tracks. Most parents could do this and didn't even know they were throwing a form of a spell.

"Yolkhai Estsan!" I intoned, sucking air into my lungs and holding my breath.

Like the Navajo sky goddess, whose name I used, I lifted off the ground.

There was no stopping my giddy smile, although I bet the sky goddess wouldn't have been very impressed with the mere four inches of air underneath my feet.

"Hah!" I was airborne!

I took a tentative step forward and nearly fell flat on my face. Thankfully the top bookshelf was in reach. I grabbed it.

For a few seconds I wasn't sure if I was levitating or hanging by my fingertips.

"Maybe that's why witches use a broom." Tentatively, I let go of the shelf, careful not to knock down any of the books or glass jars.

Walking hadn't worked so...I slid one foot forward, trying not to lean over too much. It was like swimming against a current with a plate balanced on my head. "And what will happen if I activate the motion spell?" I had the spell worked out, but if I added it to the sneakers, my feet might take off and drag the rest of me behind.

"Definitely need to put the spell on something longer." I still liked the rug idea, assuming I could stay on top of it. Then there was the whole problem of knowing when the spell was wearing off. I didn't want to be mid-flight when it ran out of controlled air currents even if I was only four inches above the ground.

The lack of height reminded me that I wanted to try helium in the mix. Unfortunately, I had planned on stepping on the helium to snap the capsule and have the chemicals mix. Four inches up in the air there wasn't anything to step *on*.

Using the shelf to hold still, I lifted one foot and snapped the capsule.

It was an instant success. "Ow!" My head hit the ceiling with an audible crack.

There was no point in trying to walk again because there was nothing to grab onto this high up. Maybe there was a balancing spell I could use, or maybe I could put the magnetic spell into my shirt in case I fell over.

I canceled the spell and got myself back on the ground.

Instead of helium, I was probably better off using warm air currents. Maybe that was why witches were often seen on brooms at dusk. Warm air currents rising from warm earth at night would be useful.

I skimmed through a few books. If I lived closer to the ocean, I would have had more currents to choose from, along with the tidal pull. New Mexico had a lot of beach, but very little ocean. "Stabilizers..." I ran my fingers down the page. "This one could work. Certainly long enough to get in or out of a building."

The shop was too small for a bigger experiment. I needed to be outside. A nice lonely desert location would also make it easier to hear the magic, to listen to the sand shift across the mesas, and feel the moonlight dance in the shadows. There were ancient voices out there, a power that ran through the earth as sure as lodestone attracted iron. Using earth elements in spells was a form of channeling--sort of like burning gasoline for power, only the extraction methods and packaging were different.

I packed what I needed and headed for my favorite spot deep in the hills, about a two-mile trek into nowhere. I rarely practiced with lights, which was the only reason I preferred a full moon. In my perfect arroyo, the piñon trees, scrub oak and pines were thick. The red stone cliffs sheltered me, giving me room to fly around without worrying about being seen.

I set the spell and attained the four inches without trouble. There was nothing to grab onto except a handful of juniper needles. I used the second spell quickly, sending myself up to the tops of the junipers so that when I added motion I didn't end up planting my face in the side of a tree.

"Easy, easy," I whispered. Breathing with exertion and exhilaration, I set the final spell for motion. The shadows moved beneath the trees. The eerie glow of moonlight on the rocks made everything red, but I wasn't afraid.

I was flying! Almost.

I had been right about the shoes. The sneakers didn't have a lot of area, so as the wind swooshed beneath my feet, I only drifted forward slowly. I had a plan for this problem though.

Smugly, I muttered, "Wind at my back…"

Swoosh! The wind was strong. "Uh--aaahhh!" My face went forward. The flat of my shoes went vertical. I headed straight for the ground. About to eat dirt, I pulled in my knees just in time, getting my feet under me. The magnetic spell in the shoes bounced off mother earth. Unfortunately, the spell at my back was still going strong. I changed one earth face for the other, rushing at the red stone cliffs with amazing speed.

My shoulder collided with the red surface. I pulled my feet in again to try and bounce. It worked only too well. I shot backwards, six feet away, straight into a pine tree. The wind at my back pushed me up through the tree and straight for the moon.

I tried to protect my face, taking pine needles across both arms. Sap tangled in my hair. A branch hit my cheek. My eyes stung either from the branches or cold air.

"Moonlight madness!" I cursed. If I dissolved the spell, I'd crash back down and have to endure the same punishment in reverse.

I tried slowing the spell by dispersing it.

It didn't work. I hadn't set up a dispersal spell ahead of time. How do you disperse wind anyway?

Live and learn. I stopped the wind spell cold, afraid that with the way my luck was going, I'd hit a weather blimp.

I fell. It wasn't too difficult to pull my legs back under me, but this far from the ground, the magnetic spell under my sneakers didn't work until I got close to mother earth. I could no longer move forward or backwards.

I glanced off a tree branch, only to have one spelled foot bounce off a high boulder. I tilted.

"Aeeii!" I righted myself, but the shadows fooled me into thinking I had more time to find a landing pad. At six feet above the ground, the repel spell kicked in so hard, the impact knocked me over backwards.

That was it. I couldn't get my feet back under me in time. With all the grace of a bound earthling, I kissed mother earth, hard.

Chapter 9

I wasn't expecting Lynx, but he was waiting in the shadows when I arrived home. Wisely, he didn't sneak up on me.

"What's for dinner?" he asked around a huge yawn. Using the porch light, he pointedly inspected the scratches and bruises on my face, but I ignored him. I did not try to walk without limping because both ankles hurt wretchedly. My left shoulder had a huge bruise where I had hit the cliff, so I used my other hand to open the door.

"I ate already. You can find something in the fridge. I bought apples and bananas yesterday."

Lynx immediately helped himself to a soda. When he turned and saw me in the full light of the kitchen he said, "You never take me on the fun ones."

Not needing any caffeine, I poured myself some ice water. "I talked to your client. I took the case."

He nodded, unconcerned.

I sat down before I could fall. "What gives? Another client?"

He pulled a box out of my cupboard and started shoveling my supply of animal crackers into his maw. "Hah." It took several minutes of chewing before he could speak. "You pay me to be ears."

"And?" I was leery, especially after having missed so much news. Knowing Lynx, he might now start telling me who was running for governor and expect to be paid.

He chewed some more. "Not sure its news or not, but it sounded funny."

"What did you hear?"

He licked his lips, gulped soda and said, "Street says there's a guy looking for a witch. Willing to pay big money."

My mind froze as I thought of my late-night visitor. My voice squeaked when I asked, "Was it a vamp?"

"Huh?" He stopped chewing and stared at me. "Why you ask that?"

I took a deep breath. It wasn't possible to sound casual after my initial reaction, but I shrugged and tried to act cool. "Well, who was it?"

He grunted and chewed some more while watching me carefully. When I didn't offer more information, he answered the question. "I think he's a cop. He's offering too much to find you in particular and asking too little about the spell he says he needs."

I wasn't sure I liked that answer much better than a vamp. "A cop."

Lynx nodded and upended the box of crackers. "Might not be looking for you. He's an amateur, describing an old witch, but the best. All the dummies think witches are old."

The old part made me think of White Feather. Had he gotten the map and decided to call me out into the open? "What made you think he was looking for me in particular? Maybe the guy just needs a potion."

"That's the funny part. He asked about protection."

"So?"

"Guys don't go around asking for protection, not the way he's doing it, you know?"

I could see his point. Protection wasn't a spell most men would ask for, at least not publicly. "Is he Indian? Maybe he has a spirit after him."

"Nah. Could be a Mexican dude with a voodoo curse, though." He shrugged. "I don't know. I was gonna ignore it. He didn't seem like a real client, more like a big talker, gonna hire him a witch for protection."

"What made you think he's a cop?" It made little sense for White Feather to try and find me openly. He had to know that finding the real me would ruin our relationship, and unless he had some other source of information in the paranormal world, I was his best edge.

Lynx smiled. "The cop part I know."

I groaned. When Lynx *knew* something, he wouldn't tell his sources unless I could convince him the circumstances were life or death--for him. "What does he look like?"

Lynx shrugged and climbed down from the kitchen chair. "I only saw him in the dark. He's tall. And he hasn't been doing all the asking on his own about this witch. He's definitely the one hiring, but there's been a couple of other whispers about "a friend of mine lookin' to hire a witch'." Lynx took one last longing look at the refrigerator, but he had already checked it and knew there wasn't any leftover takeout. "Maybe not even you he wants. He didn't ask for you by name, but it sounded like he had someone specific in mind, you know?"

No, I didn't know, but before I could complain, with a quiet snick, the doorknob turned, and he was gone.

Chapter 10

You don't have to be a witch to feel the power and presence of Santa Fe. Ancient cultures lived in its hills; men fought and died for their homes, their dreams, and their way of life. Feet traveled across this earth from the Indians, to those who forged the Old Santa Fe Trail. Each person left behind a tiny essence that created the aura of Santa Fe. The air breathed of life and dreams, ancient and modern.

The plaza was at its busiest after church on Sunday so it was hard to feel the aura, even though the tourists were a part of what made it what it was. After putting my newly blessed crucifixes and water in the trunk of my car, I hurried across the buckled and cracked sidewalk towards the center of the square. The earth beneath my feet radiated heat, the mundane kind, making me glad I had worn shorts. I wondered if there would be a signal from White Feather.

I didn't dally until I heard my name. "Adriel!"

My feet stopped churning. Even my sister used my chosen nickname rather than my birth name. It nearly killed her, but she had seen too much to deny she could do me harm by revealing my real name. "Kas," I replied, turning to face the open patio where she sat.

"You haven't been by to see Mom in a while."

No complaints that I hadn't stopped to see her and her husband, Gary, but, oh, she nagged me about Mom and Dad. "No, but I called them..." I couldn't remember exactly when. "Last week," I finally decided.

Her dark brown eyes matched mine except for the hazel streaks in my left. Despite being two years younger than me, we might have looked like twins except for the fact her ebony hair had burnished orange streaks, the less-than-attractive result of following the recent highlighting trend. "You could be more attentive," she pressed.

"And you could be less obnoxious."

She waved one bejeweled hand imperiously. "Off on your important gutter business, no doubt. I wouldn't want to take up your time."

"No problem. I am busy at the moment, but why don't you stop by for dinner when you aren't swamped with your other social engagements?" I might not have the extra money required to sit at plaza patio restaurants sipping coffee and nibbling cakes, but I got by. Of course, it wasn't the amount of money, it was the way I earned it that bothered her. I had chosen an ancient profession, one she had no respect for--one she believed "our ignorant ancestors resorted to."

She sniffed. "It would be better if you came to our house for dinner." She glanced behind me as though searching for someone. "I'll call."

Her wave was probably supposed to be a casual "good-bye" rather than a shooing-off, but it felt that way anyway.

Whatever. Not everyone could marry a husband who raked in the dough. She called him a water specialist, and while he did do some exotic fountain designs, the bulk of his work came from installing fancy water-efficient toilets in new houses and remodeling the multitude of old ones in Santa Fe.

Kas was right about one thing though; I needed to call my mother more often. If I had, I would have known about the werewolf killings. It was exactly the sort of thing my mother would gossip about.

Mindful that my sister was watching, I crossed the center part of the plaza without slowing. I was relieved to see the monument in the middle contained no signal from White Feather. If he were truly eager to see me, he would have left a signal. He was either planting a false trail in the rumors or it wasn't White Feather doing the chasing.

There were other people besides Lynx who might have good information about cops looking for witches. I headed out of the plaza for the kind of restaurant my sister would not be seen in. Not that Tino wasn't respectable. It just happened that he owned restaurants and bars for the underground.

The Owl was a bar, but contained more private rooms in the back for a meal and business. Only those of us known to Tino were invited to the back rooms.

The Monastery, his higher-end eatery, was rumored to house the ghosts of past monks, but I knew it was only bats living in what was either an old chimney or *perhaps* a refurbished belfry.

Tino kept the groupies away by owning places like "El Ojo," better known by its English name, "The Evil Eye" and "El Lobo Negro," often translated unkindly as "The Black Mongrel." The groupies went to his trendy places and had their fortune told by people who couldn't read a tarot card if the instructions were printed on the back. Very avoidable and not a good place to pick up legitimate business.

I slid into a booth in one of the back rooms at The Owl. I always sat near the alley-side. There were no windows, so I had to settle for sitting near the door. The dim candlelight was rumored to be from illusion candles, throwing magical shadows to make it harder to recognize a person in the future.

When Angel shuffled over to take my order, I said, "Green-chile cheeseburger. Tino in?"

"Nah, there were some gang problems over in El Lobo." Angel only resembled her namesake in that her hair was shocking white. Even if she somehow grew wings, I doubted they would be strong enough to help her five-four, hundred and sixty pounds into the air. "You want a diet coke or water with your burger?"

"Make it water. I don't need the caffeine."

"I'll have your coke then," she suggested.

"Sure, add it to my tab. If Tino comes in, let me know, would you?"

"You looking for business?"

"Not really. Just wanted to catch up on gossip. I'm a little worried about the women who have been found," I waved my hands wishing I didn't have to say it, "dead."

Angel nodded vigorously. "Ain't we all, mi Dios!" Her eyes flicked left and right. "I *serve* some of those folks, you know? What if one followed me home?"

"I'm guessing you'd curse his skinny little butt and be fine," I said with a smile.

Her dimples showed momentarily and then disappeared. "My curses don't always take right away," she confided, as if I didn't already know. "It's hard when you're nervous and don't have it prepared for the person beforehand, you know?"

"You could prepare it beforehand. You don't have to know the guy. If you're scared, remember to put it into the curse."

She tapped her pad. "I usually know the person, right? I find out what matters to him, like if they have a big old boat or something. Then I curse it."

"You don't have to know a guy to know a couple of things that would bother the heck out of him. Like any other fight," I advised, "you kick 'em where it hurts."

"Well, yeah. Yeah. I could do that. I'm pretty good with pain."

"And then you throw your fear into it. You push it right into the guy. You make sure that curse sticks with everything you've got."

She brightened and her pen tapped harder. "I could prepare it ahead of time! Shoot, I could put all my frustration in there because I can't lose any weight, you know?"

I laughed. "Now that would be a world-class curse!" Angel wasn't good enough to make a living selling curses. She relied on a few simple ones she had learned from her grandmother. When she stuck to those, she did okay. Anything else had a tendency to turn out badly--like the time she cursed a customer's food. Tino had to throw out every morsel in the place. The guy she was mad at walked away. He wasn't dumb enough to eat it and neither were the rest of us.

"Maybe your mother can help you or ask your aunt," I suggested. "You'll need to practice to get it right under stress. And don't rely on line of sight if you don't have to."

She sighed. "I wish mi abuela were still around."

"I know." My stomach growled, but I ignored it for the moment. "Did you know any of the ladies who were attacked?"

She shook her head. "No way. They weren't regulars." She leaned in. "Rich folks. Messing around where they ain't got no business. Tino's really worried. This stuff could hurt his business!"

"Is the gang activity over at El Lobo related, you think?"

She nodded vigorously, her straight white ponytail swishing. "Absolutamente! What else could it be? The normals are out lookin for a wolf!" She made a stabbing motion.

My stomach rumbled again, either in protest or hunger. It was loud enough that Angel heard.

"I go, I go," she laughed. "Maybe I'll even make mine a diet coke today on account you gave me such good advice!"

I smiled and nodded, knowing she'd lose more weight if she stopped asking customers for additional tips in the form of food and drinks. She had convinced herself that if a customer bought her a drink she was obligated to drink it and didn't have to count the calories.

Tino didn't show by the time I finished stuffing myself with delicious salty fries and a succulent cheeseburger. I thought about stopping by The Monastery but I was too full to even pretend to eat more. I was also still tired and sore from my canyon run. I worked enough nights without throwing extras in. There would be time later for me to search out information on whoever might be trying to find me.

Chapter 11

It was always good for me to be well-rested before I did reconnaissance. With proper sleep, I tended to be able to carry off the impression of "tourist," as opposed to "insane bag lady." Bright and early after the first good night's sleep in a week, I gathered a floppy straw hat, binoculars, bird book and canvas shorts. With tourist disguise in hand, I drove to White Rock to start work for Vi on her love spell problem.

If there had ever been a white rock to give the simple little town its name, it was well hidden among the winding mountain roads and canyons that formed the edge of the Santa Fe National Forest. Centuries ago, the craggy earth had shared its secrets with the Bandelier Indians, sheltering them inside the magnificent cliff walls near Frijoles canyon. Life danced in the twisted pine trees and clear streams; jagged rocks spoke of the earth's throbbing inner heat. Any spell spun where the earth was so full would be long-lasting and powerful.

Sheila's estate wasn't hard to find on the Pajarito Acres side of White Rock. The town consisted of no more than two or three subdivisions spread along the top of the deep canyon walls that housed the Rio Grande. Each estate sat on a minimum of an acre decorated by spindly desert grasses and shrubs. Junipers and pines mixed with yucca, gamma grass and wildflowers. Her neighbors weren't close enough to notice much that might go on.

Vi had given me good directions and assured me that the woman worked regular hours at Los Alamos. Maybe Sheila did, maybe she didn't. I still had to scope out the place if I was going to put my plan into action.

Location was the only thing that was easy. With my "bird watching" binoculars, I could see cameras fixed on the corners of Sheila's house. The woman had cut down or purchased what looked like jagged juniper boughs and formed it into an ugly fence all the way around her property. Maybe she had convinced the neighborhood that using local fauna was environmentally friendly, but to me it looked like a good excuse to line up very pointed sticks so that no one could climb over without being impaled.

Given the fence and the cameras, there was a good chance that if she had something valuable, like signed papers granting her money, she would keep them on the premises. Unfortunately, given the cameras I had a feeling I would need a professional for the locks.

My best bet was Lynx, but he was only twelve or thirteen years old. I couldn't involve the kid in breaking and entering. I had given him his first job and the idea that he could work for real money. He had taken the idea and combined it with his alley life, becoming a professional of a far more dubious nature than I had ever imagined. Just because he was quite excellent in his chosen field didn't mean I should push him further into the lower echelon side of things by involving him in breaking and entering. He deserved better from me.

Of course we wouldn't be exactly stealing anything, we'd only be taking back what had already been stolen--a signature.

I mused on the ethical situation on the drive back to Santa Fe. The fact was, I needed someone very, very good. I couldn't risk getting caught. Lynx was good. I was not. Lynx was also for hire and experienced.

Hmph.

The first thing I did when I got home was replicate the levitation spell in my hiking boots. After that, I got to work on an invisibility spell. It was more of a blending and avoidance spell than complete invisibility. All scents were carried on airwaves and some scents were simply more visible than others. The herb pack I made wafted a smoke-like illusion. Like a wisp of fog, it formed shapes, moving with the environment. It didn't smell bad, but like garlic repels a vampire, the spell tended to make people want to avoid it.

When I tested it, I found that the spell wasn't much good in broad daylight. I drummed my fingers. If I created a different spell, one using reflection of light rather than tendrils of smoky smells, it would work better in the daytime.

I might need both. Or if I were lucky, neither.

I mixed the new spell and made an extra pack of each for Lynx, but my conscience hammered away. It was not fair to ask Lynx for help in this matter. Of course, one way or the other, I had to at least contact Lynx because he was the person I used for messages--including a "look for me if I don't show up after a certain time" type of message.

I moved the cactus pot on the porch to the location that indicated I wanted to talk to him. If he showed before tomorrow when I left, maybe he could teach me a couple of mundane lock tricks. I had a few spells that worked on locks, but the woman was a witch. I didn't want to use magic to get into her place, not if I could help it.

Still, I prepared those spells also. Then, since it had been a while, I called Mom. She was more than happy to tell me that no more bodies had been found.

"Only the three?" I asked, my mind racing.

"Three isn't enough? Three too many!" She went on to lecture while I wondered about White Feather. Had he not followed the map? If he had, why wasn't the other body in the news?

When my mother switched to a rumor about the governor, I eased myself off the phone with a promise to stop by soon.

Lynx showed up for dinner, not unusual since I tended to eat late, and he tended to always want food.

"What's the job?" he asked in reference to the signal.

I warmed another tortilla for the bean burritos I was making. "Well, it's complicated."

Lynx sniffed the heady aroma of the bacon grease I used to fry the beans. "More distractions needed?"

"In a manner of speaking. Actually, it's two jobs. You can choose either one."

"How about both? I charge you triple to be in two places at once." He grinned happily.

"You want your burrito smothered in chile and cheese?"

"Cheese," he responded, knowing that I'd give him chile anyway, because it was the only vitamins the kid received from my less-than stellar cooking.

I put the burritos in the toaster oven and set it to broil. "It's for your client. I'm going to retrieve some papers that belong to her."

Lynx stilled. Slowly, a large grin spread across his face. "You want me to retrieve the papers?" He wiggled in anticipation, his little butt almost falling off the chair. "You've never given me such a big job, boss!"

I had no idea, not one, until that moment, that he thought I didn't trust him with big jobs. "Lynx, I'm talking about breaking and entering! This is *not* a big job, this is--" I gulped. "Illegal. And I can't ask you to do that. I need to ask you instead to...take action if I don't come back in a certain time."

His face clouded with disappointment. "You don't think I can do it?"

I snorted. "Of course you can do it. And it would be better for me if you did it because I can't use spells to get the doors unlocked!"

He considered this, along with the plate of food I put in front of him. "If you can't use spells, who you gonna get to open the door?"

"I'm going to have to figure out a way to open it without spells."

He took a bite of food and tried to talk around it. "So why you ain't going to ask me?"

"I covered that part," I snapped. "*It's illegal.*"

My own mouth was full when he said, "But why you ain't gonna ask me? That's what I want to know."

"That *is* the reason, Lynx." I calmed down and tried to be patient. "You are--" I was going to say "a kid," but he had never seen himself as a kid. "I can't go around asking people to do illegal things."

This seemed to confuse him even more. "Why not? You got some spell set on you that won't let you?" His face lit up. "So, hey, now that I understand the problem, I can volunteer, and then you aren't asking, and I can do the job, right?"

I closed my eyes. Eating seemed to be the only thing that made sense. I chewed for a while before trying to explain. "Lynx, it's not a spell. I don't ever want to ask you or anyone else to do something illegal."

"Whatever," he replied. He had settled the point in his mind, even if it didn't make sense to him. "You're still going to hire me to do the job, right?"

The kid did not care why I might or might not be comfortable with the situation as long as I hired him. I could try all night to explain why it was wrong for a grown-up to exploit the skills of a twelve-year-old thief, but the word "illegal" held no meaning to him.

"Yes, Lynx, I'll hire you." I swallowed and then forced out, "to help me break into Sheila's house." If there were truly justice in the world, lightning would now strike me dead. Of course, there wasn't, so I kept on breathing.

"Great. I give you a discount on account it's your first big job."

"I'll hire you, assuming I can afford it. I've never hired anyone for this type of thing before."

"Yeah. I didn't know why. But I'll do it right. I'm the best," he bragged, looking up at me quickly through his hair before using his drink as a shield. After he gulped the entire can of soda, he wiped his mouth with the back of his hand and asked, "Is tonight the job?"

I shook my head. "No. We're doing it tomorrow morning."

He blinked a couple of times and then smacked his forehead. "In daylight? It's no wonder you don't do this kind of job much. You don't do these things in the *morning*."

"Tomorrow, Lynx. Be here at seven-thirty in the morning. Sheila has a day job and that's when we'll go."

He shook his head. "I was gonna give you a discount on account you never done this sort of thing before, but now I'm thinking maybe I'm gonna have to charge a premium." He scooted off the chair. "Seven-thirty." He picked up the last bite of his burrito and swiped it around the plate. "In the *morning*." Still chewing, he carried his plate to the sink.

With a final disbelieving shake of his head, he slid out a barely opened door.

I put my head on the table. I was officially a corrupting force on today's youth. Even if he was already a goner.

Chapter 12

Between asking Lynx for help and nerves over the job, I managed only a few hours of sleep. I was up early packing my rattletrap Civic when Lynx showed up.

"Okay Lynx," I said sternly, palming a pack in front of his nose. "You need to wear this. Wear it across your back, down your shirt. It will keep people from seeing you." I handed him another pack. "Store this one. It will only work if you snap it and we're somewhere dark. I don't think we'll need it."

He laughed, his face contorted as if he were giggling, only he made no sound. "No one sees me if I don't want them to. Do you ever see me leave?"

I saw shadows when he moved outside. That was close enough. "Sometimes." I ignored his sneer. "This will help. No one will *want* to look at you. That way if someone is shooting at you, maybe they'll aim wide."

He sobered up immediately, studying the package of herbs carefully. I despaired that he was trying to guess what was in them, but after looking at the outside, he put the dark pack in his pocket. Taking a braided wool yarn from around his neck, he expertly secured the daylight pack and put it around his neck. "Okay, boss."

I picked up my own bundle. "Your batch is from the same as mine. You won't be much affected by the spell on me so long as you're wearing your pack."

He looked me up and down and then sideways. "You got a kinda glimmer thing. That's good. I'll know it's you if we get separated."

My heart jumped uneasily. "That won't happen! You're going to stay right with me."

He smiled, his eyes narrow, but readable. He'd abandon me in a second.

After we got in the car, I said, "One more thing. If you really need to stay hidden, crush the pack you're wearing between your fingers. There's another spell inside. If you break the outer packing of the first spell, it'll release a second one, even stronger."

"That's what I like about you," he said. "You always make double sure. You always have a backup."

Too bad his respect for my preparations evaporated right after we arrived in White Rock when I parked the car.

"We ain't parking on State Road four," he yelped. "I don't care if you can make the car invisible!"

"No one will notice it. Her house is yards away down one of the nature trails. We can get right to the side of her property."

"You didn't case the joint properly. You need to park at the community club or Overlook Park." His finger stabbed the map that was lying across the cup holder between the front seats. "No one gonna notice your car in a park. You don't need no spells, you just use your brains. I still don't know why I agreed to do this in daylight."

"I told you I checked with Vi. Sheila works normal hours and shouldn't be home until after five. There are hiking paths all over Pajarito Acres. If anyone asks questions we're hikers who got a little lost." I pulled the car off State Road 4 and onto Monte Rey Drive South to shut him up. North Monte Rey was closer, but he was griping too much. "Our get-away car is going to take longer to reach from here."

"If we get away," he muttered, following me out of the car and donning his own backpack. There were enough trees and long grass that we weren't very noticeable.

I checked the map a final time and started walking. It was already warm, and I was nervous. "This must be almost a mile away."

He showed his teeth. "You don't need me to help you break in, you need me to make sure she doesn't find you here. You don't know nothin' bout this breaking-in stuff."

"Just get me past the cameras and locks, okay?"

"You coulda given me more to work with by letting me do this at night." He cursed some more while we tramped closer.

My planning wasn't the problem; Sheila's property location was. Los Alamos land hugged the side of her house right across state road four, and the back of the house faced Potrillo Canyon, a natural drop-off cliff. We ignored the "no trespassing sign" on the southeast side of her property. To get near her spiked log fence, we climbed a neighbor's chain-link fence.

Lynx didn't slow down for the chain-link or Sheila's spear-tipped juniper boughs. He had a far easier time with the fences than I did, which was good because he was able to start on her camera system as soon as he was over.

"Can't you cut one of these logs and let me through?" I tried to find a handhold on the juniper fence and failed. The wires binding the logs were too tight for me to rest my feet on and there was nothing to grab except spiked logs.

"I ain't cutting anything. You think I brought a chain-saw? Hurry it up already!" He took off over the broad expanse of rocky ground, running low. Every now and then his blurry form would stop and climb a tree to disable another camera.

I heaved myself up into a nearby juniper tree. No way could I vault over the fence like he did. I clutched my backpack and muttered the flying spell. I canceled it the second I was airborne because I knew what the thing could do to me.

If Lynx had seen me, I'm sure he would have been impressed. The spell shot me twenty feet away from the fence before dropping me on my butt.

I got up and hurried toward the residence. Lynx was waiting by the open back door. "You know, she has a maid," he whispered.

"She's supposed to be gone by now. She only does one hour every weekday morning."

He tilted his head and grunted. "I knew that, but I figured you didn't even know about the maid."

I rolled my eyes and followed him inside the kitchen. "Of course she has a maid." I pointed to the spotless granite countertops. "I assumed that from where she lived. Then it was only a matter of checking the service she hired."

"What if she used someone personal?"

"She didn't, okay?" We were both still whispering. "Now help me look for the papers I told you about."

He shrugged. "This floor plan has a safe, you know."

I peered at him suspiciously. "How do you know that?"

"I tol' you. I looked up the lay of the land when you asked for my help."

"This place was custom built!"

"Don't mean the plans ain't filed by that builder sometime, somewhere. Once you been in a house by one of them, you pretty much know the rest."

I wasn't sure that built-in safes had to be recorded by the architect, but Lynx was the professional thief. I didn't care how he found out. "Fine. Let's check there first."

The kitchen opened into a living room that appeared to had been furnished by an interior decorator with a taste for deep maroon. Wooden mini-blinds were closed to outside light, and a special blind fit the half circle over the front entryway. The hardwood floor gleamed, threatening to show even a slightly wet or dirty footprint.

Lynx led the way soundlessly past a beautifully detailed antique buffet. I started to follow, and then gave the buffet a wide berth. Old things kept things, especially when made of ancient hardwoods. I had seen a china cabinet once that flickered oddly in the dark as though the blood of a murdered man ran down the side. This thing felt like that, dark and moody, waiting for more death.

I slid behind Lynx through the living area and up the stairs. He drifted soundlessly across thick beige carpet to the end of the hallway. At the door to the master bedroom, he surveyed the room silently for a minute. His ears twitched underneath his hair, I just knew it.

The canopy bed was made of wrought-iron. The rest of the furniture was an expensive black panel wood that reflected our movements. As we crossed the room, it was like walking in front of a black mirror.

I shivered. The silver at my wrists tingled a warning. I wanted to be on fresh mother earth worse than the silver.

While Lynx walked into the closet, I waited in the doorway and studied the decorative tapestry that formed a loose canopy over the antique iron bed frame. I couldn't decipher the woven design on the curtain, but recognized enough characters to be certain that a protective spell had been added. "Must have trouble sleeping at night." When I looked at the design out of the corner of one eye, two snakes appeared to be moving up and down the fabric.

I hurried to join Lynx in the master bedroom closet.

A neat row of shirts, organized by color and fabric, lined most of one wall. At the back, there were pants and along the other side, dresses. The dresses appeared to be organized by designer labels, from Klein to Ralph Lauren. The rest of the clothes must have been more expensive because they were hidden behind cloth cover bags.

Lynx had pushed aside some of the shirts and was tinkering with the breaker box. "What looks like breakers act as an alarm if anyone flips them wrong. Don't worry, I know what to touch." He swung the box back on hinges and turned the dial. Impatiently he swatted his hair back from his ear.

Not more than a minute, and he had it opened.

I crept closer and peered inside. The first thing I saw was an open-faced jewelry box. Thick black velvet embraced a long row of amulets. It took my breath away and not because the pendants were of gem value.

This lady wasn't new to the coercion game. Worse, she kept the trophies. Assuming any of these people were still alive, the mere existence of the amulets was probably hurting them. No doubt she had used the things to get what she wanted and then kept them in case she wanted more.

Lynx cursed succinctly, "Witches."

While I should have been insulted, I knew what he meant. There were witches and then there were witches.

Several folders rested in the safe, tucked to the side of the jewelry. What I first took to be ancient Kachina dolls stuffed in the back of the safe were clearly not. "Voodoo," I gulped.

This was not a place to tarry. I set my backpack down, got the replacement papers out and pulled on silk gloves. The silk would protect me from magic to some extent. "Don't touch anything," I warned Lynx in case he thought he could help.

"I ain't no dummy."

The first folder contained mostly pictures. "Blackmail too?" I shook my head and moved on.

The papers I needed were in the third folder. I read the headers on the other documents; they were all lab related, but nothing had Harold's signature except the ones I already knew about. There were no signs she had marked them or bespelled them, but I was very careful. They went into a special lined box before going back inside my backpack. I placed fake papers back inside the safe so that Sheila might not guess what we were up to in time.

"Okay, that's it." I slammed the safe shut and turned to find Lynx sneering.

"You going to leave that stuff there?" he asked in disbelief.

I crossed myself. "I don't know what those spells are for--who they are tied to, which are active or what would happen if I destroyed them. It could kill someone."

His flat expression told me what he thought of being alive while someone held him in the palm of their intent.

"I need one more thing." I headed for the master bathroom, but it didn't take me long to figure out that Little Miss Sheila was a clean freak. There wasn't a hair in the place. Inside the top drawer, I found a hairbrush. Lynx watched over my shoulder. I handed him the brush. "Any chance you can tell if the hair on this is hers?"

He sniffed it. "Human," he declared and handed it back. He went into the bedroom and sniffed the pillow. "These were washed today."

"I'd bet they are washed every day." I eyed the hairbrush. She was a witch of the worst sort. What were the chances she would leave this lying around when the rest of the place was so clean?

I opened three other drawers. There was a stack of brand new toothbrushes in one and another hairbrush. The real brush was probably in her purse. "She can't use a new toothbrush every day!"

"She can't take every bit of herself away," Lynx agreed. He was on the floor now, inspecting the clean tiles.

"No, she can't, but a hair on the floor could belong to her or the maid or you." I tapped my foot impatiently. There was nothing for it. "Open the safe again. Damn."

He had it opened in a heartbeat.

I stared back inside with distaste. Sheila had handled each of these items. I couldn't chance taking one, but I bet she had fondled the things. "Check the bathroom. I need a pair of tweezers, some sort of soft brush--" I pointed to the dressing table. "I think there was makeup over there. See if you can find a makeup brush. I don't care if it is hers or not."

He disappeared and returned shortly with the tweezers. I selected a smooth dark pendent, wishing my silk gloves were heavier--or lined completely with silver. My bracelets let loose warning currents when I snagged the pendant. Whatever was nestled inside moved. My skin tried to crawl off my arm.

Several deep breaths calmed the nausea, but it didn't erase the fear or disgust. I managed to squeak out, "I need you to find packing tape, the clear kind."

"What's a lady like her gonna have packing tape for? I bet someone does all her packages for her."

"Check the study, will you? Maybe the kitchen. Everyone has a junk drawer somewhere."

I left the safe open and took my prize to the bathroom. I found a tin of perfumed powder in the bottom cabinet.

Lynx came back. "Found it." He handed it to me and watched me balance the amulet while trying to tear off a piece of tape.

He put his hand out. "Gimme."

"Fold a piece over for handling it. Don't get your own prints on it either."

He eyed me with disgust, muttered, "witches," and turned his back.

When he handed me the piece of tape it was sliced neatly.

I looked down at his hands, but they looked perfectly normal, stubby and smeared with dirt. "Thanks." I took the tape, patted the amulet with the powered perfume, sneezed into my elbow and voila! A partial print on the side and a smear on the front showed up. I lifted them both onto the tape. "Another piece please?"

He didn't bother to turn around, but I respectfully kept my eyes on my work. As soon as I had both of the prints, I handed the tape back to him. "Put this back. Leave no signs, okay?"

I had her fingerprints--or rather the oil from her hands. It was weak, but it would likely be enough. I cleaned up the mess very carefully, put the amulet back and shut the safe. I hurried back downstairs and found Lynx in the kitchen near the back door. "Ready?" I asked.

Instead of opening the door and slipping out, he said quietly, "I found something."

My feet froze. "What?"

"I'll show you. When I was looking for the tape."

He walked past the sink and pointed to the cherry wood cabinet underneath the countertop. "You told me to check the kitchen, so I was opening all the drawers and cupboards."

He pulled open the cabinet door. There was a locked door behind it, solid steel. It looked like the door to a miniature bank vault, complete with combination lock and handle.

"Wine cabinet?"

"Nah. Most people have a glass door on wine so they can show off. And this is taller than the standard."

"Maybe she has some really valuable stuff."

"Want me to open it?" Lynx asked greedily.

I swallowed. "I have the papers. I don't think--"

He turned to the door, disappointed and moving fast. I guess he figured if he could get the door open before I finished the sentence, it wasn't a "no."

The lock snicked quietly. "I'll check it out. You wait here."

I blinked. I would have called him back, but he had disappeared down a stairway.

Chapter 13

Peering after him down the dark hole did no good. The inky blackness didn't bother him because he could see better than me in the dark. I leaned in and found a light switch.

Not much help. Lynx had already gone beyond where I could see. "Lynx!" I hissed. "We've already been here too long." I looked at my watch. It was nearly eleven. Though I had expected finding the safe to take longer, I had used up any leeway by collecting the fingerprints.

"Lynx?" I called again down the stairs. "Lynx, get back here!" How could I let the kid go into possible danger while I stood there like an idiot?

My skin crawled. I wasn't sure if it was because I couldn't stand myself or I was afraid. I got my answer soon enough when a loud bang sounded below.

I was on the third step down when Lynx nearly bowled me over as he rushed up the stairs past me. His face was dead gray as if he had seen the ghost of his alcoholic mother. Unfortunately, I knew for a fact that Lynx wasn't particularly scared of ghosts, although I think he avoided jobs that involved them.

"Lynx?" I stared after him as he flew through the outside door. He moved so fast, he outran his illusion spell. "Lynx!" I didn't know whether I should follow him or worry about what he had seen--and maybe left behind. "Dammit."

I dithered, but in the end, I ducked down the stairs. The corridor leading down had probably been cut from rock, but it was carefully finished with a dark paneling. Hopping steps as fast I could go, I nearly fell when I grabbed the brass handrail for support. My silk gloves didn't provide good purchase.

If Lynx hadn't run out like his tail had been on fire, I'd have convinced myself it was nothing more than an ordinary wine cellar.

A door at the bottom gaped opened.

What other evidence had he left behind? The lights weren't on in the room, but a quick sweep with one hand found a switch.

When I hit the switch, I wished I hadn't.

I should have asked Viona what Sheila wanted to research, but at the time, I had been more concerned with what the woman was using to coerce Harold. "Oh my...God in heaven." I crossed myself. My hands shook so badly, I couldn't hit the light switch again.

A noise at the top of the stairs made me get it right on the second try. Was Lynx coming back? I couldn't be sure. Had the lights still been on, I don't think I could have forced my legs inside that room filled with hundreds of mal-formed, diseased, and grotesque rats. The creatures were missing eyes, or had too many...there were things that didn't even look like a rat anymore. I wished my heart would beat louder to shut out the hundreds of squeaks coming from the cages.

No wonder Harold hadn't wanted to sign for Sheila's research. From my one glimpse, it looked as though the woman was strongly inclined towards abusing her test subjects and looking for creative ways to kill--not heal or understand disease.

The lights went on. It wasn't Lynx. Sheila, platinum hair pulled back from her face, stood to the side of the doorway, holding a gun. She wasn't as old as I expected; probably only mid-forties. Her nose was slightly hooked, and with the current snarl on her face, she was easily unattractive. Her eyes searched the room quickly. For a fraction of a second, I forgot about my illusion spell.

With the next breath, I smashed the inside package containing the stronger daylight spell.

I was mist; humidity, a reflection off the glass cages. *Oh Lord, don't let her shoot. Don't let her accidentally let any of those* things *out.*

If she shot through a cage and one of the rat-looking things with what appeared to be a human arm came at me--then again, if I stood here long enough she was going to figure out that I was there. The illusion spell would keep her from looking at me, but as a witch, she would see through it eventually. I had another awful thought. What if she closed the door and *locked me inside?*

That was it. She could shoot me if she wanted. I moved behind a row of cages, watching my feet so that I didn't make any noise. She hadn't entered the room yet, and it didn't look as though she was going to. If I didn't get back out fast I could be trapped.

When her arm moved to the door, I ran. I stepped hard on the helium and tilted myself forward, muttering the words for wind.

Like a rocket, I shot past her. She was sideways, against the door, about to close it. The wind behind me curled through the doorway, and she crouched down instinctively.

I didn't cancel the spell even when I was past her. Hands out, I pushed off the narrow stairwell, wishing she had left solid rock rather than finishing the walls with slippery wood.

A bullet bit into the ceiling, but the wind at my back shoved me up the stairs so quickly, I'm not sure it could have caught me. One day, I was going to tone down this flying spell, but not today.

I should have canceled it the minute I was in the kitchen, but I could hear her behind me. The back door was closed. Probably locked. I hit the ceiling and had nowhere to go.

Frantically, I grabbed at the wall, the wind still pushing me, forcing the air out of my lungs. I clawed at a high cabinet door. The rest of me, powered by wind, went sideways, shoving my feet over my head.

Sheila came through the small doorway shooting. Thankfully, she was focused on the back door.

I aimed my feet as best I could and let go.

I hit the window over the sink, feet first. The sound of shattering glass didn't stop even when I was through.

I looked back in time to see the window next to where I had gone out burst apart in a rainbow of glass. The window was below me--and getting further away by the second. I was gaining altitude at a frightening pace.

"Exitor," I mumbled.

The blue sky turned into a flash of green and brown. The fence was close enough that if wind had been blowing just right, a spiked limb might have snagged me.

I hit hard, but it barely slowed me down. My shakes were so bad, I moved across the dirt like a jelly blob, making progress as some sort of an amoeba.

My stomach was a pit of fear. Had I left any blood on the glass?

Frantically, I felt my face. One silk glove had been nearly torn off, and the sleeve on my left arm had a ragged slash. I pushed it up. There was no blood on my arm...yes, there was a thin scratch. It didn't look bloody, just red.

There was no time to do anything about it. I dodged around trees, jumped over rocks and wished for the wind at my back, but I didn't dare.

There were no more shots fired, not that I could hear. It would be hard for her to target me through the fence and the invisibility spell. Maybe she would be looking up, the last place I had been before canceling the spell.

My arm throbbed even though there was only a minuscule scratch on it. There was little to no chance she would be able to find a single piece of glass or splintered wood that might or might not contain a scrap of my blood. I got myself back to the car by a circuitous route.

I checked every inch of my body that I could see. No blood. My eyes watered in relief. I didn't want that lady getting *anything* from me. Shivering violently, despite the ninety-degree air inside the car, I sat without moving for several minutes. My backpack may have lost a few fibers.

The whole thing, my jeans, my shirt, even my underwear had to be burned. I needed a mirror to make sure there were no cuts on my back. There was no McDonalds in White Rock, and I didn't have time to drive to Los Alamos to the one on Trinity Drive to use as a restroom. After another frantic check in car mirror, I started to calm down. "Hair." I had probably lost a few hairs despite my braid. Would she find them? Could she be sure they were mine? Her hair was white. Mine was about as far from blond as hair gets.

"Okay, one thing at a time." I looked at my watch. "Lynx, my friend, where did you run to?" It was now past eleven-thirty.

He had been running for…twenty minutes, half hour?

He could probably get himself back home, but I couldn't leave him out here in his present state of mind.

I started the car and drove up and down the streets until I hit the only main drag in town. At a gas station burger joint, I ordered four cheeseburgers, a chocolate shake and French fries. I ate the fries and drank the milkshake on my way back to the neighborhood near Sheila's house.

I dug out the tracking spell from my backpack. It was set to Harold to find the papers he had touched and signed. Thankfully, I hadn't needed to use it.

Lynx was a smart kid and too careful to leave stray hairs in the front seat of my car, but he had been there recently enough that I could change the spell over. I removed Harold's hair from the fork and stashed it carefully in a silk sleeve inside the box with the papers. Using a pocket knife, I whittled away any remaining evidence of Harold. When I was finished, I rolled the branch across the seat. Lynx had sat here last, and it hadn't been long ago. It should work.

I grabbed water bottles from the trunk, left the burgers for Lynx when we got back, and headed out. I didn't think he'd go into the Los Alamos territory, not after what we had seen, but there was still a lot of wilderness to cover. There were trails all over the neighborhood. There were houses too, but he would avoid those.

Then again, he hadn't been running with a plan.

"Lynx, sit yourself down and get a hold of yourself," I ordered the empty air. It was noon. At least it wasn't dark out.

The willow branch didn't want to leave the vicinity of the car, and it first tried to go back to Sheila's house. Since I knew Lynx wasn't going back there ever again, I ignored its pull until it started indicating the canyon.

"Lynx…" I wondered if he had tried heading back to the car on some route he had picked. It was possible there were trails right from Sheila's house down into the canyon, although most spots were far too steep--for humans.

I made my way back to the car and parked in a different spot before studying the maps again. There were trails into the canyon. He had mentioned the park…I traced routes.

There were at least two trails into the canyon that looked viable. The one by the park was too far away, but there was another exit from the canyon at a place marked Red Dot Trail. With my link to him, if he was in the canyon I should be able to find him, although he had better be heading my way to get out rather than deeper into Potrillo Canyon and Los Alamos land.

Cursing my luck and still wondering if Sheila could trace us both, I emptied what I didn't need from my pack and headed down. The trail was bad. It looked like it had been hiked one time a hundred years ago by a desperate gold miner who needed to get to water.

The canyon trapped the air and the sun beat straight down. My hands were too busy helping me ease over steep rocks to wipe the sweat away.

Periodically, I stopped to drink water. It was hard not to sway, to give into vertigo. The shattered, jagged boulders from years of rock slides, the Rio Grande snaking below and the mountains of Santa Fe in the distance would have taken my breath away if I'd had any left to spare.

Luckily the steep down was little more than a mile. The canyon eased off its death threats as I got lower. A few trees started to grace the gentler slopes and the map showed springs.

No one could have been more grateful than I to find water there. I cooled off and tried the spell on the willow branch.

Nothing.

I tried it again when I hit the Rio Grande. I couldn't be certain if the vibration was hot wind off the water or a tease, but I headed deeper into White Rock Canyon, staying alongside the river and hoping.

I passed at least two old Indian sites. They were all over the mountains in this part of New Mexico, although these looked like nothing more than mud spots that might have been temporary shelters. It was in a crevice of one such shelter where I found Lynx, huddled and maybe crying.

I made sure he was aware of my presence before I said, "Lynx, it's time to go home."

He whispered something I couldn't hear. A breeze picked at his torn shirt.

"Are you okay?"

"That lady, why you mess with her?" He was breaking all the rules by asking questions about a job.

"She's the one who put the love potion on Vi's husband. We had to get the papers back to help Vi's husband."

He lifted his head. His eyes were dry, but I couldn't tell much else. "Those people at the labs, that's pure evil!" He crossed himself.

I almost laughed. Lynx was not a Christian in any sense of the word. He made fun of me for going to church on a regular basis. I made the sign of the cross back at him. "You'll note," I pointed out dryly, "that those animals weren't at the *labs*. They were hidden inside her home."

He shook his head. "Burn it. Burn the whole place down!"

"Lynx," I dared to reach out and shake his shoulder. "Your client hired you to get rid of a coercion spell that was going to help that lady obtain funding to continue her work. Vi and her husband were against it. We got the signed papers that might have given Sheila money. Not everyone at the lab is into that stuff."

His eyes flashed so wide, I could see the white. "Evil!"

I shook my head. "If people at the lab were doing her kind of research, she wouldn't have had to use a potion to befuddle Harold's mind so that he would sign. Besides, I read the headers on the papers she wanted him to sign. The experiments are nothing like what she has going on in her home. My guess is she needs access to funds and will stop at nothing to get them."

"What's the difference if it happens at the lab or not if she gets money to do it? Burn it," he said again.

I sat down next to him, my back against the hard-packed earth. The sun was shifting, but still hot. It would be a relief when shadows stretched across the ground, eating the light and heat. "She probably takes chemicals from the lab, but that doesn't mean she is supposed to. Our client was trying to stop her. Not all scientists are made of the same brain." I held out my hand. "Not all witches make the same potions."

We sat that way for the better part of an hour, until close to three o'clock. I offered him a water bottle, but he ignored me.

Finally, after another half-hour he stood up. If his pants sported any new holes, I couldn't tell them from the old ones. "It wouldn't do no good to set them free, would it?"

I shook my head, not having to look up very far to meet his eyes from where I sat. "I went down to shut the door, Lynx. There's nothing there to save."

His hands balled into fists.

To distract him, I teased, "You could have at least run in the direction of home. This way we have to walk all the way back to the car and drive home." I handed him the water bottle.

"I didn't charge enough for this job." He took the water and slugged the contents noisily.

"What are you going to do with all the money you make anyway? Your prices are too high. You need to cut me a break now that you see all the dangerous work I have to do."

He drank until the water was gone. With a satisfied burp, he handed the bottle back and started walking. "I'm gonna buy me a house," he said. He picked his way along, dodging a cactus and never missing a step.

"A house?" I wouldn't have been more surprised if he told me he was building a rocket ship to leave earth.

"Sure," he said. "Soon as you have a house, no one tries to put you in protective services. They figure you have an adult, and they stop asking questions. See, even if you run a," he tilted his head, "a business like mine, so long as you run it out of a house, it's legitimate."

"Uh, Lynx--"

He waved a hand. "Sure, some of it is illegal. But with a house, you can pretty much cover up anything by acting like a normal, you know?" He flashed his white teeth back in my direction. "Just like you. You do your witch stuff, but you act like a normal, and everyone leaves you alone."

"I don't pretend to be a normal, Lynx."

"Yes, you do. So do all the others. The ones that pretend the best survive."

I started to argue, but couldn't. Witch or not, there was a lot of pretending that went on in life.

Chapter 14

We were on the first uphill stretch, perhaps a quarter of a mile from the Rio Grande when Sheila hit. My back arched all on its own, a spasm as though I had been knocked hard from behind. The small cachet of herbs that had allowed me to be almost invisible burst into flame. "No!"

I threw my backpack off and started dumping things out of it. My shirt came off as I danced around, shaking the backpack. Lynx grabbed the pack from me and started helping.

"Fire," I panted. "Get a fire going, hurry." I tried to point out the lighter that had been in my backpack, but violent shivers took hold, making my aim useless. My jeans got stuck on my hiking boots, and I had to slow down to get them off. "Hurry," I screamed in an agonized whisper. "Hurry!"

Lynx scooped together a few juniper needles and yanked on blades of dry grass.

My turquoise necklace had been warm from my skin, but it was on fire now, fighting the cold that shook me.

"Lynx…"

He kept breathing life into the flames he was starting.

There were things I needed to tell him, but maybe he was right to prioritize one task at a time. I pushed through the remains of my pack and found a bundle to help the fire. I threw the dust onto it.

"Shirt and backpack first," I chattered. I bit back the "hurry."

I pushed my hiking shoes close to the edge of the flames. They were mostly leather and would take the longest, but they were not likely to have supplied Sheila with whatever part of me she had found. I was damn lucky she had chosen revenge over tracking me. Or maybe she had tried to track me, and it hadn't worked, but I doubted it. Whatever she was doing was strong.

"More of that powder?" Lynx asked, surveying the small flames.

I was tempted, but I didn't want to start a grass fire in the canyon. "Just--" I thought of something. "Can you make it back to the car?" I had to stop and breathe slowly before I could continue. "I parked near the trailhead. There's a blanket in the back and a case with some supplies." It was over a mile straight uphill to the car. It would take me the better part of an hour to make it, but I was pretty sure Lynx could travel faster than I could.

Lynx looked skeptical. "What about the fire? You sure you can take care of it? What about me? Can she find me?"

I tried to shake my head, but the rest of me was shaking too. "N..no. I don't think she knows there were two of us. You were gone."

"Okay." He picked up the keys from the mess and was gone before I could tell him about the cheeseburgers I had bought him.

I got as close to the flames as I dared, but it didn't help. The cold came from inside. As I slowly fed one pant leg into the fire, the shirt finished burning. The backpack was a mess of melted nylon, smoldering on one side. "Come on."

Teeth chattering, I sorted through my things. Hating it, I doused myself with the last of the water. It nearly killed me, but it helped slightly. There was water back at the Rio Grande, but I couldn't chance wandering around. Not only that, the currents there could be dangerous.

I finally pushed the jeans fully onto the flames. It nearly smothered the fire. My hands were too unsteady to hold the lighter, so I waited, shivering and talking to myself. I lost track of time, but kept the fire going. At one point I was so cold, I burned my fingers before I realized what was happening.

Lynx called out before coming into the circle of smoke. He didn't realize I wasn't capable of setting a spell right now. Besides, I wasn't about to use magic. If I were looking for a witch who broke into my house, I'd key to any magic in the area. A spell could lead her to me, or worse, make her spell stronger.

He handed me the blanket and the small zipped pack where I kept a few extra herbs. I stuck some willow bark in my cheek, but it would take a while to help, if it did at all.

"I saved you a burger," Lynx said.

My teeth chattered as I tried to talk. "I..d..on't--"

"It might help?" He broke off a chunk and handed it to me.

I stuck it in my mouth, but chewing was almost impossible. "Got...to... go." I said. At least that's what I was trying to say. I was so cold, I couldn't think.

Lynx shoved my boots further into the fire. The rubber on the bottom smelled horrible as it burned. We both moved out of the smoke, me huddled against a tree trunk under the blanket; him keeping watch.

"Soon as it burns down, we'll get." He took off his shoes and tossed them my way. "I don't need them."

It took me a while to tie the blanket under one arm, squaw style. The shoes went on okay, but I couldn't tie them. Lynx leaned over and did it for me. His eyes were narrow and yellow with the firelight behind him. I was either very cold or the kid was half-changed. If I hadn't been freezing to death on a hot summer day, I'd have been impressed. Few shifters could control the change enough to only take on some of their animal aspects.

"You better eat this." He handed me the rest of the burger. I wanted to tell him about the fries and shake, but it was too much trouble.

He had also found my rain poncho in the car. He tied off the arm and neck holes so that he could fill it with the stuff that had been in the backpack. "Any of this need to burn?"

I shook my head, still chewing my second bite of burger. Nothing in the backpack could have been left behind at Sheila's house. The bag itself was probably what caused the problem. No doubt some of the fibers caught on the broken glass. Maybe some of my shirt too. I didn't want to look at my arm, at the reminder of the scratch. The thought of her hunting through the glass and maybe finding a tiny scrape of my skin, hair or blood...

Lynx added more juniper needles, dried leaves and a log.

"Don't...have time!" I said.

He stared at me. From across the fire, I could tell he was scared. "Is she coming here?" His voice cracked. Maybe it was the fire.

"Don't know. Got to get this spell...off me." My brain was numb. I couldn't figure out what she was doing to me. With regular voodoo, she could cause me pain. If she had my blood...she could try to control me or call me back, but this was some other type of torture. It almost felt as though she were trying to kill me outright by stopping my circulation.

I looked down at my hand. The fingers were cramped, blue. Did she think she could stop my heart? *What did she have of mine?* My body shuddered harder and dizziness took over.

Lynx smacked the back of my shoulders. "You're breathing funny. Fast. Then stopping. Are you gonna die?"

Yellow eyes peered into mine. "Burn it...faster," I gasped out. I wasn't sure if I was hyperventilating on my own or if Sheila had enough of me to stop my breathing.

Lynx obeyed, shoving the backpack further into the flames and feeding the mess with more dead pine needles. "Shirt and pants are gone completely." He poked at the fire with a stick. "Backpack needs to melt more."

As did the shoes. We didn't have time. "I'm going...for Pajarito Springs. Give it..." How long would it take me? "Give it what you can, then put it out." I stood up. Dizziness pushed me back down. "First cold water," I instructed. "Then..." I closed my mouth, knowing it was hopeless.

"What herbs do you want?" he asked.

He was a smart kid. "Not in my packs," I panted.

"I know. But I can get them."

"Sage. Corn pollen, white and blue. I have white in this sachet, but not the other two." I stared at the packet and tried to remember what to do with the pollen.

He stared off and breathed in deep. "Sage I can do. The other will have to wait." He came over and gave me the stick he had been using in the fire. It was sturdy.

I felt slightly better when I started moving. Sitting had only made me colder. I clutched my turquoise necklace and walked. Since the path was uphill, I tried running a few times, but the shivers unbalanced me.

I made the spring. Off the main crossing, there was a giant boulder, a scant waterfall, and a pool of water probably formed by some kids blocking the stream. Great on a hot summer day after the steep hike down, but I did not want to get in. Cold spring water might cure me, but it could kill me first.

I unwrapped the blanket and took off Lynx's shoes. I bit back a scream when my foot hit the damp earth. Scrambling backwards, I fell. At that point, nothing on earth could have convinced me to get in that water, but I was clumsy. If I hadn't been, I'd probably have died.

Screaming, I slid into the water, unable to get my feet under me.

The minute my head went under, I knew the truth. The water blocked the spell. Running over the rocks, across me and over the slight dam, the water took some of the spell that was stuck on me and washed it away.

My teeth chattered, but I forced my head back under, too scared to chance muttering a spell of my own.

I felt the sage when Lynx threw it in. He didn't bother to collect a few leaves. He tossed an entire bush in, roots and all. A branch dragged across my neck before fingers of it tangled in my hair.

"Lynx, what in the--" I came up sputtering.

"There's a lot of spring water in this stream. I didn't have time to harvest leaves."

No point in arguing. I pulled some of the leaves off, breathing in the heavenly scent. It made me sneeze. I gagged and pushed my head back under, still holding the bush.

Under water, I felt my way to the bank and pushed the torn roots into the soil as best I could. I didn't chance breathing the sage too deeply again, but I broke off a small piece to keep.

Sputtering, I crawled out. The blanket was mostly out of the water and Lynx held it in one hand while dragging me out with the other.

"I'm going to have to make good time up this mountain," I told him.

"You go. This mess needs to disappear." He waved his arm to encompass the slide marks on the soil. He was right. A blind man could smell where we'd been and anyone else could see it.

I got moving. Before I was halfway up, my teeth started chattering again. There was no more water on the way up to save me. I took the little pack of corn pollen out and clutched it, but I needed water to block her. I should have used the pollen at the stream, but I hadn't been thinking straight.

By the time I made the car and got in, I was talking to myself and answering too. Part of me muttered, "Find Sheila," and the other part of me screamed, "No!" Sheila must have given up on killing me and decided to go with an easier spell--force me back to her lair.

I wasn't going. I'd rather she kill me.

After starting the engine and getting the heater going, I sat there like an idiot, my teeth clenched around the sage twig. I wasn't sure I should drive.

Lynx confirmed it when he got to the car. He had to wake me up. My face was drenched in sweat, but I was still cold. As Lynx dragged me into the backseat he said, "You're burning up."

"Just...a fever," I tried reassuring him. "Fighting..." I didn't know how my body was fighting, but it was fighting. Either that or Sheila was tiring. No one could run spells forever.

I fell into restless slumber in the back seat, knowing that distance would make the spell lose some of its grip.

I hoped.

Somewhere along the drive, Lynx asked, "Do I take you to the hospital or another witch?"

"No!" The hospital might help, but I couldn't afford that from either a magical standpoint or a pocketbook one. Sheila might expect me to go to the hospital. I wasn't taking any chances on her finding me. "Got to...break the fever. Water--"

"Cold or hot?"

"Don't speed," I coughed. "You have a half naked woman in the back." I sat up. Dizziness pushed me back down. "First cold water. Then...the herbs." I closed my mouth to keep from biting my tongue during the hard shivers.

"Same herbs you mentioned before? I can get them from your store room or somewhere else if I have to."

"Sage. Corn pollen, white and blue," I repeated through clenched teeth.

"Okay."

As far as my brain was concerned, the rest of the ride didn't happen. Next thing I knew, I was on the shower floor, cold water spraying all over my face. The blanket was gone, and I was still in my bra and underwear, shivering so hard I thought my teeth would crack. *"Lynx,"* I yelled. "I'm going to kill you."

It didn't take me long to find my feet and get the water shut off. Whether I liked it or not, it helped. Water could very well be the best purifier there was. Many spells, especially long-distance ones, couldn't travel through it. Reluctantly, I turned the water back on. "Cold," I howled. "Cold, cold, cold!"

In the tub next to the shower, I could see that Lynx had started filling it with warm water. I could jump from cold straight to hot. "Dammit."

I rinsed off, letting the water bring any vestiges of fever down and hopefully kill most of the spell remnants. Through the glass I saw Lynx come back in. My teeth still chattered, but it was real cold, coming from without, not within.

"How much of this stuff do you want in there?" he asked me.

"Quarter cup of sage and tablespoon of each of the other."

He sprinkled it properly, tossing it respectfully away from his body and muttering the proper words. Even though he didn't have a witch bone in his body so far as I knew, he apparently had paid attention to a few rituals.

I managed to get myself into the tub.

He left me in peace to try and recuperate. At least I think he did. It was all I could do to finish the required rituals. I tripped over my poncho full of backpack things on my way to the bed. If I hadn't, I might not have noticed the fresh picked sage leaves scattered around my bed.

Crawling under the covers, I found another surprise. My pillow now housed a dirty, disgusting packet of herbs. I recognized the woven pattern on the band meant to serve as a wristband. Lynx had left me his own protection packet, one I had made for him years ago as part of an early payment.

Dirty as it was, I clutched it in my hand and fell asleep.

Chapter 15

Viona was expecting me even though it was after five o'clock the next evening before I could drag myself to her house. Eager hands reached for the papers before she bothered to invite me inside. She stared at her husband's signature granting the request for funds.

"I'm not sure when she was planning on turning them in," I told her, "but it looks like we were in time."

"Next week," she murmured, using her free hand to push straggles of hair away from her face. "We had until next week. All the budgets are getting done, and this would have gone into the head office with all the other requests as though he had approved it." She gulped in air as if she had forgotten to breathe.

"Will you be able to convince your husband that we've replaced the papers with fakes?" I was more concerned about Harold now that I had an inkling of how Sheila directed her talents. I feared for Vi's life, that of her husband and every field mouse that happened to be close to where Sheila lived.

Vi must have heard something in my tone because her eyes left the papers in a hurry. "What do you mean?"

"If you tell your husband we planted fake papers is he strong enough to tell those above him that Sheila turned in fake papers with a badly forged signature? Remember, the papers I left behind have a signature because we don't want Sheila to notice a blank line. Harold will still have to point out that he didn't sign the papers."

"Didn't you reverse the spell? Won't he return to normal?" Her shrill voice nearly split my eardrums.

I pushed past her into the entry way so that we could close the door. The way her voice carried, the entire valley would hear her business. "I believe I mentioned that the plan was to get the papers back to stop the worst of the damage. I did not say it would solve everything."

"What do you think I hired you for? Can you reverse the spell or not?"

Having seen the lengths Sheila was willing to go, I had no doubt that we were not up against a single, simple spell. "I don't think so."

"I'll hire someone else!"

"You could, but your husband has been badly used. He was likely reeled in over and over until Sheila proved to him that she was master and he slave."

She raised her chin and started to speak.

"Abuse like that leaves scars," I said softly. "Those scars are now separate from the spell itself. You mentioned that your husband had withdrawn. How bad has that gotten?"

Her brown eyes didn't waver, but her chin came down a notch. The tailored pantsuit she wore didn't go with the worn makeup and the pinched lines around her mouth. When she finally answered her voice was small. "He's not eating unless I force him. He goes to work, but I don't think he does any work. He sits. I've gotten him anti-depressants and an appetite stimulant."

"Does he go into work as though drawn there or out of habit?"

"At first it was..." She leaned heavily against the wall. "He was depressed, listless, but he went to work as though soldiering on, as though it might kill him, but he would carry on."

"When did it change?"

She waved her hand. "He--after the papers. I think he was fighting her then."

"He probably thought that by telling you about the first set of papers he might break Sheila's hold over him." I paced a step away. "She likely noticed the fight."

"She planned on me finding out!"

"How is he now?" I asked.

Her shoulders slumped. We stared at each other for a few moments. I reached out, but didn't quite touch her. Instead I turned and led the way into the living room toward the leather seats.

"Harold missed work several days, refused to go," she said from behind me. "That's when we went in for the anti-depressants. He went back to work. Then it got even worse. I don't know what happened." She was crying openly now.

"Compulsion spell, I would imagine. He goes to work now whether he wants to or not."

Vi put one foot in front of the other and came toward the living room. She ignored the tears dripping off her chin. "He goes."

"My guess is that after he defied her, she reeled him back in again, sexually and in other ways to prove she was boss. At that time, she probably got..." I didn't want to be too graphic. "It's like voodoo. She will have taken things from him to make the ties stronger. And then called him back like a puppet until his will was broken."

"It's not about sex," Vi mumbled, covering her mouth with her hand as though to keep in a scream.

"It never was. Unfortunately, sex is a very common way to break a person down." There was no easy way to say it.

"Can't you steal back whatever she took from him?" she begged. "Can't you find this thing, this hair, his fingernails--" she choked off because I was shaking my head.

"No." I delivered this sad news knowing that by now his blood had to be involved. "There's no good way to know where she stored anything she took, but best guess is it stays on her person in what is called an amulet." I had to swallow to keep from gagging. "Since your husband is her current focus, I doubt she ever takes it off, especially at work. He would know the object, at least subconsciously. She would show it to him, display it openly. It's part of the torture."

"He's destroyed," she whispered. "She's completely destroyed him!"

"That's why I replaced the papers with fakes. He might benefit if he is able to tell his superiors that the signature on the new papers is forged. It will give him a sense of control, and it will catch Sheila by surprise." There was no point in mentioning that Sheila had found me in her house. She had no reason to believe I had gotten in the safe and no reason to suspect the papers had been replaced. If she did notice, Harold wasn't any worse off than he had been before I got involved.

Vi finally reached into her pocket for a tissue. "Why can't you steal this amulet thing from her person?"

Now I did choke. It took me two tries to get out, "Even if I did, destroying the amulet could kill him depending on how tightly he is bound."

"Maybe he'd rather be dead than owned." The anger was back in her voice, and I wasn't sure if she was speaking for her husband or for herself.

"He could die as we try to release him with or without destroying the amulet. You'll have to live with that."

"He's almost dead now." She sank down into a chair, wiping at her face. "If you can't cure it, what can be done?"

I sighed. "If we do this right, we can wean him away over the next few weeks." I reached for my backpack, but I no longer had one. I dug what I wanted out of my fanny pack. "We want to make sure he's at work to stop that funding from going through. Part of his healing will be regaining control. Every step he takes to defy her is going to help fix this." I didn't tell her how hard it was to fight a blood spell. "I have a pack for him."

She sniffed and wiped her eyes, but made no move to take my offer. "Add more witchcraft?" She shook her head.

"Don't worry, it's nothing like her spells. I made it fresh this morning--a mix of sage, sweet grass, tobacco and cedar. The elements in the packet will begin the purification process and offer a small buffer. It isn't protection exactly because it won't stop her since she is already within the borders of his mind. It's more like a wall to buffer the pull that he probably feels all the time."

"Can't you cut the pull completely? Snap it in half, burn it, destroy it?"

I shook my head. "Not without damaging him, not at this point. In the end, I'm not going to be the one to do it either. I'd recommend a medicine man who can do a spiritual ceremony or a priest willing to perform an exorcism. Your choice, really."

"Exorcism?"

I shrugged. "There are ceremonies that will break the ties. But we can't do it too soon or it will kill him. First we have to strengthen his mind and teach him to fight her."

"Oh...damn her."

"You'll need to spend time with him," I said. "Hold his hands, walk with him--force him to re-accept himself and you--someone other than *her*. Part of, let's call it possession, is isolation. He has no source of command, of strength, other than her, including what used to be his own strength."

"He won't let me near him."

"I know. But we have to make him see that he isn't protecting you by doing so, he's hurting himself more. He's taking away his own best weapons. Like the spell contained in the herbs I'm going to give you, you are a source of strength."

With a deep breath, she put her hand out flat. She didn't look at me or the herbs.

I put the pack in it. "One other thing," I added. "She's probably left reminders here, objects that he brought home that contain auras."

"Items that help control him, you mean," she spit out.

"I doubt she does much active controlling from far away. If she does, he'll have to leave here completely. Otherwise as we start edging him away, she'll know and tighten her control. That could end up destroying him. The longer we can keep her from knowing we're fighting, the better."

"His briefcase." She bounced up and disappeared down the hallway. "He hasn't let it out of his sight."

"He's here now? Why didn't you say so? I could have told him all this!"

"He doesn't believe in witchcraft," she threw back over her shoulder, still moving.

I let out a frustrated breath. "Great." It was always easy to obtain cooperation from people who didn't believe what was happening.

I followed her into what should have been a sunny study, but all the blinds were closed. I almost missed the hunched man behind the desk. If he slid any further in his seat, he'd be a puddle on the floor.

"Witchcraft?" he mumbled. "No. Bad." Small eyes blinked in confusion. His mostly bald head didn't turn my way.

I went to the large wooden blinds and dared open them a crack. As expected, he shrank back and let out a cry as though struck. "Light is another good start," I said.

Before I could open the blinds completely, I felt a prickle against the back of my neck. The protective silver at my neck and wrists tingled. Without moving, I looked around the room. Vi was stuffing papers into the briefcase.

"I don't know what is current and what isn't," she said.

"Leave it," I commanded. I had fully intended to do a purge of the house, but something in here had reacted badly to the light. It may have acted as a signal. I closed the blinds. "Let's go."

I grabbed Vi's arm and drew her towards the door.

Sensing danger, she reached for her husband. "Not yet," I snapped.

We backed carefully out of the room. Harold's eyes fluttered closed.

"What?" she whispered.

"Come on. I want to find a safe place to move him. But first, we're going to need a few things." I had a disturbing thought. "Do you do your own grocery shopping?"

She nodded. "About half the time."

"Good, you won't look too suspicious going shopping. First item I want you to get is a frog. In its own aquarium."

"A frog?"

I nodded. "Let's get some paper. I have a rather long list."

We went into the kitchen, a place I figured would be safe, because Sheila wouldn't bother with every room in the house. What were the chances that Harold cooked?

I took out the compass I had spelled earlier in the day. The oil from Sheila's fingerprint acted as the indicator, and I wasn't after north. Instead of pointing calmly at anything contaminated by Sheila the arrow went haywire.

"Hmm. Did your husband cook a lot?"

"Before this all started he did."

I hunted around a bit, looking for an item that might be tied to her, but the spell acted funny, spinning wildly. "Has Harold bought anything new for the kitchen lately?" The compass refused to give me a single direction. My skin prickled, much as it had in the study. "Let's go."

I didn't have to grab her arm this time; she was on my heels.

As soon as we left the kitchen the compass stopped spinning. "Interesting." And a pain in the neck. There was way too much of Sheila around or she had found a way of confusing the spell I was using.

"Where did you put his briefcase?"

"I left it when you--what is going on?"

"There's more of Sheila around than a couple of spells. In order to control Harold, she had to leave something that was her essence, but it's stronger and more prevalent than I expected. I thought perhaps Sheila had sent your husband home with objects, but it looks like she was actually here."

Vi bristled. "That's not possible."

I shrugged. "Your husband could have disabled the alarms for her. He wouldn't even have had to be here at the time. I'm pretty sure you weren't here because whatever she did took a lot of time." I was whispering now. "Let's see if I can find a place she didn't mess with."

The hallway was a mess. I knew the study was, so I headed back to the living room. The compass gave me better vibes except for one plant. "Is this new?"

"No." She picked it up with instant distaste. "Back yard?"

"Keep it by the door just in case. Keep it watered too." I wasn't sure it would live in the heat, but if it died slowly enough, it wouldn't matter.

Once the living room was "clean," we sat down, and I gave her a shopping list.

She read it twice, and then her back straightened. "We get him out of that study *today*."

I smiled. "It might be late tonight, but it should be doable." Then I had to warn, "This isn't the cure you know. It's only the beginning."

She didn't answer because she was too busy grabbing her purse and heading out the door.

Chapter 16

After Vi left, I started in the master bedroom. I was surprised to find almost no aura of Sheila until I remembered that Harold didn't sleep there anymore. Sheila had put enough objects around the house to force Harold into the study. Knowing his location would allow her to call him if she wanted him--and if not, she could soak him in nasty spells since he was sitting there docile and half dead.

If someone like me tampered with her setup, no doubt, she had spells to warn her. She could fight back instantly--unless I was very, very careful.

After a thorough search, I finally found a single rune under the bed, but it didn't look as though it had ever been activated. "I *hate* runes."

They couldn't be erased; they had to be undone. That could take hours because I'd first have to understand the damn thing. I could probably block it with cedar when Vi brought planks back, but I didn't like leaving it there. I swallowed hard. Sheila was damned evil. I didn't like being in a house that was her focus. My muscles still ached from whatever she had thrown at me the day before. I was still very afraid and nervous.

"I'll cut a hole in the damn carpet." I didn't have as many supplies in my fanny pack as I usually carried in my backpack, but I had brought the most important things. If Vi followed my instructions, there would be a few pertinent extras when she returned.

I took out protective herb packets and an extra silver ring for my right hand. The bracelet on my left wrist had a special silver chain wrapped and hooked around one side. I unhooked it, looped the silver chain around my middle finger and secured it. Silver and turquoise were my protection; my tie to mother earth. The chain loops were a series of unique shapes, including a medicine bear and a bat carved from silver under a full moon. The bear was a powerful protector and healer; the bat a shield and stealthy friend.

The chemical links in Sheila's rune had to be broken, but unfortunately, I hadn't seen this particular rune before. I studied the lines, looking for a weakness, looking for a door. The start and end places might work, but a weak link would be better...or where the lines were too close or a bit crooked.

Maybe...

I sprinkled sage over the area. That alone would probably keep it from activating, but Vi had a good maid. She might vacuum the sage up.

I was about to cut the carpet when the sage started smoking. "Aztec curses!" I scooted as quickly as possible out from under the bed. I threw open a window and tried not to breathe any of the wisps floating out from under the bed.

I shoved against the heavy oak frame, but it barely budged. I wondered what my chances were of getting Harold to help.

"None," I muttered in despair. I pushed again, more frantically this time. The house could start on fire. Even if it didn't, I didn't want to breathe those herbs mixing with God knew what.

I finally dragged the mattress off the top, sat on the floor with my back to the bed and pushed with my legs. It moved enough that I could see part of the rune.

The master bath was the closest source of water. I soaked a sponge and ran back over. After three trips, the carpet stopped smoking.

More water could help break the rune. On the other hand, Sheila was likely to know I had messed with it. "Aztec curses and Mayan sacrifices!"

Using the sponge, I soaked the spot. Very carefully, I ran the diluted mess back across where the sage had been. Diluted rune! I hadn't thought of that. I quickly soaked the edges so that the dried chemicals spread. No way would Vi and Harold want to sleep over the spot, but it gave me another idea.

I found a phone and on Vi's behalf, ordered carpet cleaning. "Yes, today. I've spilled something. Of course I'll pay extra."

The earliest they could make it was tomorrow.

I hung up muttering, "Damn runes." Sheila would probably notice her missing rune, but if she checked, hopefully she'd confuse it with the carpet cleaning even if it were a day late.

To be more certain, I made a second pass in the bedroom and pushed the bed further away. Next, I tackled the bedroom where Harold had been sleeping.

I couldn't even go in the place. The back of my neck itched. The silver on my arms went cold and then hot.

There might have been a rune across the door, but I couldn't be sure. Sheila was beyond scary. Without going in, I identified a few bad objects, but I let them be.

A carpet cleaning in that room might dilute any runes, but it wouldn't help much. To be consistent, the cleaners should go in there, but I didn't want to ruin so much that Sheila would feel a need to come back and replace anything.

The study wasn't too bad at first, but anything near the desk was at least as bad as the room where Harold slept. If I'd had a choice, I'd have burned the briefcase, but it was too dangerous. I left it and the rest of the room alone.

Two other rooms had questionable objects. The spells on them had worn down, but I didn't see any point in leaving them inside the house, so they went out with the plant.

Vi came back as I finished removing things to the porch. "I got the frog. " She panted lightly as she pushed a wheeled aquarium across the tile floor.

"Good. We can get your husband out of there." None too soon in my opinion. The place was giving me serious willies.

"This will work?" She stared at the frog.

"Hang on." I went into the guest bath by the study. "He's been using this bath, right?"

She nodded.

"This is his toothbrush?"

Another nod. Inside a drawer I found a comb and a couple of stray hairs.

Returning to the hallway, I checked the frog and applied the spell.

"Call him out of there," I instructed, standing by with the aquarium. If we didn't pull this off correctly, we wouldn't get a second chance.

"Harold," she whispered.

Expecting her most strident voice, I jumped at the eerie whisper. Strangely though, it worked. Harold's eyes snapped opened.

"Time for dinner," Vi said. "You know I'll come get you if I have to."

The pain behind the words spoke of a physical battle. I didn't want to watch. Like a puppet, Harold jerked to his feet.

"I eat, you leave me alone," he rasped out.

"Agreed."

I nodded at her to be ready, my hand on the aquarium. "Timing," I whispered.

She stepped back away from the open doorway.

"Harold buddy, come through the door sideways, would you?" I kept my voice low.

He didn't react.

Vi repeated the order. "Wait, Harold. Stand there a minute. Turn." She touched him.

I couldn't have done it. He was a broken man. "Possessed" barely scratched the surface of the murk that surrounded him. He flinched backwards at her touch, stepping back into the room.

"Come to the edge of the doorway," she said. "I won't touch you if you come through sideways."

He stood there as though unable to process the command. My stomach clenched.

"I'm not hungry." He turned back to the desk.

"Harold." She stepped into the doorway, blocking me. "The therapist gave me the medication. We can force you. There's always the IV."

"Let me die."

"Later." She stepped back out of the doorway.

"You go through this every day?" I whispered.

She shook her head, her eyes focused only on her husband. "Not always so bad. It was worse before the medication." As Harold jerked back to the door, she stopped talking. She put her hand out in the middle of the doorway. To avoid it, he turned sideways, edging through.

Vi was in my way. For a second, I panicked. Her hand and therefore her body blocked me from seeing where to push the aquarium. With all that I had triggered this morning, I couldn't take any more chances.

I shoved her sideways, hard, and then pushed the aquarium into the room.

"Ooomph." She hit the wall on the side of the hallway. Harold took a blow from one corner of the aquarium, and I ran over his toes.

"Pull him all the way out!" I shouted in a frantic whisper.

Halfway on the floor, she couldn't do it. I shoved the aquarium with one hand and grabbed a papery arm with the other, forcing him across the threshold.

Shivering, I stood perfectly still for a moment. The frog didn't like the movement. For a time it would be stressed, but that would likely match Harold's dinnertime and not be unusual. If my spell worked, Sheila would still sense Harold in the study and keep her focus on the spells in there. Harold would be out of her direct and constant bombardment, yet close enough Sheila might not notice.

"Okay, let's get him away from here."

If it hadn't been for the fact that Harold had to be available to deny his signature on documents, getting him out of the state probably would have been best. As it was, we had no choice but to hide him right under the witch's nose.

We dragged him into the living room and deposited him under a sunbeam. He blinked against the light, but otherwise didn't move.

"Food first," I suggested. "Meanwhile I'll work on the bedroom."

"You want him to eat here rather than in the kitchen?"

"I don't like the kitchen. There's something wrong with it, but I don't know what."

She halted in her motion to go there.

"It shouldn't hurt you."

"Shouldn't?" she parroted.

I shrugged. "I don't know what it is. I don't like the idea of feeding him in there, and I don't want him eating anything already in there. That's why I had you get fresh groceries and takeout."

"Oh. The maid left enough prepared food for dinner." Her voice trailed off, but her feet headed to the garage. She had rallied nicely now that she could take action.

I followed her. She pulled groceries out of the trunk. I helped myself to the cedar.

"I hope you like hammering." I waved one of the planks in her direction. "Have him sit on this board. Put it under the chair or the couch." I looked up. Her hands were full of bags. "Oh, never mind."

I took the box of planks into the living room. The cedar was cut in thin strips, ready to be slotted together for lining a drawer or closet. I situated Harold before carting the rest of the boxes into the master bedroom.

While Vi spoon-fed her dying husband, I cleared the entire closet in the bedroom. The cedar panels slid nicely together. All I had to do was hammer them in place. All fifty or so. More like a hundred. I'd need to do the ceiling too.

Cedar was a great blocker of evil spirits. Harold was too controlled to stop Sheila if she figured out what was going on, but with the cedar blocking her sensing, the frog would be the strongest Harold link and should keep her focused there.

I was maybe a quarter of the way done lining the closet when Vi came to find me. Her husband trailed listlessly behind, held captive by a strong hand. "He didn't go straight back to the room," she crowed happily. Her eyes shone.

"The frog," I explained. "I tossed some of Harold's hair and his toothbrush in the cage. The compulsion spell that commanded him back there so that Sheila could keep soaking him in spells has been transferred to the frog temporarily."

Vi blinked. She looked at her husband and then back at me. "Are you saying you turned a frog into my husband?" The noise she made sounded strangled.

"Not--" I realized with amazement that she was giggling. "Not really," I sighed. "Sit him here on these boards and let's finish this."

We worked late. I told her and Harold how they were going to slowly fight Sheila's magic. Harold drooled, but that was a vast improvement over answering Sheila's call. Or so I told myself.

"He'll have to sleep on the floor tonight," I announced when we were finished.

"I have an air mattress."

She trotted off and came back with it a few minutes later. She stuffed it into the closet and plugged in a pump. "This closet looks like a coffin."

"Think of it as a cellar. The cedar will block negative vibes and evil spirits." My back hurt. My eyes hurt. I closed them for a moment of peace. "Did you get the sage pillow from the shop I told you about?"

"In the car." She didn't move to get it so I did.

When I came back, I handed it to her and said, "Sage is a purifier. The scent will seep into his brain and hopefully create pure channels, ones that aren't contaminated by Sheila." I shook my head. "In time, it might heal some of the damage. If you go to a shaman, he will use sage to try and help Harold connect back to his spirit--his soul."

She grabbed the pillow and began arranging it. "Harold, use this."

"And remember to feed the frog at the times we talked about," I stressed. "If Harold leaves the closet, make sure he comes right back, especially at night. If he goes back in that study or his other bedroom, his stronger essence will pull any spells off the frog and back to him."

"Okay."

I knew without asking that she would stay in the closet with him. It was probably the first time in a long while that he wasn't actively fighting her. The shock of leaving the bubble Sheila had created for him had left him numb.

"How long?" she whispered.

I had no answer and was too tired to try for a guess. Without another word, I left the closet and drove home.

Lynx must have stopped by to check on me because he had moved the cactus pot on my porch enough for me to know he'd been here. I slid it back to its regular spot, an indication everything was fine. It wasn't really, but he'd at least know I was alive and doing my job.

Chapter 17

It was time to visit Tino. Not only had I not gotten the original information I wanted about the werewolf attacks, there was the little matter of the vampire visit. On top of that, there was Sheila. It was the last problem that provided me with my own evil little idea to ensure my safety from the dead. I was pretty sure Tino could help with all three problems.

Tino didn't feel quite as negative as I did toward vampires, at least I assumed that was the case since I knew he could get a message to the walking dead.

I ate lunch at The Owl, but Tino was at The Monastery. It bugged me that I was having such a hard time connecting with him. Was he avoiding me, or did I only notice because I had tried to talk to him more often than I normally did?

I finished eating and made my way over to The Monastery. Since I had already eaten, I took a leather stool at the bar and ordered chips and salsa with an ice water. The salsa was too spicy for carbonated drinks, and I never drank spirits in Tino's places. I wasn't sure why. They were either the safest places in town or the most dangerous because of all the magicals around.

"Tino in?" I asked the waitress.

"He's in the back."

I gave the coded hand signal indicating I was on the approved list. I also asked her politely to tell him I was here so that anyone watching wouldn't notice the signal.

While I waited, I considered my plan again. By sending a message to a vampire, I was playing with fire. It was even scarier because I was making up the facts. I assuaged my conscience by telling myself that Sheila deserved some attention from a vampire. She was playing puppet games with an innocent man. She had abused subjects in her lab, and she was certainly capable of figuring out how to track a vampire. All I was going to do was suggest that the vampires ask her about her talents. If she felt hunted, well, that wasn't my fault.

I shuddered, just as Tino came out from the kitchen. He gave me a half grin from behind the glare of lights. I waved the chip in my hand.

"Yo," he said. "Hear you're in hot demand, stirring up a lotta trouble."

Tino had to be descended from other than the Mesoamerican Indians because he was the only six-foot tall, bald Mexican I'd ever met. In addition to shaving what little hair he had on his head, today he was without any other facial hair, making his dangling Quetzal earring more noticeable.

"I wanted to ask you about all this demand stuff. Who is looking to hire me?"

"There's been those asking around. Mostly in El Lobo and El Ojo."

"I don't think I've ever taken a client from The Mongrel or The Evil Eye," I said, swapping his Spanish to English. "Not usually serious clients."

He shrugged and chewed on a skewer. A normal sized person would have been satisfied with a toothpick, but that would have been nothing more than a splinter in his large hands. "Didn't figure you'd be interested so I didn't go out of my way to contact you."

"Is it a cop?" I asked.

He pondered that one. "Not the guy doing the asking. Not professional enough." His forehead moved, and if he hadn't shaved, his eyebrows would have raised. "Could be a cop, now that you mention it. Sending in someone to do some checking. Not a very good cop if he asked for you around there."

"The cops don't know much about your better restaurants," I pointed out.

"Any cop trying to hire you doesn't know much about you or any of my restaurants if he is looking for you at El Lobo or El Ojo."

"True." I smiled. "Get me a name if you get another chance at it. You have my permission to set up a meet if you have to dangle the offer in order to get more information."

He shook his head. "You are looking for trouble."

He didn't know the half of it. "I also have a message to send." The counter top was of sudden interest to my restless eyeballs.

"Sure."

"This one might be a little harder than normal," I confessed, picking at my napkin. "I don't know the guy's name. I know he's looking for a witch, a strong witch. He doesn't know the witch's name."

I glanced up and got the raised invisible eyebrows again. "The message is for a dead guy. A vamp, a real one."

Lucky for him, his eyebrows had already left his head. Slowly he took the wooden skewer out of his mouth. "I'm listening, chica."

"This vamp, since I don't know who he is, you'll have to get the message to any vamp. You tell them the witch they are looking for might be named Sheila. Over by Los Alamos." I didn't need to provide a last name. These guys hadn't gotten to be walking dead and stayed that way by being stupid. Besides, the information wasn't exactly golden.

"That it?"

"That's it."

"You planning on getting paid for this information?"

"Are you kidding?" My eyes bugged out.

He nodded and smiled. "Wanted to be sure. I take the message, but I ain't touching any bypass. I didn't think you did business with vamps."

"I don't." I glanced around quickly. Do they--" I had to stop and get air. "Do they come in here?" While I couldn't go around wearing garlic and generate any business, I could certainly wear more silver. Carry a gun. More knives. Carry a stake as part of an umbrella. Who cared that it never rained in New Mexico?

"Nah. What they do that for, chica? Those suckers, they don't need to eat, not my food. Take some air, kiddo. You ain't lookin' so good."

The thought of a vampire lurking in a corner booth...I wasn't Tino. I was five-five, maybe five-six in the morning with my hair sticking up. I didn't run that fast. I didn't have a safe restaurant to offer abnormals as a place to do business. "Okay, okay. It's just--" I choked. "I don't do business with vamps, okay?"

"You giving them this message. Some might say that is business. You better off getting the message to them through someone who does business with them."

I shook my head rather frantically. "No. Not business. Passing along information that is of possible interest. She might not even be who they are looking for. Make that clear, Tino. I don't want any trouble."

"No trouble," he repeated. "No payment, nothing more than a tip. You want, I keep your name out of it. Just an anonymous tip."

That wasn't fair to Tino. I knew my doors had protection, but I wasn't sure that his did. I was scared enough that I wasn't sure what to do. "Give them the name. If they ask you where the message came from, tell them."

"You a brave bruja." He picked up another skewer. "It still be better if you go through one who does business with them."

I caught the hint this time. "You don't do business with them either?"

"I can get them a message. They don't need to eat here. I don't stop them from coming in if they want, but," he looked right into my eyes and said again, "It's best to have someone who does business with them. That way your name stays out of it. That way it's just business."

He didn't say her name, but Matilda was the only person I knew who did business with them. If Tino didn't actually do business with them, what the heck was my friend Matilda thinking? I forgot to breathe again, and Tino started waving a napkin at me. When that didn't work, he reached across the bar and pounded my back.

"Ooof." The air in my lungs came out in rush when my chest hit the bar. "Geez, Tino. You trying to kill me?"

"You better not take no more messages for those kind," he advised. "You ain't looking so good."

"Yeah. I know." The thought of my childhood friend working with vamps--it was too much. I trusted her. She was my friend. But vamps. Yeesh.

I had done what I came to do and almost bolted before I thought of my other question. "Oh, one more thing. What do you know about the women being murdered?"

Tino sighed. "You have all the hard questions today, chica. Why you want to go messin' in bad stuff?"

"I don't, but one of them was my client. I didn't know about the others. Then I found out there seems to be a pattern."

He nodded. "Came down through El Lobo. Fancy pimp goes by the name Arturo. He started offering dates with, you know. Not the night creatures you just mentioned, but you know."

"You ignored him?"

"Of course. Those guys with false promises, they a dime a dozen. Maybe not even that much, maybe only worth a peso."

"Only his offer was for real," I said. "He must have had contact with a real shifter."

"More than one after he set a few women up. I hear he has two or three, maybe more, that want in on the action."

I groaned. "You're telling me that even after the deaths, business is booming?"

"He don't need to come into my places anymore. Business goes looking for him."

"You'd think the murders would have slowed things down." I would have been more incredulous if I hadn't dealt with Dolores. The woman had no sense, and the danger seemed to have driven her as much as the possibility of a date with someone "special."

"You want to stay away from that business, girl."

"I know." Good thing I had already eaten because it looked like my stomach was going to stay bottomed out for a while. Finding out that the shifters were still in business was very bad news. I couldn't help but believe that whoever was trying to track me at Tino's restaurants was doing so because of my link to one of the crime scenes. As if that weren't bad enough, I had to talk to Matilda about the vampire.

Hunted and hunters. Oh goody.

Chapter 18

Since Matilda's shop was near the plaza, I decided to first check and see if White Feather was trying to meet me. If he wasn't, I fully intended to set up a meet and clear the air. If White Feather wasn't the one trying to find me in the bars, he might know who was doing the looking. I probably owed him a few details on the body in the mountains too.

Because I was nervous, I used items from the trunk of my car to look less like myself. I often went past the signal location without a disguise, but not right now, not with all that was going on.

The plaza was full of people, which was the best time to visit. I walked along the Palace of the Governors. The hair from my blond wig was tucked underneath a ball cap. A special pillow around my waist added a layer of fat. While the extras provided a great disguise, I was uncomfortably warm. The bright New Mexico sunshine was frying me.

Despite my discomfort, I stopped to buy a fabulous strand of silver from one of the Indian sellers. I usually bought my silver before it was set into jewelry, but some Indians imparted a unique magic when they designed items. I wasn't too proud to obtain the extra degree of quality when I came across it.

I wandered aimlessly around the cottonwoods that were part of the center park. Strolling near the fenced monument for those who fought in New Mexico's Indian wars, I avoided eye contact with an old man who was propped against the iron gate. As I neared the chains that locked the gates, he stopped nursing his brown paper bag. In one quick motion, he reached over and grabbed my pants.

"Hey!" I shouted. "Leggo." My heart beat double-time. I hadn't put the padlock on the chains yet so no one could possibly know I was the witch who met with White Feather.

The old man confirmed it. "Oh mi Dios, mi Dios?" He held out a hand, stained from dirt and tobacco.

I reached into my jeans and dropped a dime onto the ground. It was far enough from his hands that he had to release my pants to get it. Backing up, I deliberately came in contact with the gates again. White Feather hadn't left an extra padlock, so with a flick of my wrist, I left mine.

White Feather usually marked his padlocks with a colored line to indicate the church at which we would meet. I was fancier. When he removed the padlock, candle wax inside the lock was spelled to make sure the smell would remind him of San Miguel Mission.

I headed to the south end of the plaza as though the experience with the bum made me seek safer territory. As I crossed the road from the middle of the square, I looked back. To my surprise, the bum was gone.

A quick scan of the park didn't find him.

A dime wasn't enough to buy anything, but the bum was no longer sitting at the monument.

I was very tempted to go back and see if my padlock was gone. If I didn't, I'd never know if the bum was a plant. If I did, it would look suspicious to anyone watching the monument for action. Biting my cheek, I went down Washington, keeping an eye on the monument. No bum. The guy was definitely gone.

I meandered to Old Santa Fe Trail and Loretto Chapel to set a false trail before taking back alleys to my car.

No one followed me. There was no way they could have kept up with me without being obvious, but I was still bothered.

Instead of going to Matilda's, I headed home. I needed a backup plan for meeting with White Feather because the meet I had set up didn't feel safe. Normally I specified the place and White Feather unlocked the place. If it were unlocked, I knew he was there. If not, I knew he hadn't gotten the message or couldn't make it. This time, I wasn't taking any chances. I wanted a change of routine and in an area where I had more control.

"Sheep for slaughter," I muttered.

At home, I went straight into the lab to work on a spell that would dissolve paper. My biggest problem was that every spell I looked up called for pulling humidity from the air and turning the paper to sludge. New Mexico didn't have enough humidity for such a spell. I sat and rewrote the formulas to do the opposite. The spell would evaporate the moisture out of the paper within twenty-four hours, causing it to crumble to dust. If White Feather hadn't read it by then, he wouldn't be reading it.

Once the paper was properly spelled, I wrote White Feather instructions for meeting me at The Owl. I told him when to appear and what to wear. No disguises. I didn't have time for it. I needed him in a place where I had friends, and where I knew the escape routes.

The instructions done, I grabbed a couple of illusion spells, my levitation spell, and some self-defense packages. I hoped it didn't come to that.

Passing back through the plaza, the padlock was gone.

Fine, the meet was on, but instead of me, White Feather was going to get my note. In the church it would be too easy for him to arrest me. In The Owl, I could get away.

I headed to Matilda's to take care of business, but time was short. I had to place the note inside the church before closing time since I didn't plan on being there at midnight.

Worrying about the plan kept my mind busy while my feet took me to Matilda's shop. I touched the door and checked to make sure the front was empty before entering.

Matilda pranced out from the back and smiled when she saw me. "Adriel!" Her red hair was gathered into a spiked bun and held in place by long strings of beads. I did my best to avoid getting slapped with the dangling decorations when she gave me a hug.

I hugged her back, harder than usual because I was afraid. I didn't want to involve her with the vamp, even if she was already involved. "Hey. How's business?"

"Oh good. Should I close the shop for twenty so we can talk?"

I nodded.

She stepped back, her mouth opened to prattle, but no sound came out because she hadn't expected my answer. I never took her up on her offers to close shop except for the time my sister, Kas, went missing. Luckily Kas had eloped, and all ended well other than she became an even worse snob.

Matilda blinked heavily mascaraed eyelashes. "Okay." She flipped the sign around and hit a button that engaged automatic locks. "What's up?"

"I have a message. For a vamp. I don't know his name. He's looking for a witch, one who is capable of tracking a vampire, one that wants vampire blood."

"Patrick?"

"I didn't ask him his name," I said nervously.

"Hispanic? Wears his hair in a short ponytail? Short for a vamp?"

Most Hispanics were on the short side so I wasn't sure that part of the description counted, but I nodded. "That sounds like him." The image in my mind scared all the blood out of my face. "Look, I'm not sure I know the name of the right witch, but whoever this vamp is, he came by to check me out. I know I'm not the lady in question, so I'm throwing him--" I choked off before I could say, "a bone."

Matilda smiled. "Patrick came around asking about hiring a powerful witch. I didn't get the full story out of him."

"You sent him to me?"

"Of course not. I told him I was the best." She straightened her back proudly, ever the salesman. Truthfully, she was the best at what she did. She just didn't dabble in the same areas that I did.

"Are you sure you didn't mention my name? How else would he find me?"

She started to argue with me and then clamped her mouth shut. A long purple fingernail tapped matching purple lips. "You know, vamps can find out a lot of things. I know I didn't give him your name on purpose. But he's a vamp. They have more glamor in their pinkies than I could produce with a lifetime of spells."

The thought didn't seem to bother her. "You're telling me he may have glamored you into telling?"

"It's possible.   Goes with the territory. I have nothing to hide, and neither do you. He knows that, so I don't know why he'd bother. If I found out, it would ruin a perfect working relationship." She frowned.

I didn't want to get into the logic of how she was going to pull out of a relationship where she could be glamored into cooperating. I delivered my message. "Tell him that he may want to look into a witch named Sheila. Of Los Alamos. Make sure he knows it isn't an accusation, just a person of interest." I wasn't sure I cared if Sheila turned up dead--so long as she wasn't turned into a vamp. The woman was enough of a bloodsucker without someone giving her that kind of power permanently.

"Okay," Matilda agreed easily. "She's a person of interest."

"Exactly."

Tapping her fingernail against her mouth again, Matilda asked, "Do you really think he used glamor to get the names of witches from me?"

I shrugged. "How would I know? You're the vamp specialist."

"Hmm. Maybe I should set up some traps."

"What?" I shouted. "You aren't trapping any--"

She waved a hand at me. "Not to trap the vamp, silly. To leave evidence if one tries to glamor me. A tape recorder would work so long as the vamp wasn't suspicious. It would be better if it were more sophisticated though." She stared around her shop, assessing possibilities.

I shook my head and left her to her idea of protection. It didn't impress me much, and it probably wouldn't even set the vamp back a pace. My heart feared for her. My heart feared, period.

Unfortunately, I didn't have time to argue with her. I had to get myself to the church and leave the note for White Feather. It was almost five o'clock, which was closing time at the tourist traps.

Chapter 19

The San Miguel Mission was an ancient church said to have been built on even older native structures. For certain, the church had burned down at least once. The remains were sealed underneath the floor when the new foundation was laboriously rebuilt over two hundred years ago. In my mind, such rebuilding trapped the strength of the place; a sense of time and power emanated from the cool adobe walls.

Hiding inside past closing was hugely risky, but if I didn't, the note was likely to get thrown away. I had been too rushed to think of putting an avoidance spell on it for anyone other than White Feather. Besides, the church was cared for by the Christian Brothers. Setting spells against those of any holy order was risky because half the time they didn't work.

My goal was to reach the inaccessible choir loft at the back of the church. It was inaccessible because there were no stairs and hadn't been for over fifty years. No one knew what had happened to the stairs, so the loft remained, untouched and more importantly, unchecked at closing.

Unfortunately, the only way I could get there was levitation, and I wasn't that good at levitating. Even if I managed the spell, anyone could walk through the low door from the gift shop and catch me mid-flight. The good news was that the door to the church was kept closed to keep the gift shop noise out.

I entered the gift shop and did my best to look like an aimless tourist, picking through the brochures. My wig was back in place and hopefully my dark eye shadow made me look older, flattening my features, and drawing watchful eyes to my deep red lipstick.

"Can I help you?" The Hispanic woman behind the counter had a better disguise than mine. Like a thousand others in the area, her dark hair was threaded with gray strands. She wore enough silver and turquoise to be a walking jewelry advertisement. She could have been a mom, a grandmother, an aunt--or all three.

"Uh, just looking." I glanced at my watch. Ten minutes to close. The lady probably wanted to leave on time. I ducked into the church through the very low doorway. Empty--except for one man kneeling in the front pew.

He was probably the Christian Brother waiting to tidy up and lock the place. What would he think if he turned around and caught me halfway up to the old choir loft? I dithered for only an instant. I peeked back through the gap in the door to the gift shop. The couple who had been shopping was leaving.

I turned to the confessional, thinking to hide inside, but there were no doors or curtains because it was no longer used in its original capacity. I could kneel in it, but the Brother would see me.

If he caught me, could I get him to hear my confession? If I distracted him and then went silent…there were rules on hearing confessions, and I didn't think a Christian Brother was able to absolve sinners. Besides, the confessional was tucked under the loft. There was no way I could levitate through the boards, and if I stepped away from the confessional, I'd be in his line of sight.

The Christian Brother finished his prayers and stood, catching me staring.

"Hello." He spoke low and inclined his head.

I had a crazy moment where I thought he was White Feather. I knelt quickly at the back pew and dropped my eyes. This plan was going all to… whatever.

The Brother turned then and went into the sacristy to the right of the altar.

He had seen me. Hiding anywhere at ground level was impossible. It was now or never.

I moved out from under the loft and activated the spell. Unfortunately, I had forgotten a very important fact. Not only do spells not work well against holy orders, they weren't that great on sacred ground either. Churches were sacred ground. They had their own magic. Not that what I was doing was necessarily a sin; the spell used all natural elements, and it was for a good cause. But anytime magics mixed, so did the results.

The levitation spell hit resistance. Instead of drifting quickly upwards, I ricocheted sideways. My head connected with the white plaster wall hard enough to rattle the hanging depictions of the Stations of the Cross. "Oomph."

Before I could fall, I grabbed out, barely grazing the loft railing with one hand. The spell hadn't been deactivated, and I started rising again. I pushed myself away from the wall and grabbed again.

This time, I snagged a handful of wood. It was the only thing that kept me from shooting even higher. My head felt as if the contact with the wall had left nothing but plaster inside my skull.

Through the dim black curtain forming around my eyes, I dragged myself down and canceled the spell. Lying flat would have been best, but my head hurt so badly, I ended up on the choir floor in a helpless ball.

The Christian Brother came out to see why the light fixtures were shaking. "Hello?"

Luckily the loft had a cloth draped around the railing. I didn't think he could see me. I know I couldn't see him or anything else other than a few shooting sparks in front of my eyes.

"Amy?" He rattled the massive wooden plank that barred the door out the back of the church. That or my head was pounding from pain.

"Amy, did you drop something?"

I couldn't hear Amy's reply. From the buzzing in my ears, I think I had a concussion.

There was no way to tell when the murmuring stopped and my head cleared. I lay in a stupor, trying to decide whether I should move.

I must have passed out because when I could see shapes clearly again, the church was very, very quiet. What time was it? If I had stayed too long, it could be midnight and all this subterfuge was for nothing. White Feather would show up and arrest me. Assuming he could get up here.

Standing was an effort. The digits on my watch were blurry. It was either quarter to six or quarter to seven. I couldn't quite tell which. Either way, I had time to leave the note and make my escape. "Hello?" I tried tentatively. "Hello?" a little louder.

No one came rushing from the gift shop or the sacristy. Good.

There was one problem. I was stranded. No way was I going to try levitating my way down. With my luck, I'd shoot myself out the bell tower. "Ooogh." I sat back down, trying to figure out which of my spells would help. But I couldn't use them. No way. I wasn't sure what had gone wrong on the way up. It could have been bad driving on my part, lack of testing or...Something Else.

I feared Something Else enough that I stood myself up, muttered, "Help me Lord," and put one shaking leg over the ornate railing.

I wished I could use levitation. I did not want to damage the beautiful hand-crafted railing. Carefully, ever so slowly, I got my tip-toes on the inch or so of support on other side of the rail. I slid my hands down until they were at the bottom. My butt hanging in the air, I let one foot go and then the other, dangling with both hands wrapped tightly around a single square chunk of railing. The wooden floor wasn't so far away. Four feet, maybe five at most?

So long as I didn't land on my head, I'd live, right?

"Lodestone..." I couldn't help it. I muttered the ingredients for levitation, just for confidence.

I think Someone heard because I'd swear there were g-forces pushing me down. Like a lead statue, I fell.

Splat.

"I'm going to die," I whimpered. Rolling off my bottom, which now hurt almost as much as my head, I crawled to the confessional. I slipped the letter out of my jeans and onto the chair where the priest would sit. Since confessionals were part of our routine, White Feather would at least look inside.

"I should have left it here in the first place. Maybe the Brother wouldn't have even seen it." I secured the letter under the stole that rested on the chair and hoped White Feather would find it. If not, it would disintegrate by morning--or if Something in the church interfered, maybe it would grow wings and start singing out my crime.

While I waited for dark, I called myself names. Originally I had intended to use a blending spell to sneak back outside, but I wasn't touching another spell on church grounds, at least not this church. The wooden pews did not make for comfortable bedding. I wasn't certain, but I think the bell tower had bats. That was better than mice in the walls or…whatever.

By ten o'clock I judged it dark enough outside that I could avoid being noticed. I was dizzy from what I thought was hunger and frustration. It wasn't until I got home and saw the matted blood on the top of my head that I realized I had left evidence of the worst kind. If anyone wanted revenge against me, my blood was all over the wig I hadn't even noticed had fallen off my head in the choir loft.

I hoped Someone would take offense at anyone collecting the wig for use in a spell. I hoped Someone would protect me until I could go back and retrieve it. Given what I had gone through, I had no idea how I was going to do so.

Chapter 20

Lynx was a night creature. He rarely stopped by in the wee hours of dawn because it was the end of his day, not the beginning. When the coded knock worked its way into my sleeping brain, my head hurt so badly that I thought the knock must be part of a bad dream. When it repeated, I sat up and wondered if the vamp had figured out the coded knock.

I fumbled about, gathering what protection I could on such short notice. I was beyond bleary-eyed as I made it to the door.

Lynx was no more pleased than I to be on my doorstep at five a.m. "I have a message and a client," he growled.

"And I have a headache." If I tried to sit down, my butt would hurt too. I was pretty sure I owned a robe, but I hadn't been able to find it quickly. My sleep t-shirt was supposed to be for the gym. When Kas gave it to me she said, "You aren't ever going to need sexy clothing because witches don't get dates."

The thing was comfortable, and I loved it. The shorts I had thrown on weren't, but that was because a heavy silver dagger weighed down one pocket.

"This can't wait," Lynx said when I tried to shut the door. "It's Zandy. You might remember him from the thing with the Dolores chick. He says you owe him. He already knows who you are, did his own research."

I peered outside, trying without success to see anyone else in the gray light. "Zandy?" I repeated dumbly, starting to wake up and not liking it. Lynx did not normally bring customers to my doorstep. Part of Lynx's job was to set up meetings so that not just anyone found out where I lived.

"Look, the guy knows where you live, but he wanted me to put in a word for him."

Lynx wasn't smiling. I rubbed my eyes. I yanked on the tops of my shorts to keep them from sliding down under the weight of the dagger. "Now is not a good time."

"You got that right."

Angry. Lynx was angry. "Then why are you here?" I was awake now. Lynx angry and doing something against his will was not a good thing.

"I can set up the meet if you want, or he will show up here. Which do you want?"

"Wait a minute! I haven't even said I'd see the guy! Why should I?" True, I was quite curious. I might even get more information from this Zandy about the other three dead women. But Zandy was a killer--and I was a witness to that fact.

"I agreed to put in the word he wants to meet with you. He said you would help him."

"Help him? He wants to hire me?"

Lynx shrugged, his hands in his pockets. "I deliver the messages. You pay me. He only wanted me to put in a word for him. I did it."

Before he could leave, I grabbed him. "Did you get paid to deliver this little message? By him, I mean?"

Lynx gave me his flat eyes, refusing to answer the question. "You want I should take a message back?"

I let him go. "If he knows where I live..." My head throbbed. "It would be better to meet him at The Owl." I looked at the clock and groaned. I had just set a meet there for tonight with White Feather. It probably wasn't a good idea to lead a werewolf who was also guilty of murder to the same place. "Moonlight madness! Have him come here. Today, one o'clock. Tell him to mind his manners." I glanced at a wall calendar. It was nowhere near a full moon. His powers would be diminished, and he wouldn't be too edgy. I cursed again. I turned back to complain to Lynx, but he was already gone.

Maybe my sister was right. I needed a better job. Or at least better clientele.

Grumbling, I returned to my bedroom, but was unable to fall back to sleep. I needed to research werewolves to make sure I had enough protection to be able to talk to this Zandy guy without getting killed. I needed to get my wig back because if the wrong person found it, I would be better off dead.

I rolled out of bed, whimpering. I showered. I slugged back medicinal tea. Zandy wouldn't show until after lunch. That gave me the morning to get my wig back.

I drove to the plaza and made my way to San Miguel. It didn't take me long to get inside and position myself on the same hard bench I had used the night before. The only problem was that my mission was impossible. Tourists came and went while I knelt and prayed for ideas.

Even dressed as a maintenance man I didn't think the Christian Brothers were going to let me drag a ladder inside the church. I couldn't use a spell for a disguise, and I certainly couldn't use levitation again.

The only good news was that no one paid any attention to the loft. It was inaccessible and therefore not interesting.

I rested my aching head on my arms. There was no way for me to get up there in broad daylight. The only person I knew who could get into the church at night was White Feather. I had come full circle. Had I met him last night as originally planned, I wouldn't be in this mess.

Feeling very sorry for myself, I drove home. Talking to my mother helped, but only marginally. I couldn't tell her about my problems, but I could catch up on the news. At least tonight when I saw White Feather, I wouldn't look stupid because I wasn't caught up on basic news.

Lunch did nothing to perk my spirits up. All I had in the house to eat was garlic. A deep search of the cupboards yielded some dried pasta and a can of tomato sauce. As spaghetti went, it was way below average, but I put in lots of garlic with the hope that it would at least give the werewolf pause if he tried to attack.

At a quarter 'til one, I positioned myself behind the living room curtains. I listened for noise from the back door in case the werewolf tried any tricks.

At five after one, I moved a chair next to the window. By one thirty, I was almost asleep. Luckily the werewolf wasn't shy or quiet. He approached my front door as if he owned the place, hopping up the steps and knocking loudly.

Zandy looked a lot better than the first time I had seen him, but my first impression was correct. He was very young, somewhere between seventeen and twenty. His ratty blue jeans and tight shirt were stretched and torn as though he had shapeshifted with them on. He swaggered away from the door and leaned against one of the porch supports. His relaxed position didn't last long. He must have felt the silver I had pounded along the outside of the pole because he jerked away.

When I opened the door, he stared and blinked for a few seconds before announcing, "I need your help."

"You had my help," I replied. "The way I see it, we're even at best and maybe you owe me one."

He frowned. "I don't think we're even."

"Fine, then you owe me."

He shook his head vehemently. "No way, lady. *You* owe me!"

I stretched my lips across my teeth. It was as close as I could come to a smile. "Afraid not, tiger. Not only could I finger you for Dolores' murder, I also could have kept you at the scene of the crime until help arrived. You didn't have much fight in you as I recall."

"I didn't kill her on purpose! It was your fault! You sold her the shirt, and she hurt me with it!"

I shrugged. "Your life wasn't in immediate danger from the shirt, and no jury around is going to believe that your life was in such danger you had to kill her. I make products--like gun manufacturers make guns. Dolores purchased the product and misused it. That doesn't make it my fault she purchased it, nor does it make it my fault you killed her."

"She forced me to do it!" he snarled.

I remained calm, although I didn't like the depth of the growl. It sounded as though his vocal cords had changed to coyote. "She had a role in her own death. She played with fire and when it exploded, it cost her life. I don't deny that. But I merely sold a product. *You* killed her," I emphasized. "And I allowed you to leave." I crossed my arms. "I repeat. If anyone owes anyone, it is you owing me."

His throat worked. "I didn't kill them other bitches! You have to help me!"

"You may not have killed the other women, but I do *not* have to help you."

He eyed me for several moments, undecided. "Will you help me?"

"I have no reason to get involved."

"You're a witch," he said. "I could tell everyone."

I walked out onto the porch and took a seat in one of the metal chairs. It was laced with silver. The only other chair on my porch was not, but I didn't invite him to sit. I said, "Now that would be bound to hurt my feelings. You haven't a shred of proof and even if you did, do you really think anyone would care?"

That stumped him, but it didn't keep him quiet. "I could--"

When he didn't finish, I did it for him. "You could tell people that I made a shirt that burned your skin? Hmph. That would be rather incriminating for you, I would think."

He flung long tawny hair over his shoulder with a toss of his head. "No one knows I'm a," he stuttered to a halt again.

"I'm sure several people know. Dolores knew. I know. There's at least one policeman out there who knows. If Dolores knew, she could have easily told someone."

"She could have told them you're a witch too!"

I shrugged. "Perhaps. But it's how I make my living anyway. Being known as a witch isn't a huge deal. Most people assume I'm a con artist; others want to do business with me. Now your problem, that's a little different."

His eyes grew desperate. "Will you help me?"

"Why should I?"

"Because! Why shouldn't you?"

"How many of those women did you know? How many did you have sex with?"

He shook his head and worked his mouth opened and closed.

"Don't bother to deny it," I snapped. "You weren't in Dolores' room to have coffee. She wasn't likely the first full human you wanted to have sex with, and why should I believe you stopped there? Maybe you kill all your dates."

"I didn't kill them!"

"Why should I believe you? Maybe it got out of hand. Maybe after Dolores you decided you liked the killing part."

"I never had sex with her. And I never killed anyone!" He dropped his eyes because we both knew better.

"Zandy, you can call it what you want, but you killed her. Self-defense, anger, surprise, it doesn't matter. She's dead. If you killed those other women, you're in even worse trouble."

"I didn't!"

I waved my hand. "But you keep putting yourself in a position to get into trouble. This thing you are--this animal--it's not a sex toy to turn women on so that you can play around."

"You don't know nothin' about it. You don't know nothin' about me!" A man might have clenched his fists. Zandy flexed his hands, an animal reaction expecting claws as weapons.

I stayed relaxed on the outside, but was ready to move if I had to. "Look Zandy, I imagine it's a lot of fun. The girls flock to you as something new and dangerous. Not to mention forbidden. But it will get you killed. You have to worry about angry fathers, angry boyfriends, and the law. And you better wake up and start worrying about who is killing them if it isn't you."

He made a noise in the back of his throat. Again it sounded too much like the growl of an animal. "I don't care who it is as long as the cops don't think it's me."

"But what if the killer isn't a werewolf? What if it's someone who kills the women because they had sex with a werewolf?"

His brain might have turned the thought over, but it stalled pretty quickly.

"That would make you the enemy, Zandy. That would mean the women were being killed because the killer has a thing against werewolves. Maybe he'll come after you next."

Zandy nodded. "That's why I need help. I got people after me. The cops. They think I did all those women."

I rolled my eyes. "You need more than help. You need to stop dating these women and stop playing this game."

He eyed me through the messy strands of hair that blew across his face. After a minute, he said, "I'm not the only werewolf that does this stuff, and I ain't the one that killed those other women. No one is gonna make me take the fall for them."

"But you're still in the game, still splitting the profits with Arturo. As long as you do that, you're adding to the evidence against you. As soon as they tie you to Dolores, you're in for the rest of them."

"Well, let them pick someone else to blame. How about they pin this on your buddy Lynx? He's not so innocent. He thinks he has a big master plan, but if Arturo finds out he's horning in on his territory, he'll have more problems than I do." Zandy let out a hard breath of air. "I bet you'd help him. Or is it all shifters you have something against?"

I snorted. "Don't pull the prejudice card, Zandy. I'm a witch. I hire out my services, I don't give them to bleeding hearts who have gotten themselves into trouble. You want me to lie to the police? That isn't for sale. You want someone to find the real killer? That isn't a job for a witch. You're right when you say you need help, but it isn't my help you need."

"Where am I supposed to get help?"

I shrugged. "You're going to have to turn yourself in on the Dolores thing. There's no other way."

He shook his head. "Whoever did those other women, they can fry for Dolores too."

"Maybe," I agreed. "Or maybe you'll fry for all of them."

"That's why I came here. To settle this."

"What is it you want me to do?" I asked again. "I only know what I saw. I can't undo that. Neither can you."

"You could fix this," he insisted, waving his arms. "Get rid of the evidence against me. Make it disappear!"

He wasn't trying to solve the problem, he was trying to hand it to someone else. "No, Zandy, I can't. Magic can hide things, but it doesn't make them go away. It doesn't change what they were."

He slammed his hand against the wooden support pole hard enough to rattle my porch. I was positive I saw claws. "Zandy, you have to control yourself," I warned.

He stomped off the porch, jumping across two steps. "You wait, bitch," he called over his shoulder. "All I need is enough money to find out who did those other women. Then I just make sure the police know about it."

"You can't keep trying to earn money the way you are, Zandy."

"So I freelance. Maybe your buddy Lynx is right. Maybe that's the best way, just offer private protection services. No one to know where you've been, no one to be a witness." He flipped his middle finger at me, broke into a trot and was soon out of sight.

I might have re-iterated that the problem was not a witness, it was the crime, but since he hadn't heard me the first time, I didn't bother.

"How did my life go to hell so fast?" I wondered. "One protection spell, and suddenly I'm up to my ears with appointments and none of them are making me any money."

Zandy must have threatened Lynx. Otherwise, Lynx wouldn't have agreed to help Zandy meet with me. But what had he threatened Lynx with?

"Lynx, you are a pain in the rear."

With my meeting already set with White Feather, I didn't have time to go looking for Lynx. One good piece of news though. I might be able to find Zandy again.

On the wooden support pole of my porch, several strands of tawny hair floated in the wind. I collected them carefully.

Chapter 21

In the figments of my dreams, White Feather was a Viking, a wise Shaman, and one time he was an Italian mafia ghost. In reality, he was taller than I imagined, but his shoulders really were very broad. He must have hunched while in his monk getup. Halfway across the back room in the Owl, when he glanced my way, his eyes were in the shadows.

I walked closer.

When he turned fully from the bar and focused on me, hints of ocean green with flecks of sky blue watched me approach. He set his drink down to greet me.

I checked the only other table with occupants and nodded at Angel, who was tending the bar, before accepting the outstretched hand White Feather offered. His hair was beautiful. Women would kill for the black waves he had combed casually back. His nose was too strong for him to be absolutely handsome, his lips too stern.

Despite offering a firm handshake, he was wary, and I didn't blame him. Not only had I led him on a treasure hunt to meet with me, I looked like hell. Because he was taller than me by a good eight inches, he could, no doubt, see the hefty scab on the top of my head. There were still scratches on my face from when I learned to fly, and I hadn't had a full night's sleep in a while. All in all, I wasn't too surprised by his first question.

"Are you homeless?"

I blinked. "No."

"Did the witch send you?"

That one got me. Since there were no other single women around besides Angel, he had figured me for the meet, but he hadn't recognized me as Merlin. "In a manner of speaking," I hedged. I hadn't worn a disguise tonight, thinking it would set him up to distrust me, but since he didn't recognize me, I went with it.

We moved to a booth, and I had to wonder if Tino really used illusion candles. The dim light caused shadows to flicker across White Feather's features, making his face rather more gentle than it had seemed by the bar. He rested muscular arms on the table and studied me.

I forced my concentration to business. "Have you been trying to track down Merlin? Word on the street is someone is pretending to want to hire Merlin and that someone is a cop."

"Why would I track her down? I already know how to contact her. At least I did until she started playing hide and seek."

"That's the whole point. Merlin needs to know who is looking for her and why."

He shook his head, resting back against the booth cushion. "From what I can tell, there's a lot of looking going on. Have you been in El Lobo lately? The place is full of people trying to buy witches, werewolves, you name it. How can she tell someone is trying to find her in particular?"

His question was legitimate. I still wasn't sure I was dealing with anything more than my own paranoia. "Word is that it's a cop looking for her, and you're the only cop she deals with."

Even in the half-light, I could see color flush his cheeks. "And she figures that since she gave me a map and very little else to find a woman in the woods, that it must be me." He grunted. "Maybe she feels guilty. Seems to me that she should."

My mother hadn't said "boo" about a fourth body being found. "Assuming you followed the map, why isn't it in the news?"

"Saving the details for the investigation. Do you know how many false tips come in? There's only one person who knows about--" He looked around the restaurant, but Angel was still tucked behind the bar. The other two men eating were across the room well away from us. White Feather leaned across the table anyway. "Only one person knows about that spot in the mountains. So far the loonies claiming responsibility for the other three deaths don't know about it."

"More than the killer knows," I said. "I knew, and I didn't kill her. The guy who told me knew."

"And Merlin knows." He shrugged and sat back. "Okay, so it isn't a huge secret. But at least some of the loonies don't know about it."

I could see where keeping it quiet could help him. "Why is a cop looking for Merlin?"

Instead of answering, he said, "Are we going to eat anything? Or do they only serve food in the front?"

"Sure, the food is good here. Do you want me to order for you or do you want a menu?" Angel wouldn't interrupt business unless I specifically asked her to come over. It was one of the rules of the place.

"You come here a lot?" He seemed doubtful.

"Enough." I had to be careful or he was going to guess that I was Merlin rather than a low-paid messenger.

"What's good?"

"The burgers. It's only a question of whether you want cheese and green chiles."

"Fine. Everything."

"Yeah." I held up two fingers to Angel. She nodded and disappeared into the kitchen to place the order.

He watched without complaining, his eyes missing nothing. "I don't think a cop is looking for Merlin."

Before I could reply, Angel headed our way to take our drink order, although White Feather already had his. When she arrived with her trusty notepad, I said, "A diet for me." I automatically answered the plea in her eyes, because she couldn't speak normally with White Feather sitting there. "And a regular coke."

She beamed and hurried off. I really needed to stop adding to her tips this way.

I turned back to White Feather. He watched me with curious eyes, his hands resting on the table between us. "I heard a cop was looking. If it isn't you, can you find out why a cop is after her?"

"None of the cops I know are looking. The cops don't even admit we're looking for a werewolf. Come on--" he stopped. "What did you say your name was?"

"Adriel." I smiled. It would be a lot easier than answering to Merlin. "I don't think you told me yours either."

He weighed that for a moment. "I like White Feather."

"Okay," I agreed. Names were important, and I wasn't one to push on that issue.

After another moment, he added, "You can call me Jason if you want." His eyes shifted away.

"Okay. Either works."

He made eye contact again. "The cops aren't looking for Merlin."

"Are you sure?" That had me stumped. Lynx was positive a cop was searching for me. He was rarely wrong about the underground. Tino hadn't considered the possibility of a cop until I suggested it, but he thought the idea had merit.

"I can be fairly certain of it," White Feather said. "We've got our hands full tracking down this other problem. If someone is looking for Merlin, it could be any of the loonies looking for services. The word I hear is that Dolores did some injury to the werewolf who attacked her. Even Merlin told me the guy had been burned. There are a lot of people interested in getting that same protection or any protection."

"Dolores died. Doesn't seem to me the spell would be all that popular." But I could imagine a sulking Zandy complaining to his friends about how badly he had fared in the deal. Was the kid too stupid to hide the fact that he had been at the scene? Had he dared brag about it?

White Feather shrugged. "With these people it doesn't matter. A motorcycle gang has been offering a chaperon service. I heard another rumor about a shifter organization offering protection from other werewolves."

My blood chilled. "Really." I thought about what Zandy had told me, something about Lynx offering services. It seemed everyone wanted in on the new business opportunity. Out of the corner of my eye, I noticed Angel signal the food was ready. I ignored her.

White Feather sighed. "I'm not in the right crowd to fool anyone into thinking I'm going to date a werewolf, so no one is going to tell me much about protection."

"Most cops don't hire witches either," I said. Lynx had been adamant about whoever was looking for me being a cop, but Tino hadn't been sure. Which was it? Or was more than one person looking? Maybe the vampire had been the start of the rumor. I drummed my fingers on the table, trying to decide if there was any other information along this line that White Feather might help with.

"Look," he said, "if you're worried, why not stay away from Merlin for a while? She's obviously up to her ears in this stuff. It might do you good to keep away." He reached a hand across the table, although he didn't actually touch my arm. I could smell his cologne, a rich combination of soap, outdoors and probably shaving cream.

I signaled Angel, moving his attention from me to her as she bustled back to the kitchen for the food.

Neither of us said anything even after she brought the tray and set everything down. He took a few bites, and we studied each other while we ate. He was more handsome than I originally thought, but it could have been the candles. He had fox eyes, watchful, but with a hint of playfulness.

"You do much work for Merlin?" he asked.

I nodded. "Full-time. I'm afraid I can't walk away."

Those blue-green eyes looked, oh, so disappointed. "It might be dangerous."

"I assure you that it is."

"Are you a witch apprentice?"

I never considered myself fully-learned. "Yes."

He smiled. "You any good?"

I couldn't help but smile back. "Merlin only works with the best."

"Whatever protection she sold Dolores, if you don't know how to make it, have her teach you," he said with sudden seriousness. "I think it would have worked if Dolores had used it right."

"How do you know?"

"These women are playing with fire. Dolores was teasing the wolf or trying to tame him. She shouldn't have done that."

I silently agreed. "What about the others?"

"Those murders feel different, but the cops are putting them all in one basket."

"If…" I didn't think Zandy would ever come forward. "If the cub that did Dolores came forward, it wouldn't really help, would it?"

Hope kindled. "Do you know who it is?" He reached out and grabbed my wrist. With my hands halfway to my mouth, I almost dropped my burger. The shock from his touch wasn't just hormones. The silver around my neck sang, earth responding to earth.

I didn't move. He let go. "Sorry. Didn't mean to grab you so hard."

He hadn't. I let out the air that had gotten stuck in my lungs. Did he know he was a warlock? Power often sang loudly, but a direct line was rare. I'd felt it in the desert, in the wind across my arms, usually when there was lightning in the air. He was like that.

It took me a moment to catch my breath. My blood had responded automatically; like the silver, it surged towards that magic, wanting to sing too.

"Do you know who it is?" he repeated, more calmly.

I finished taking a bite. It gave me time to find my feet. "It's a kid really. I could tell you who it is, but it won't solve your problem because even if you got him, it would leave the other killer out there."

He concentrated on his food for a while. "It would solve one of my problems." When I looked up, his eyes were hooded, hiding secrets. There was anger there now.

"I have no loyalties to this particular werewolf," I assured him, "but I don't think it will do you any good at all."

"Believe me, it would. I need to know, even if it is only one murder."

"You want to arrest him, knowing he might end up keeping the police from looking for the other guy? That would leave the other murderer out there!"

"Never mind," he snapped. "This is dangerous business, Adriel. Tell Merlin that. Tell her she's better off not selling protection to young ladies looking for a good time."

"Or anyone else that comes looking for it right now." The vampire and his warning came to mind.

We finished eating. He paid for dinner. On the way out, he touched my elbow and started to say something, but then stopped.

I held my breath, but other than the very nice feeling of being close to a man and the clean smell of him, there was no heady zap.

He knew he was a warlock. Only someone who knew power could tamp it down to almost nothing.

Chapter 22

I abhorred nightclubs and not just the ones that attracted groupies looking for magic. I did not like body piercing, tattoos whether they were magical or not, and I hated loud booming noises that substituted for music.

Even though I could have used the cactus pot to reach Lynx, after my meeting with White Feather, the timing was right to hit the nightclub. If I were lucky, not only would I find Lynx, I might also get a handle on who was looking for me.

As soon as I walked inside El Ojo, I felt out of place. My jeans were not tight enough. Sneakers probably weren't high on the list of favored shoes either. I could have lived with being ignored, but it wasn't terribly helpful when after information.

My plan was to sit at the bar and listen to the place, maybe ask a few questions. While the earplugs I had purchased at an all-night Walgreen's cut the obvious noise in half, it was still too loud. The noise negated magic, mother earth and any intelligence required therein to work spells. I felt vulnerable.

Grumbling, I worked my way through throngs of people. A lady with fingernails as long as the beer mugs on her tray swayed by too quickly for me to grab anything. Apparently there was a signal or some sort of dance required. I watched as an over-muscled zealot bumped hips with her, grabbed a drink and managed to slither his arm up against her while he paid.

"Gross."

Muscle-man could have used a few more clothes. His ripped Nike t-shirt showed off his wares, but it wasn't doing a thing to catch the sweat. "Gross," I muttered again, moving on.

I wiped at my own sweat, glad I hadn't worn heavy makeup. A wig would have been the death of me. Given that the look of the day here was "bursting out," my summer knit top failed miserably as a decent disguise. "Too bad."

In due time, I managed to find the bar and crowd my way to the inside long enough to decide that ordering a club soda would only mark me as an idiot. "Lookin' for a friend," I shouted at the bartender, putting money on the table for a beer that I wouldn't drink. "Kid named Lynx. You seen him tonight?"

The bartender, a muscle-man with more clothes than the one on the dance floor, shook his head. I don't know if that was because he didn't hear me or he didn't care. "Do you know where I can find a witch?" I yelled next.

He used his chin to point towards one corner. I took the mug he deposited on the bar and pushed my way out of the crowd. In the process I tripped, spilled beer and ruined someone's bust-out blouse. The woman screeched at me, but I did what everyone else did; I ignored it and moved on.

I kept a death grip on what was left of the beer so that I didn't have to go back to the bar.

The corner where the witches were doing business was busy. One lady was reading palms in a booth partially obscured by sheer curtains. The hand she was generously interpreting was mashed between her breasts. No way she could see it well enough to read it. The paying patron didn't seem to mind. Every time the witch leaned forward to divulge information, the guy gasped and grabbed the nearest plump object for support.

To her left, two more restaurant-style booths were set up with heavier gauze curtains. A peek into booth number one revealed a woman who was having a seizure or pretending to be communicating with the dead. From her pale make-up, maybe she had even come back from the dead, who could tell?

In disgust, I tried to discern how anyone would go about looking to hire someone other than the carnival freaks. My skin positively crawled in this place of negative magic. It was my last instinct and apparently the only one left that worked in a place like this.

I set my beer mug down and pushed toward the back of the place. Tino had back rooms in his other places. Why not here? Surely that was where a conversation could take place, because the dancing bodies and front office were nothing more than a petting zoo.

The first door I found led down a hall to restrooms. The lengthy corridor was an extension of the petting zoo, only slightly quieter. As I turned to go back the way I had come, a shadow flitted back against the wall. It could have been my imagination or one of the lovers shifting with passion.

I scanned the moving bodies, but no one stood out. If someone wanted to use the bathroom, they weren't moving toward those doors.

The next door off the main looked like a game room. Business might be conducted there, but if someone wanted to hire me, why look in a place with electronic games?

My ears were ringing despite the earplugs, and though I hadn't touched the beer, I was woozy from breathing in too much smoke.

The third door I tried led to another hallway, but I was so dizzy I had to stop and lean over. There was no telling what I had breathed in. Lowering my head helped. I tried to tilt it sideways in order to watch the dim corridor around me.

Bodies came and went, mostly through the doors on the ends. Black shadowy people moved in my direction, and one went past me to a door further down the hall. Empty eyes flicked in my direction, but the guy didn't slow down.

As I turned back to face the main area, another shadow moved against the wall. I leaned over, trying to see better. My skin was still warning me. Someone was following me.

Slowly, my head still down, I shifted along the wall, feeling my way. I stayed up against it so that I could see someone approach, but there were angles, doors, and other halls branching off. I peeled each foot from the sticky floor as quickly as I could without running outright.

I shouldn't have come here. For some stupid reason I thought that because Tino ran the joint, it would be respectable. Bottom line, it was a bar, and it was open for business. Tino wasn't selling quiet family nights here. I wasn't sure how it affected my opinion of my friend, but I didn't have time to worry about it. The shadow at the top of the hallway detached itself and moved towards me.

I scooted around the nearest corner and realized that I had left one building for another. Joined buildings weren't uncommon in Santa Fe because most original adobes were very small. Proprietors often bought a series of adobe shops and combined them in order to have larger real estate.

I dodged into what appeared to be another main party room with more couples dancing to different music.

Running wouldn't help me blend. Walking and moving in the crowd wasn't going to help much either. I worked my way across the dance floor, weaving between couples and trying to avoid being noticed. Halfway across, an arm came out high, hitting me in the chin.

I stumbled and knocked into a lady, who promptly fell on the floor.

Ignoring the chaos, I kept going forward until I found the hallway to the next set of bathrooms. From around the side, I looked back.

There were no familiar faces, but it didn't take long to spot more than one person surveying the crowd. Bouncers? Or someone looking for me? One guy, built like a small tank, stood by an entrance or exit. Another guy doing some serious looking at the crowd was smaller than the bouncer type. He was dressed business-casual rather than tucked-in muscle shirt. He shook a hand here and there, working the room as he studied the customers. It was impossible to tell if the guy was working his way toward me or if he actually needed the restroom.

I moved backwards only to find that the hallway was a dead end.

Without being too obvious, I got behind the next guy who came out of the john and stayed very close. Once out of the hallway, I headed for the only other door in the place, a small door in the shadows near the rear of the building.

Too bad the fire alarm went off when I went out the back way.

It didn't occur to me until I got outside that El Ojo was right next to the cemetery on Cerrillos road. The graveyard had long been closed due to lack of funding, but what did that mean for a cemetery? Big deal; more people wouldn't be buried there. Not like anyone already interred was going to complain about being abandoned.

The first fence wasn't bad because it had wooden support boards across the sides and top of the chain link. It also wasn't very high. The second fence was harder for me to climb because it was normal chain link. I was in a bigger hurry too because my original follower plus a bouncer was staring out the open back door of El Ojo.

You'd think the neighborhood would care about all the bar noise, but on the other side of the cemetery there was a school for the deaf. The two guys behind me could kill me and celebrate loudly. Even better for them, I was already in a cemetery, no burial necessary.

From behind a decaying mausoleum, I watched the bouncer looking guy step outside and slam the door behind him. In the last swatch of light before the door closed, I saw the glint of a gun in his hand.

When he started to climb the fence, the gun clanged against the metal. He stopped, tucked the gun into his pants and tried again.

Witches didn't carry guns. I always had spells, but none were all that lethal. Some spells could turn that way depending on my desperation, but in general I didn't want to use my talent to kill anyone. Frankly, I'd rather use a gun, but didn't happen to have one on me.

The guy after me did.

It would have to do for both of us.

My magnets for levitation were still in my shoes. Since I wasn't about to go flying around the graveyard, the magnets would work nicely for a different spell.

A place to set the spell and infinite time would have made things easier. Obviously, I wasn't going to get such a luxury. The guy looking for me walked with his arms flung out as if he were a human drag-net, and I was going to run right into them. His breath rasped loudly enough for me to hear, but I couldn't tell if he was a shifter using his sense of smell or tired from climbing the two fences.

I took off one sneaker, checked the outline of the tombs around me and prayed no one or nothing evil had been buried here.

Muttering carefully, I used a spell that would only resonate with iron and other metal materials. *Nothing* plant, nothing that might have come from say, bones or degraded ashes-to-ashes type earth.

I tried to draw most of the energy from myself, but magnets were of the earth, and they automatically resonated back to like energy.

The feeling from the ground was downright creepy. Worse, it smelled.

I didn't want energy from this place.

Shivers ran up and down my back. The spell barely touched the surface of the earth, but in a place like this, it didn't take much. The mustiness that rose to my fingertips and my shoe made me want to gag. It was probably nothing more than energy from rusted iron responding, a screw, hinges…I gulped.

Mr. Net-man was almost on top of me before the spell had enough strength to pull the gun toward me. It floated rather faster than I expected, but the speed was probably a good thing, because Mr. Net lunged.

The gun batted against my hand. I snagged it and rolled away. There was no time to put the shoe back on, but I kept it tucked under my arm. I was not leaving anymore pieces of myself for anyone to find.

"Dammit," Net-man snarled when his arm barely missed me.

He didn't give up. He reached over the top of the tombstone.

I somersaulted behind the next one, crouched and fired over the top. The bullet parted his hair and probably took a piece of his ear.

Net-man stood with his arms wide opened for a split second.

I kept my arms steady on the tombstone, the gun trained right at the breath of air emanating from his lips.

Net-man pulled in his arms and changed course. He weaved like a drunk toward Cerrillos road at the front of the cemetery.

We had both come in the side, but apparently he wasn't going to try and get back inside the club.

"Your aim ain't that great," Lynx informed me from behind another gravestone.

I nearly shot him. I would have shot at least the tombstone, except he was there one second and gone the next. Trembling, I set the gun down and hugged myself. "I didn't have time to aim right for him, idiot!" My eyes searched the eerie darkness.

"What are you doing here?" Lynx's voice came from behind another stone.

"Looking for you."

"In the place of the dead? You think I spend much time here?" He appeared behind me, a neat trick since I was slowly turning, checking every direction possible.

I nearly throttled him, but settled for catching my breath.

"You couldn't leave me a message?" he asked.

"That would have been a better idea."

"It's dangerous here," Lynx said. "You shouldn't have come. There are people looking for you."

"Who are they?" I hissed.

"You need work that bad? You don't usually take hires from here."

"No, it isn't the work."

"Come on." He grabbed my arm and pulled me up. "You ain't equipped for that place." He looked down at my flat shoes, at least the one still on my foot, and up to my shirt, which hadn't budged. I wasn't showing any more skin than when I started, but I was dirtier.

He snorted with disgust. "You maybe better hire yourself some protection if you're going to be cruising around without trying to blend in."

I found my shoe, which had fallen after all, and put it on. The gun wasn't going to do anyone here any good, so I picked it up also. "I heard you might be selling protection services," I said, trying to keep the sarcasm and annoyance out of my voice.

Lynx didn't answer, he just kept walking. With no choice, I huffed after him. "Who was that guy?"

Lynx walked me to my car, climbed in and said, "He's the one I told you about, the one talking around about working for the "government." A cop."

"Cops don't go running after people for no reason." I got in the driver's side.

"You did leave the club by way of the back door. Could be he thought you stole something."

I shook my head. "No way."

"Probably not," Lynx agreed. "But you were asking funny questions about witches, and I hear was looking for me also. That's gonna get some attention even if he didn't know you were a witch." Lynx gave me his twisted smile. "At least you found me. I'm charging you dinner in addition to my regular rate on account I had to go find you in the graveyard."

I glared at him, but didn't argue. He was as bad as Angel about getting food tips, but I wouldn't get any more information out of him until he had eaten.

There weren't many places open all night in Santa Fe except the nightclubs. I pulled up to The Owl's drive-through. Technically the sign said, "Closed," but we knew it was open all night. I ordered him a burger and fries.

"Make it two."

I ignored him. Growing or not, the kid didn't need two burgers at two a.m.

I let him get his mouth full before I started pestering him. "I came for two reasons. I was trying to figure out who is looking for me. I thought maybe it was a vampire, the one that came knocking, but that guy didn't look like a vamp."

Lynx almost choked. "You 'ot--" he gagged. "Vampires--"

"Don't worry, the guy and I already talked it out," I said. "But he did find me after you said someone was looking so I figured maybe it was him at the clubs, maybe not. I also thought maybe it was my normal police contact, but my contact swears no one on the force is looking for me."

Lynx swallowed and peered at my neck.

I smacked his head lightly. "It was days ago, dummy. I'd have already made you into fish fry if I was going to go after you. The guy was checking up on a bunch of witches."

"Hmph." Lynx went back to eating.

"If it isn't the police, and it isn't the vamp, who is it? Who is that guy?"

"Dunno. The guy says he is looking for the best witch money can buy, and he asked about you by name at least once. He could be for real, but I still think he's working for somebody else because he isn't the only one putting out that message." Lynx shrugged. "I tol' you, it's like a bigger search, not one normal looking for a single spell."

The description sounded like what the vamp had said, but I had already told the vamp to look elsewhere. Of course, who knew how long it would take Matilda to tell the vamp about Sheila? Even if the vamp looked into Sheila, in the meantime the vamp could leave the offer open.

"Fine," I sighed. I pulled up to the house. "Next issue. I hear from your buddy Zandy that you're competing against Arturo or in this dating service or something." It was none of my business. After stating my suspicion out loud, I had nowhere to go with it.

"So?"

I got out of the car and slammed the door. He got out also, but didn't come up onto the porch.

"Lynx, there has to be a line. You can't go selling sex like some kind of whore!"

"It's not only sex. You think you're the only one that can offer protection? Besides, yours didn't work so well."

"There was nothing wrong with that spell!"

He shrugged. "Sure, I know that. But the normals, they worry about stupid stuff. If they want to hire me to protect them from a date gone stupid, I ain't gonna tell them that your spell works."

It took a great deal of patience not to snap at him. "How do you convince them they need protection? Wait," I stopped him. "They already know they need protection because there are four bodies littering the landscape."

He nodded. "Yup. And I'm the bodyguard."

"What happens if Arturo comes after you looking to put you out of business?"

His eyes flattened. I'm sure his ears went back. "Who cares what he thinks? He runs a business, and I run mine."

"How did you get into this business of yours?" I demanded, thinking of the complications.

He closed his lips stubbornly.

I rolled my eyes. "Lynx! I am not trying to steal your business. You said yourself that it's easy enough to convince the normals that they need protection. Shoot, Dolores thought of it all by herself."

"Yeah." He loosened up enough to admit, "The ladies still want dates, but they want more reassurance."

"Don't you realize playing bodyguard could get you killed?" I was pretty sure that Lynx wasn't a werewolf. Even if he were a Lynx as his name implied, who hired a cat to go against a wolf?

"They pay for a shifter, and they get one. I'm quick enough to get them out of danger."

I gulped. "Do you change for them? To prove it?"

He shook his head no before I could envision cameras and evidence. "Nah. Mostly they don't even meet me at all. I do the hiring like you do, through an intermediary."

My eyes closed. "Zandy."

"Yeah." He sounded unsure for the first time.

"Let me guess." I opened my eyes. "Zandy needed to be able to convince a date that he was safe so he hired you."

Lynx shifted his gaze away. "Not exactly."

I waited.

"Arturo needed some proof that Zandy wouldn't go nuts again. I offered to hire myself as protection."

"You work for Arturo?" I shrieked.

"Freelance. On that one case I do Arturo a favor. But I do protection on my own."

"What's to keep Arturo from having one wolf protect against another?"

"People trust it this way more."

The numbers still weren't adding up. "But for the others, is Zandy your go-between?" Lynx didn't answer. I sighed. "You're working for Arturo and Zandy." I paused. "And charging them both." I knew I was right even though his face didn't change. "It's no wonder Zandy told me that if Arturo found out about you, you'd be in trouble."

Lynx grinned, showing a flash of tooth in the starlight. "Aw, come'on. Zandy, he's a lot of talk."

Yeah, and Lynx thought he was freelance. He was up to his ears in this stuff. I didn't like it, but there wasn't anything I could do about it. Well, maybe one thing. "Lynx, you gotta draw a line in the sand. You can't be hiring yourself out to both sides."

"Says who?"

"Says me. I am not hiring some guy who can't reasonably draw a line where there should be one. I don't want a guy working for me that is basically a…a…pimp." There, I'd said it.

"Fine by me." His voice was a low hiss. "I can make more in one night from one of these jobs than a month on yours. When those ladies hire, they pay *big* bucks. They want the *best* and that's who I am. Maybe you should find out who is looking to hire the best. Maybe you'd make more money that way too."

"That's little more than whoring--" He turned his back and walked away. "Lynx!"

The night swallowed him without any help from his talents.

He was gone. And mad.

And I couldn't blame him. Who was I to try and tell him where to draw the line? But my God, these ladies were dangerous. Couldn't he see that?

I paid him close to two hundred a month on a normal basis, and that didn't count the extra work he had been doing for me lately. One night at that price?

I shook my head. Money that big was going to attract a lot of attention.

Dammit, it already had.

Chapter 23

My work calendar went from the pot into the fire the very next morning. As if it wasn't hard enough to fraternize at bars, Vi called first thing in the morning and demanded I attend a political schmoozer.

"I don't think me going will help your husband," I told her.

"Harold has to be there. I want someone in the background to counter any spells that Sheila sets to humiliate me or Harold."

"Why don't you both stay home? Harold doesn't need anyone yanking on his chain right now, and I assure you, if she yanks and he doesn't respond, we're going to have a bigger mess than we already do."

"There is no way he can get out of attending. Every political hack thinks he deserves special attention before awarding a contract to Los Alamos. It's Harold's job to be seen, to rub the right egos."

"Have him take someone important out to lunch instead," I suggested.

"He has to go! As it is, he's going to be missing a few days of work, and he may as well not have a job if he can't keep doing what needs to be done."

"Why will he miss work?"

"Because we went to a shaman like you recommended. It's done wonders for him, but the shaman said Harold wasn't ready for a sweat lodge yet. We have another appointment with the shaman next weekend. If it goes well, we plan to stay through Tuesday."

"No sweat lodge? What did the shaman give him then?"

"Nothing. We hiked out to some ceremonial cave over by Bandelier Monument. There was a lot of adobe. The shaman said the mud would be good for him."

"Ah. The ruins blocked Sheila."

"All I know is Harold was happier than I've seen him in a long time. We ate enough food that he actually put on a couple of pounds. I want to go back."

"That's good news. The longer Harold flies under the radar, the better he will get. He can build up his resistance, but only if he isn't being noticed. I'd have to advise against the party."

"I'll pay triple your regular rates since you know how dangerous this could be."

Lately people were willing to pay a lot of money for witch services. It should have been a stroke of luck, but all it did was convince me that things were going in the toilet. "Vi--" I hesitated. The truth was best. "I can't guarantee that I can stop Sheila from controlling your husband. She still has some very powerful pieces of him. I can't compete with that."

Predictably, she went from professional to shrill. "You're not as good as she is, are you?"

"Depends on how you define good. I would never bind someone like she did. That doesn't mean I don't understand the spell, it means I wouldn't use it."

Silence on the other end.

"There isn't anyone who can necessarily stop her," I said. "If the shaman thinks Harold wasn't ready for a sweat lodge, well, that means we have a long way to go. We can protect him, and we can wean him. Eventually the spell will weaken. But the best thing is for him to stay away from her."

"He has to go to this party. It's his job!"

"Maybe if you weren't there, Sheila would be less likely to create a scene?"

It was her turn to hesitate. "I thought of that."

"And?"

"And she might cause a scene anyway. Just to embarrass him. That's why I need you there. Surely you can counteract some of the spells she might try."

"It's possible. But if she realizes we're fighting her, it could undo all the progress we've made so far. I'm not sure he could withstand a second trip down that lane, especially if she isn't careful about how she does it."

"And we can count on her to be careless," Vi agreed bitterly.

"It's likely."

"I want you to go." She swallowed noisily. "And use your judgment. Deflect the spells at least a little."

"Even if I have to let some through, and he is embarrassed?"

She choked back a sob. "Even then. He might lose his job, but he'll live." There was another stretch of silence. "Right?"

I didn't have a good answer for that question. Some people couldn't live with embarrassment. I didn't know enough about Harold or what had been done to him. The parts I did know scared me. "He's been through a lot already. We had better prepare him for the worst."

Vi sniffled. "I'll send a courier with the invitation. I need your address."

I gave her the address of Matilda's shop. "I'll pick it up there. And remember. I can't stop her outright."

Vi took down the address before saying, "You know, I think you're afraid of her."

She hung up before I could explain that Sheila was a very scary witch. She had a piece of me already, I just didn't know what it was. If Sheila figured out who had broken into her place, I'd become the sudden focus of her attentions, and that was a war I didn't need.

I clamped down on the fear and headed for my closet, hoping I had something appropriate to wear to the gala event.

Chapter 24

My head was in the closet, but my mind was in my workshop. I needed some spells at the party that had no part of my aura anywhere near them. Since that wasn't possible, I would only be able to produce a version of stink bombs--little more than smoke and mirrors.

That sort of thing wasn't my forte, and I hardly had time to design them anyway. Fumbling through my closet, I cursed. I had to find a dress, get my hair done up fancy, and pack spells. In addition, I was pretty sure I couldn't show up in sneakers, and I couldn't find my heels. "Moonlight madness."

I only had one dress. I hadn't asked if the party was formal or semi-formal. Unzipping the dark periwinkle silk from its garment bag I declared, "Semi-formal it is." A long evening gown would have given me more places to hide spells, but I didn't have time to shop for one.

"How am I going to get the levitation spell to fit inside high-heels?" I pawed through the bottom of my closet. At some point, I probably owned heels that went with the dress, but I had no idea where they might be. I did find an old, extremely dusty backpack, but no heels.

Sighing, I sat back. "And I bet no one will appreciate it if I show up covered in garlic bulbs either. This gets better and better. Only a half-wit would show up anywhere near Sheila the witch."

My dress didn't come with pockets. That meant sewing in flat pockets against the liner and carrying a sheath strapped to my thigh. I had to have spells. Luckily spells was a favor I didn't mind asking of Matilda.

She was the queen of stink bomb spells. Some were of her own making, some she bought from other sources to make sure she had the best inventory around. I couldn't ask for a better way to spread false auras.

I called her and told her to expect the invitation to the party. "I also need some spells."

After I gave her a list of what I thought would help, she said, "Stop on by. I'll have my very best ready!"

"Okay, I'll be over in about an hour, maybe two."

On the way to her place, I stopped at Wal-Mart and bought the best heels I could find. There were two walk-in places nearby for hair; I picked the closest. The new hairdo wasn't the best I'd ever looked, but it wasn't the worst. At least with my hair pulled up on my head, the scab and bump were hidden.

When I got to Matilda's she had spells galore laid out on the glass counter. She locked the door behind me and waited for my reaction.

"Excellent." I gave her a thumbs up and began loading up one of everything. "I don't want your aura on too much of anything."

She reached out to touch one. "Are you sure? I can always use the business."

"Not this business you can't."

"You aren't using this on a vampire, are you?" Her eyes went wide, and she reached out to grab my arm. "I got your message to Patrick. Are you telling me that he isn't leaving you alone?"

"Good to know he got the message. Unfortunately, someone is still looking for a good witch. I don't know if it's a vamp or not. Either way, no, this stuff isn't for a vamp. I'm beginning to think a vamp would be easier than what I'm dealing with. Trust me when I tell you that you don't want your aura on all this stuff." Sheila might still be breathing, but she was a blood-sucking creature either way.

"Worse than a vamp?"

I nodded. "Yeah, way worse."

Questions churned across her face, but instead of prying, she said, "Sit. Where did you get that hairdo? Don't go back to that place, ever."

She disappeared into the back and returned with a small suitcase.

"Uh, Mat--"

"Don't worry, I know you don't want to look like me. I don't know why, but I know it." She fluffed at her hair and batted her eyes before laughing at my dismay. "Your hair is pulled back too tight." She tugged at it delicately with a hair pick. "It makes your eyes scrunch. You look like Ms. Roman; you just gotta stand up straighter and get a ruler."

I laughed. It was in Ms. Roman's first grade class at recess when Matilda first showed her skills as a witch. She created the perfect illusion that the class bully was a billy goat--one which was promptly chased by a group of kids who were no longer afraid. Even back then she hadn't cared that she wasn't a normal. Now especially, she didn't care. Matilda put on the show, and the rest of us could barely keep up.

She busied herself around my face, pulling, tugging and re-arranging. When she was done, out came the make-up brushes. "You should wear a touch of purple around your eyes. It would bring out that green in your left."

"Eye shadow makes me look like a lizard. My grandmother told me so."

Matilda rolled her eyes. "Well, yeah, green eye shadow would do that."

"I don't need to enhance that color anyway. It makes me look strange."

Matilda smiled. "And that would be bad, how?" She spun around, demonstrating the true definition of strange. "You'd get more customers!"

"I'd get more trouble. I don't want to be recognized tonight at all, never mind with something so memorable. Trust me. There's a big bad witch out there, and I don't want her to know about me."

"Turf wars?" She didn't mean to pry, but she couldn't contain her curiosity.

I shook my head. "Voodoo. Blood spells. Bad news." Most witches were distrustful of other witches at best, feuding at worst. Matilda was a rare fit in the middle because she had carefully cultivated a reputation for not only selling wares of other witches, but keeping identities a secret. Sheila was outside all of us, in a class of her own. She was rogue, playing a normal and dabbling in stuff no sane witch would admit to. I gave Matilda the highlights without mentioning that the witch had taken a piece of me.

Matilda was silent while she took in my story. The makeup brush faltered a bit when I described the number of amulets Sheila had in her safe.

When I finished talking Matilda said, "This woman is going to bring the normals down on all of us, isn't she?"

"If we live through her spells."

Matilda gave my shoulder a worried squeeze and then handed me a mirror.

I took a quick glance and then did a double take. I almost didn't recognize myself. "Wow." Wavy strands of dark hair floated around the sides of my face. My forehead was no longer prickling and protesting against being pulled backwards. The former bun had transformed into some sort of piled mass of curls.

"I don't like the purple." The eyeshadow did indeed cause the green flecks in my left eye stand out. "It's got to go."

I started to rub at it, but she stopped me. "Okay, okay. But let me do it. We'll go with plum and browns."

With a few strokes, she redid my eyes.

I checked again. I looked...elegant. Fancy. Good enough that my own sister would have approved. I smiled. "Thanks, Mat. You're a genius."

"I know." She wagged a brush in warning. "I'm not sure changing the eye shadow is enough to really disguise you, you know."

"I'll be careful."

She gave me a look. "From the sounds of it, I had better be too."

I nodded. If accusations started, Matilda was an easy target. Everyone knew her, witch and normal alike. Witches were a finger-pointing lot with half of them pretending they weren't witches, a quarter of them in denial and most of them socially unable to mix with either normals or non-normals. The paranormal community was accustomed to being chased and maligned. They would be more than happy to turn over one of their own, especially if it took the heat off the rest.

I gave Matilda a big hug. "Do watch your back." I thanked her again for making me beautiful and headed back to my house to finish the transformation.

* * *

Dressing for the party took longer than I planned, but then, I wasn't that used to stuffing flat packages inside my dress and checking for lumps.

Before I left, I moved the cactus pot to indicate to Lynx that I needed to talk to him. I owed him an apology. He was a good employee…and friend. I couldn't afford to have a tantrum over his other business deals.

Looking at the invitation and directions as I drove, I realized that the party was at a private residence. For some reason I had expected it to be at the grand ballroom at La Posada or one of the other classy resorts. Instead, it was out on the southeast part of town where mansions dotted the mountains.

I found county road sixty-seven easily enough, but forgot to pay attention to the letter after the county road. I started on plain sixty-seven, which had nothing in common with the directions. I finally realized that I needed county road "sixty-seven f."

Even once I found "f," I went up two driveways without knowing where they would end before I found the right one.

My arrival was somewhat later than "fashionable." Luckily, according to the invitation, it was a "night to celebrate art, dancing and fine wines," rather than a sit down affair where I would have had to make a bad entrance.

A short Hispanic caterer answered the door. There were about ten other individuals dressed in the same black and white uniforms handling doors, trays of appetizers and drinks. Unlike the bar the other night, no one was bumping and grinding before taking one of the long-stemmed glasses.

Musicians were set up in the living room. Not a band mind, but musicians. There was a lady playing solo on some sort of renaissance horn instrument. It was a real horn, one that looked like it belonged on a cow. The only other instrument I recognized was a dulcimer. Happily, the music was picked up by hidden mikes and pumped through the mansion's sound system rather than giant speakers. It wasn't bad music, but a little eerie.

My next observation was that if Tino used illusion candles in his restaurant, they didn't work very well. I recognized White Feather from across the room. Despite the dark suit replacing the casual polo from the other night, there was no doubt it was he. His jacket fit nicely, the black herringbone pattern offset by a smooth white shirt underneath. Instead of a tie, the shirt had a notch at the neck forming a tiny vee.

Very handsome. Very classy. He looked my way. His eyes moved away and then back, but I was fairly certain it was the look of a man appreciating an attractive woman, not of recognition.

It didn't take me long to spot Harold. At this point in his life he was a diminutive man, the curve of his back making him look far older than he was. His little balding head bobbed up and down as he talked to another suit.

Like a first-time convict, every few seconds his eyes flicked nervously around the room.

I doubted he would recognize me, which was for the best. Not only did I not want him clinging to me, I didn't want him watching me all night. On the good news front, the appetizers were dynamite. The shrimp roll I grabbed was stupendous. There was also no sign or feel of Sheila.

Just before I headed to the open French doors that led to a garden, I caught a glimpse of White Feather again. He looked right at me, but his eyes turned politely away when I caught him staring. A part of me sighed. It would have been very nice to be at this party for fun, rather than work.

Outside, stairs wound up to a second floor balcony. At eight o'clock, most of the stunning view was probably gone, but I was tempted to climb upstairs and look.

There was still no Sheila, no bad vibes anywhere. The music could very well be imparting peace and tranquility, helping my mellow mood. A lot of old songs and instruments had such magic, especially if the musician was any good.

Artwork was displayed on almost every wall, and most of it was for sale. I checked out three piñatas that hung strategically around the room. Their bright colors made great party decorations. Given their placement they were probably part of the artwork for sale. An elaborate display of a burro with attached cart hung near the fireplace. Large paper maché fruit and vegetables looked as though they had rolled from the cart and landed perfectly piled on the fireplace's carved wooden beam.

I stood close enough to the group inspecting the scene to look like I belonged to someone.

As I turned around, I nearly ran into White Feather. He caught and steadied me, his hands warm on my bare arms. "Dance with me," he invited, tugging me from the crowd. His hand slid down my back as he guided me to the dance floor. It occurred to me that I had never answered, not verbally anyway.

"Lovely evening," he whispered into my ear, sending pleasant shivers down my spine. The music was slow, background noise. "Not as lovely as you, of course."

Luckily he was holding me close enough that he couldn't see my blush. "Oh. Thanks." We were in a waltz embrace, but instead of a relaxed hand on my back, he held me in a solid hug, my chin sideways so that my nose wasn't pressed into his shoulder.

He pulled away enough to look into my eyes. "Is Merlin here tonight?"

I sucked in a quick breath. I don't think he was certain who I was, but trapped in his arms, he felt the quick tension, the swell of my breasts as I held my breath for that little bit too long.

He smiled triumphantly. "Or did she only send her beautiful messenger?"

I should have been angry at the trick, but the real game was still in play. Of course Merlin was here, but he didn't know that I was Merlin, and I wasn't about to tell him. I lifted my chin, and smiled. "You're not supposed to use one dance partner to snag another, you know."

His teeth flashed. "Wouldn't dream of it. But I am curious, of course." His eyes swept the room, but instead of returning to mine, he looked far away. "I thought it would be best to pester her about the identity of the werewolf. You," he looked back down and smiled. "Look too good to spoil with business."

Another compliment. Flustered, I looked away.

Spinning me gently, he added, "When I saw you here, you fit in so well, it took me a while to figure out why you were familiar. It never occurred to me that Merlin would have such above-board associates." His shoulders shrugged lightly, taking me with him, my arm gently shifting against his muscular chest.

"Merlin wouldn't fit in here very well." The hunched over disguise, bulbous legs and walker would get me quickly redirected to the senior citizens bingo nightclub.

White Feather laughed, a rumble in his chest. "I don't suppose she would, now that you mention it. I guess that is why she has other people to be her eyes and ears. I didn't know they would be so," he looked down at me again, "exceptional."

The impish light in his eyes drew me out. I ignored the hint for information about Merlin. The music drifted through me like a spell. Perhaps it was the smell of him, all male, steady and firm, but I had an undeniable urge to snuggle closer.

He hadn't left much room even if I had the temerity to encourage him.

We finished that dance and the next one. The next selection was taken over by a short man playing what looked like a miniature organ with bags attached. We either had to start hopping around and clapping with everyone else or stop dancing.

White Feather reluctantly let me out of the hug, but kept my fingers for a moment longer. He brushed them lightly with his lips. "You're a good dancer."

"Uh--mmm." I caught his eyes and then looked away bashfully.

"I'll claim you again when the music slows back down."

Every nerve ending tingled, and it wasn't from the wizardry that I had felt the other night. Maybe better than magic, it was just the man that made it so. "Sure," I said lightly, watching him walk away. My eyes weren't the only ones following him either.

I might have stood there like an idiot the rest of the night had Sheila not made her appearance. Not that she made an obvious entrance. Professional that she was, she wore a dressy designer suit rather than a gown. Her white hair was done into a neat coif. I had thought her hair might be platinum blond, but I could see now that she had prematurely grayed to a perfect snow. Makeup announced an intellectual rather than emphasizing the feminine side of the woman. I thought her nose still looked hooked.

"Hmph." Perhaps I had risked coming here for nothing. Such a paragon wasn't likely to throw herself at Harold, nor was she likely to tolerate Harold drooling on her in public.

Socially perfect or not, she made my skin crawl. I had to hope she didn't feel any such reaction to me. I prayed that whatever she had used to trace me in the canyon had burned itself up. If it were a hair from my head, she would have saved some. If it were merely cloth from my backpack or clothing, I had burned all traces. She should have nothing of my aura left with which to sense me. Shouldn't, absolutely shouldn't.

I clutched the wall, trying not to hyperventilate.

She started making rounds, shaking hands, smiling and moving through the crowd. I edged outside to the garden where she would be less likely to sense me. Even if she carried an amulet--I turned back. With dismay, I noted her necklace.

Frantically, I searched the crowds for Harold. His reaction would tell me if the amulet was designed to control him. If not, it could easily be for someone else in the crowd. There were a lot of hopeful politicians in attendance and a few of the real thing. I recognized the mayor, at least one guy I thought was in the state legislature and a very popular radio announcer.

My hand instinctively reached for my own throat. There was no reason for her to constantly wear a beacon in the hopes of finding me in every crowd. Especially here. I had burglarized her home, not met her at a soirée.

I didn't see White Feather until he was right in front of me. Good trick too, considering I was halfway behind a rather fabulous sculpture of a cougar and its cub. The garden was lit, but mostly by dim, porcelain luminarios. The candles lined the walls, the staircase and a single bagged light sat on each wrought iron table.

"You wouldn't be avoiding the next dance, would you?" he teased.

I spared him a quick glance and a half-hearted smile. "Not at all." I tried for a nonchalant tone, which was ridiculous considering he had caught me peering out from behind a piece of artwork.

Sheila moved through the crowd, patting shoulders and chatting. I didn't dare take my attention off of her, although she didn't seem in danger of coming closer or going upstairs out of sight. Where was Harold?

White Feather's attention followed mine back inside as he tried to ferret out what held my avid gaze. "You wouldn't happen to be here on business?" He leaned against the stucco-covered staircase.

"Of course not."

"Not here for fun," he guessed anyway. "I wonder what could be so interesting to Merlin." He cocked his head and scanned the crowd again. "Could it be that she won't tell me the name of the werewolf because he belongs here? Is she protecting someone with political power?"

The smile I offered was strained. "I doubt it. Merlin wouldn't care about that."

He bristled. "She must have some excuse, but whatever it is, it isn't helping. Need I remind you that the guy murdered a young lady?"

"Shh," I warned, reaching for his arm. The doors to the balcony were opened to the dance floor, and we weren't the only ones out here. At least three people used the outside as an excuse to smoke. One woman sitting at a table looked our way, but I couldn't tell if that was because White Feather was handsome or because she had overheard.

White Feather stared down at me, his jaw clenched. Without turning his head, he let his eyes flick to the people around us. Deciding I was right, he put one arm around me and clasped my hand. "You're more agreeable when we're dancing."

"So are you."

His feet barely moved, which was fine because although other couples out here were holding hands, none were actually dancing. I didn't want to go back inside either. "You could help me, you know," he murmured. "All I want is the name. I could take it from there, no need for you to be involved."

He was holding me rather tighter than before, but it didn't carry the same feeling. He turned me in a spin, further into the garden. He was facing the doors. I didn't like that. I needed to keep an eye on Harold. Gently, I pulled away, but though he gave me some space, he didn't let me go. "I wish I could help."

"Will you at least tell Merlin I want another chance to meet with her?"

I sighed. "Okay, but knowing one name isn't going to solve this problem."

"He killed once. And he could do it again." His eyes sparked again, this time with anger.

"It's possible."

"Would two be enough?" he demanded. "Would you tell me then? After it's too late for number two?" He released me suddenly.

He was right. Zandy was guilty.

Before I could defend my not-so-defensible position, the back of my neck sent a warning that reached the hair on my arms. Spinning around, away from White Feather, I searched.

Sheila was easier to find than Harold because of her white hair. She sipped calmly from a wine glass. If she was working a spell, it didn't show in her eyes. They were perfectly focused, politely amused by the man standing in front of her. The man wasn't facing me, but it wasn't Harold. If she were going for Harold…

I found the broken man because he was moving towards Sheila, a glazed look on his face. He was everything but drooling, answering the call. Sheila never even had to crook a finger in his direction. There was absolutely no fight in him. He probably didn't even know he was under duress.

White Feather stiffened behind me, and I couldn't blame him. Unfortunately, I didn't have time to answer his questions right now. It was beyond rude to walk away, but I headed inside, the words of my first spell choice forming on my lips.

I was stopped cold by a sudden breeze. Strong enough to flare cigarettes, it brushed past me, scented of pines, of earth, of strong magic.

I put out a hand as though to capture it, breathing deep of its cleansing scent. The breeze ruffled clothes, weaving through the crowd, dispersing everything from odors to…I found Harold again. He stood, a puzzled expression on his face. He shuffled forward uncertainly.

The amulet around Sheila's neck glinted an unhealthy green, but the breeze dispensed the color into an unfocused smattering of light. I turned back around, my mouth agape.

"You sensed it too." White Feather took my arm again, and this time, we danced together indoors. The breeze wafted gently. I didn't know if White Feather meant that I had sensed the magic in the air or Sheila's amulet. In his arms, the earth smell was stronger. I nearly swooned.

Gads, but the man was powerful. I couldn't help but suck in a lungful of air, savoring the clean fresh scent, the power that he was controlling.

As suddenly as the breeze arrived, it was gone. I could still feel the remnants around White Feather. Like a giddy school girl, I clung to him. "Wow."

White Feather was bemused. "You have a lot of empathy, but you'd better learn to block it," he said.

I blinked. "Yeah. Good idea." I sighed, not wanting to get a hold of myself very badly. I had been listening for spells, much more receptive than normal. White Feather had hit me from behind like a load of bricks. Very sexy bricks. Glancing around, I noted that the laughter was a bit fuller, the air brighter, cleaner.

"How long will it last?" I was impressed with the warlock magic. It was so alien from the spells I used. Moving elements was not easy, but he had called a strong enough breeze that it dispersed things, including the voodoo spell that Sheila had tried to use.

"What did you sense?"

"Bad spell."

"Do you know what it was? I could smell the poison. I had no idea where it was directed."

I nodded. "A coercion spell."

"From whom?"

I smiled at him. "Not the werewolf."

He grimaced. "Werewolves don't tinker with spells. I wasn't asking after that information again."

"I know you weren't." He deserved an answer to his question. Any witch or warlock deserved to know about Sheila. "It's from the lady with white hair."

"I thought it was directed at you. Do you know why someone would be after you? Or Merlin?"

I shook my head and leaned closer to his ear. "Not me, not this time. But it's good that you blew it away from us."

He shrugged. "There really wasn't an option. The wind had to come from outside. I could hardly blow it from inside. Besides, that would have drawn the spell towards us."

"It was a good thing that you did." Having been hit by the bulk of the cleansing rush, I was still incredibly tingly. That and feeling his strong male body dancing next to me didn't require any outside magic.

"I suppose you're used to being around this sort of thing." His voice faded at the end.

Surprised, I felt a rush of warmth from his neck. "Around what sort of thing?"

He didn't meet my eyes. "People like Merlin," he finally said.

"Witches?"

He shrugged, a quick, irritated movement.

"I suppose I am. What's the big deal?"

"The big deal is that I broadcast what I am across an entire room."

He was right. Such a broadcasting could be very dangerous. Worried, I found Sheila again in the crowd. If she was perturbed, the signs had already been erased. I had been so pleased that she wouldn't be able to home in on me because I hadn't done anything, that I hadn't thought of the possible danger to White Feather. "Do you think she can tell where it came from?" I asked.

"Who?"

"Sheila."

He glanced over that way, but didn't let his eyes linger. "I doubt it. We moved away pretty quickly from where I started the spell." He grinned. "And you did a good job of jumping into my arms as though there was nothing else you were focused on." He laughed when I ducked my head in embarrassment.

He was right. I had been nearly overwhelmed, my heart singing instead of pounding with what should have been anticipation of a fight. "I am quite sure she noticed your effort." Sheila certainly hadn't reactivated her spell. Whatever reason she had called Harold, she had decided to do without.

The good news for Harold was that she had no reason to suspect he was fighting her because he hadn't been. The bad news for me was that she knew someone had dispersed the spell. The news was worse for White Feather, but at least Sheila didn't have a piece of him or his belongings.

White Feather guided me back out to the edge of the garden where we could stop dancing and watch the crowd again. The tiki torches burning on the far wall threw some light, but not enough to put us in the spotlight. I had a hard time taking my attention from him, especially when he still held me in the circle of his arm.

"I'm not normally so sloppy," he said. "But that stuff felt nasty. Who is she?"

I shrugged. "She works at Los Alamos. Obviously she's a witch."

"Voodoo?"

"At least," I agreed. "Bad news."

"Make sure you don't give her a reason to notice you."

I didn't bother to tell him that I already had.

"I think I'll go see about damage control." He squeezed my shoulder. "You'll be okay? I assume Merlin already knows about this, and she can help protect you."

His eyes were in the shadows, but I could tell he was concerned.

"Merlin will do everything she can to keep me safe," I assured him.

He bent his head. I held my breath, but he changed his mind. Instead of kissing me, he touched my cheek. "Be careful."

Without another word, he moved away. There was no sign of the power from before. I wasn't sure what he intended to do, but I was worried. I didn't want her attention on *him*.

Or Harold, I thought guiltily. I had neglected my charge. Hmm. Perhaps I could do some damage control on my own. Two auras of magic were surely harder to track than one. Or better yet, three or four.

Smiling, I decided to put Matilda's wares to good use. Sheila might backtrack to Matilda, but Matilda had enough inventory, Sheila would be more confused than anything.

I headed toward the ladies room and retrieved a few packets.

On the way back, in an idiot act with a glass of water, I dumped the water along with the spell onto a poor waitress.

"Oh, I'm so sorry!" I grabbed a towel from the waitress' own arm to help her dry the spray. Carefully, I swabbed the liquid spell. It would soak through her skin nicely.

"I'm quite all right," she said stiffly.

I kept her from drying the arm by batting her ineffectively with the towel. The woman was already invisible by a lot of social standards, and the spell was good. When I got done, I could barely look at her.

That gave me an idea for the other spell, a much more flamboyant one by Matilda. Originally I'd planned on using it on myself because it would basically make me look exactly the opposite of my normal appearance. I had hoped it would keep Sheila from getting any kind of real description if she got a bead on me.

I surveyed my options.

The downstairs bar was an overlook into the kitchen. The wait staff kept it busy by refilling trays, not to mention several people stopped to order special drinks. Heading upstairs, I found better opportunities. The upstairs room overlooked the balcony. The bar was manned by a single waiter. He had none of the appetizers to entice people over.

Most of the party-goers up here were standing aimlessly in front of artwork or were perched at a table gossiping on the balcony.

I moseyed up to the bar with my highest watt smile. "Hi."

The hapless, unsuspecting bartender smiled back.

"It's so busy in here tonight," I gushed. "My gosh, I don't know how you can stand it."

"Not a problem. What can I get for you?"

"Oh," I sighed. "I'm helpless when it comes to ordering." I leaned forward. I could have had no boobs at all, and the man would have looked down anyway. "Tell you what. Let's split a drink--what's your best?" I giggled. "You deserve it. I've seen you working so hard."

"Wine or something stronger?" he asked smoothly.

"Oh, the wine sounds good, doesn't it?" When he looked mildly disappointed, I giggled again. "But how about a teensy bit of something stronger? I *know* there are special bottles back there for certain people. Let's pretend I gave you one of their names."

He opened his mouth to protest.

"Come on!" I flapped my hand at him, catching his arm in what could have been a flirtatious caress. I whispered the mayor's name. "Or how about the football player? I bet he is on the list. Just tell your boss I said I was getting two drinks, one for each of them, and I ordered the "best" stuff."

The man checked quickly for other patrons. He got two shot glasses out with record speed. I didn't bother to note what bottle he pulled. I palmed the powdered spell into his glass. "Let me pour!" I said, waving my hands as a distraction.

"Uh, it's against regulations."

"Okay, I'll hold the glasses." I put a hand around each glass. "You pour but stop when I say." I giggled again and heaved my breasts onto the bar as though I had to do it to keep my balance.

Out of the corner of my eye, I saw two men come up to get drinks. The bartender hurried.

"There, there!" I took about a half shot and made sure he got a full one, swirling them both. Since the two suits had arrived, I whispered, "I'll sit here a moment."

"Of course." He eyed the drinks and weighed them against the two gentlemen who had walked up. I let myself appear distracted, took a sip of my shot, nearly gagged and waited.

He took care of business.

When he came back, he downed the shot in one smooth motion as he turned to put the bottle up. He winced and licked his lips, tasting the remnants.

"Mmm, you sure can pick them," I said. He must not have thought so. He picked up the bottle again and stared at the label. I distracted him with, "I might take your wine selection too." I sniffed again at my shot.

What the hell was I going to do with it? The thing had to be a hundred and fifty proof. The last thing I needed was to be wobbling around the place. I tried another sip and choked.

A helpful person nearly knocked me over patting me across the back.

I would have said thank you, but when I turned, it was to find White Feather beside me. He gave my back a firm pat and glared at the bartender. "What are you doing?" he asked me.

"Red herrings," I replied lightly.

He grabbed the shot glass and finished it for me. His eyes didn't even water. "I don't know if I have any idea what you're talking about."

The spell was good. When I looked back at the bartender, I didn't recognize him. The bartender had been overweight, but the spell made him appear much thinner. His lack of hair, well, for the night, he could dazzle the ladies with what appeared to be a full head. Of course it was the opposite of his remaining dark strands, but since he didn't even know he had any hair, who was he to complain?

It was possible that White Feather had seen the bartender before and then again after the spell. If he had, he didn't ask questions. Luckily, spells that were eaten or imbibed were different from the raw power White Feather wielded or the voodoo type. They didn't shout. They blended. Most importantly, they left an aura that didn't belong to me and didn't belong to White Feather.

I leaned into White Feather and whispered, "I'll explain later." I took the wine glass that the bartender offered and headed off to mingle.

It had been an hour and a half since I arrived, but Sheila had shown she would misbehave. The safest thing to do was get Harold out of here. He had made his appearance, I had done my duty, and I damn well knew I didn't want to fend off another attack.

It would have been easiest to give Harold something to make him ill so he could go home sick. Unfortunately, I didn't have the heart to put a spell on a man so badly used.

I searched out a phone, but the first one I found looked like an old fashioned gilded piece. I didn't want to embarrass myself by picking it up only to find it was an antique decoration. In the bathroom area, I found a normal looking one and used it to call Vi.

She argued with me, of course. "Is he in danger? What if she uses the page as an excuse to keep him just to show her power?"

"You need to get him out of here." I tried not to clench my teeth. "Trust me when I tell you that the hold she has on him hasn't diminished one bit. If she does it again, I can't fight it and what's more, I won't bother to try!" I wouldn't let White Feather try either, but I didn't tell her that.

"Okay, okay." She mumbled something and then, "But make sure he comes home when I page. I'll pay you extra if I have to."

"If he gets a page, everyone will know, and he can tell whoever he's talking to that he has to go." I hung up.

Sadly, when I walked back into the main downstairs room, Harold was standing in front of none other than the big, bad witch.

Chapter 25

"Drat." I headed for the nearest light switch. Matilda had given me several spells with "atmosphere." All I had to do was insert one into the system somewhere and maybe it would provide a distraction.

Finding a switch was easy. They were everywhere. Unfortunately, there were people everywhere too. At home I could have gotten to the wires, but here, there were too many people.

If only the hostess had hired me for the decorations, I could have set these things up ahead of time. The situation was laughable; a witch unable to find a place to set off a spell.

One look at Harold's glazed eyes, and I was about as far from laughing as I could get.

Searching for a way to dispense the spell into the air, I noticed White Feather, his head tilted as though listening. He was staring into the main room from the garden. I shook my head, a silent warning for him to leave well enough alone. From where he was, he might be able to feel the spell, but Harold was already reeled in. The aura was limited, unlike before. I had probably been upstairs when she activated it.

In desperation, I cornered the flutist. She was sitting off to the side, taking a break. "What is that flute instrument you play?"

"It's called a recorder," she told me helpfully, leaning over to pick it up and show off the long wooden horn. Between her gauzy green dress and her delicate features, she resembled a fairy.

"What was that one instrument you were playing before, the one that looks like a, uh, cow horn?"

She laughed, a soft tinkling that somehow blended with the other musicians playing nearby. "It's a Gemshorn," she said gaily, reaching into another box.

"Could I touch it?" I asked.

"Sure." She stepped further from the other players and handed me the horn. "It's from an ox."

Unfortunately, the end was stuffed with something, no doubt to control the sound. I handed it back and looked again to the recorder. "Can I hold that one?"

She obliged without any sign of concern.

Palming the spell, I caressed the wood, pretending to peer closely at it while I dumped the dust into the end.

"Could I talk you into playing it again?" I asked wistfully. "A request?"

She nodded happily. "I can play it, but I'm not sure I can play what you ask."

"Oh, I didn't mean a particular song." I glanced at Harold. Sheila had already done damage, no doubt. He was now talking. I needed to do something quickly.

"Play," I begged. I handed her back the long flute, the powder safely scattered inside. The spell was heavy. It wouldn't filter into the air quickly.

"I'll wait until Sam is finished."

"Could you accompany him on the song he's playing now?" I was more than a little frantic.

"Well--"

"Please!"

She backed up a step. "Well, I think I should wait. It won't be long."

"Or let me play it!" If I didn't distract Sheila soon, Harold was going to sell the keys to the kingdom or the secrets to blowing up the world.

"No, no, I'll uh, okay, a note or two." Watching me out of the corner of her eye, she blew a trickle of notes.

The spell leaked into the air and reacted immediately. It was too blue. She looked like she was smoking a giant blue cigarette.

The source of the spell was going to be obvious to any witch worth her salt unless I managed another distraction.

The flutist stopped playing and frowned at the end of her instrument before turning an accusatory glare my way. The horn continued to glow even though she had stopped playing.

"Harmless," I mouthed. "Honestly. Illusion."

She shook the flute, but that only made it worse.

"Play?" I put my hands together beseechingly.

A pinched look on her once friendly face, she put the instrument to her lips. The notes gave me cause to shiver. The woman had her own brand of power, and she was purging her instrument.

The other musicians glanced at us, but never missed a beat.

"Sorry," I mouthed, turning away.

With a desperate gulp, I headed for Sheila. I couldn't afford to leave Harold in the clutches of the witch a moment longer.

I got about two steps before bouncing off White Feather.

"What are you doing?" he demanded, grabbing my shoulders.

"She's at it again! Got to stop her. She's dangerous. Don't you dare get involved this time!"

The chemical from the horn finally dispersed enough to react with the lights. Once it hit actual bulbs, the room tinted blue. Art changed nuances, and people's faces were suddenly bathed in a soft blue color. The soothing scent of fresh mountain water filled the air.

I looked back. The flutist inclined her head, but not in a friendly manner. She was aware she had been used.

"Oh boy." I needed to find a better way to make friends. The woman probably would have gladly participated had I taken the time to explain.

Turning back to the problem at hand, I found Sheila and her crowd still standing near the fireplace. I watched in dismay as Harold extracted his checkbook from an inside jacket pocket. "Uh-oh."

Harold pulled out a pen and started writing a check. The man to one side of Sheila helpfully supplied a small notebook to support the pen and checkbook.

"Dammit." I couldn't afford to use magic around Sheila, but the mundane would do. I zipped around White Feather and headed straight for the fireplace. Unfortunately, my disguise spells were gone. If she spotted me, she would remember my real form.

I picked up the fire poker. Using my body to block the view of it as long as possible, I jabbed it hard above my head.

"Excuse me," I heard someone say behind me.

Candy exploded from the burro's piñata cart as I tore the poker out, letting it slide down my arm.

Tiny bombs of wrapped candy flew, startling the suit talking to Sheila and Harold. The poker "fell" over in the excitement. I giggled and fled from under the deluge as though I had nothing to do with the piñata breaking open.

Like children, the crowd reached for a prized piece of candy. One of the many, I bent to collect some. Out of the corner of my eye, I saw Harold staring down at the check in his hand. Sheila was looking straight at me. My heart skipped a beat, and I started praying.

She took a step toward me even as I dropped my eyes and scurried harder, my hand retrieving another spell from the pocket on the bottom of my dress. There was a tingle of power, a feeling of intense rage. The lady next to me gasped and grabbed her heart.

Instinctively, I blocked the power, clutching my silver necklace and reaching for mother earth through the floor for all I was worth. Sheila's power may have been directed magic or generalized, but it was ugly. Deflecting it was almost unconscious on my part; survival instinct.

The defense was, unfortunately, bound to draw her attention to me.

No matter, I couldn't stand her filthy aura oozing across me.

I don't know what might have happened had White Feather not entered the fray. Magic or mundane, his arm was no less accurate than a pro-pitcher. Two other piñatas exploded in a rich succession of candy and happy screams from the onlookers.

I moved with the crowd to the new candy, pushing the lady next to me into Harold in my rush. Harold swayed. He might have stepped back.

The feeling of evil rage stopped as suddenly as it started.

She refocused. "Harold, it's so generous of you to donate to the charity," Sheila said.

I felt a resurgence of power, but it wasn't the rage, it was a return of the coercion and control of before. "Aztec curses!" There was enough magic in the room to distract an entire coven of witches, but not Sheila. The suit who had handed Harold a supporting notebook was not even paying attention any longer. He was leaned over collecting a piece or two of candy. His face was clean-shaven except for giant white caterpillar eyebrows that were long enough to nab some candy on their own. If his beard came in white, he'd make a good Santa Claus. Maybe that was why his face seemed vaguely familiar.

Sheila's reminder about the check got Mr. Eyebrow's attention. He abruptly stood.

That's when I got my first real break.

Mr. Eyebrows had to step sideways in order to avoid stepping on another candy-hunter. Sheila moved to give him room and very nearly toppled over the person collecting candy behind her. She had to step away to avoid falling over.

No way was she looking at me and neither was Eyebrows.

I reached out and grabbed Harold's checkbook.

Faster than a gnat could buzz, I dispersed the next spell, a magical element of the smoke bomb variety. The light already shown blue, but now it bounced off white smoke that drifted into insubstantial shapes; trees, a balloon, a puppy dog. The spell was one of Matilda's wonderful illusions, blending perfectly with the party atmosphere. I prayed that it kept Sheila from spotting me half crawling, half duck-walking as I returned to collecting candy.

The checkbook went down the front of my dress. Maybe it would keep my heart from jumping out. If Sheila had seen me take the checkbook, I was toast. Almost as bad as using my own magic in her presence, thievery would immediately associate me with the break-in.

I moved several paces before standing with my candy. Someone threw more of the stuff playfully into the throng. I glanced towards the fireplace.

Sheila was staring straight at Harold's empty hands.

Before she looked my way, I reached under the slit in my dress for another spell pack. If I didn't distract her, she might have the audacity to try and track me from Harold's hands. Fortunately, he hadn't lifted a finger, so I wasn't certain I had even touched him. Still, his essence was on the checkbook.

White Feather was nowhere to be seen, but I felt another cleansing breeze, not as strong as the first one. The flutist may have taken pity on me, because I could feel magic from that direction also.

Had Sheila seen me take the checkbook? Would she remember my face?

I got myself outside.

Harold's check, the one he had started, went straight into a decorative tiki torch at the very back of the garden. To my amazement, I noted that he had written it to "Dr. Arthur Gonzales" to the tune of ten thousand dollars.

After the name, there was a shakily written HF and either the start of a "B" or "P."

After the check was ashes, I took the rest of the book and scorched it as best I could. The smoking, charred leather remains went under a bush where I hoped it would never be found.

I left via the garden without ever going back inside.

Chapter 26

With luck, it would take Sheila time to sort out all the spells. To be complete and fair, I used one of my own spells when I left. If Sheila had noticed me, she was going to have a hard time knowing when I departed. I pushed a touch of my magic around a couple talking in the garden. They would remember seeing someone of my description long after I was gone.

On the way home, I stopped at the San Miguel church to retrieve my wig. I was scared out of my mind that Sheila was going to somehow retrieve it. It was well after midnight, and I couldn't use magic because the church wouldn't allow it. I thought about ramming the car through the doors, but decided it was probably not a good idea.

I stood on the cobblestones outside the old adobe building and shivered violently. I couldn't feel mother earth. Was it because the ground was sacred or…had Sheila done something to me? What if I never felt mother earth again?

I swallowed hard to keep from crying. No one could take away mother earth, could they? What would I be if I couldn't feel her? Ever again?

I clenched my fists, concentrating as hard as I could. There was a pulse here; I had felt it before. A small keening escaped my lips, making me realize how crazy I was acting. I clamped my mouth closed. I was tired. Very tired, stressed and scared. Magic was no different than anything else. I couldn't perform the simplest of spells right now, never mind feel the energy of the earth.

I forced my fists to open, but my hands were shaking. Dealing with Sheila petrified every bone in my body. The look on Harold's face as she called him…I wasn't about to become a mindless playing card. Or worse.

Lynx could help me break into the church. I could get my wig back. I could set things right.

I ran for my car like a woman possessed and drove worse than a drunk. Panting, I ran up the porch steps, only to stop in despair. "Moonlight… curses," I hiccuped. The pot remained in its lonely location, ignored. Lynx had not moved the cactus to indicate a meeting time. He was obviously still mad at me.

Maybe tomorrow I would go looking for him. Or maybe I'd go after Zandy to tell him what I thought of him involving Lynx in his games.

I turned away from the pot and dragged myself inside. Too tired to walk into the bedroom, I collapsed on the couch.

I needed tea. Or food. I closed my eyes. It was too much work to prepare anything, but on the other hand, I was afraid to sleep in my current state. After having seen the soulless, wanton witch in action, I wanted to be on guard, I wanted my wig back...I wanted to scream and run far, far away.

For certain I had to call Vi to make sure she changed all her checking accounts and credit cards. Legally, anything Harold signed they would still have to pay for, but Vi could do her best to make it harder for Sheila to hand out Harold's dollars.

Half slumbering, I felt as though Sheila were eyeing me again, her mouth moving in words that would destroy me. Where was mother earth? My home was suffused with earth, with herbs, with mud, with silver. Why was there no comfort here?

Sheila need only raise her hand and the spell would be finished. I couldn't let her utter that final incantation or I would be under her power. I had to stop her! I had to finish this!

With a start, I jerked so hard I fell off the couch.

I was too young for night sweats, but I was drenched as though I had been running full-out.

Crouched on the floor, shivering as the sweat dried on my skin, I knew. Sheila may not have recognized me, but she had guessed I was at the party. The sweat indicated that she still had a real piece of me--skin, hair, something--and she was closer now than White Rock.

The clothes and backpack had been burned so she couldn't use them against me. I was damned lucky she wasn't strong enough to do more than cause night sweats through the adobe and silver of my house.

I got up and showered. The water blocked whatever spell was out there, but I knew she would try to reach through my dreams. I removed my dream catcher from the headboard above my bed and went into the lab. Sheila's fingerprints were still safely in a silk-lined silver box. Working with them while I was her focus was dangerous, but I had no choice but to trust the safety mechanisms in my lab.

I was so tired that if I had had to weave the entire spell from scratch, I don't think I could have done it--even though my life depended upon it.

I took a tiny snippet of Sheila's essence as I had done to create the compass for Vi's house, only this time, I wove a spell into the dream catcher's net that would specifically block Sheila. Anything bad would be trapped in the turquoise beads already a part of the catcher. With her essence woven into the fiber of the spell, she didn't stand a chance at getting through to my dreams unless she had another witch set the spell. Somehow I couldn't imagine anyone cooperating with her that closely, not on her best day.

I put the dream catcher in place and then went to the kitchen to boil water.

I filled four separate jars with the steaming water and carried them back to my room. I added crushed tobacco to the east, sweet grasses to the north, sage to the south, and cedar to the west. I was so tired, I scalded myself twice and nearly stabbed myself with a piece of cedar, but the steam would do its job. The very air in the room was now protected.

When I was finished, I finally crawled into bed and stared into the abyss until I fell asleep.

Chapter 27

By lunch time the next day, I still hadn't heard hide nor hair from Lynx. In case he didn't plan on stopping by my place out of stubbornness, I tried The Owl.

"Hey Tino," I called out to my friend at the bar. Taking a stool I said, "I've got another job, but for the alley rat. Have you seen him?"

Tino shook his bald head. Even though we never used names, he knew who I meant. "According to the rat, he won't be needing small jobs anymore. He stopped by a couple of days ago to let me know he appreciated my business, but that he wouldn't be able to keep taking on the small stuff."

"What'd you do, insult him?" Guilt at my own mishandling of the situation made me flush.

"Nah, he was in to eat, part of the standing payment." Tino shrugged. "Pretty happy about his "mother lode" as he put it. Said he was going to go house hunting over on the east side."

I stopped chewing. "What?" I tried not to choke on my mouthful of green chile burger.

"You surprised too about the house thing?"

"The house, the big job--what's the kid talking about?"

Tino gave a dry chuckle. "Who knows? All the shifters seem to be doing big business these days. If they aren't, they lie and say they are. Your friend said he was all about protection, so he couldn't mix his old business with his new one."

"Did he give you any more details?"

"Someone told him he needed a squeaky clean reputation to work the protection racket. He said it was a big job that offered to hire the best, and nothing but the best. Your buddy couldn't stop talking about how it was his reputation for being trustworthy that would give him the edge over the competition."

I put the burger down slowly. "The best?" My next sentence came out a squeak. "He's not working for a vampire is he?"

Tino's eyes blinked fast, as though his brain was reloading. Then he roared with laughter. "Where did you get that idea?"

I shrugged sheepishly. "I've been hearing about people looking for the "best" lately. Vampires, cops, whoever. It's making me nervous."

"How many people you get looking for the worst? Or average?" He chuckled.

I nodded, but something still didn't feel right. "Of course."

"Don't worry, chica. It can't be a vampire. What would they need with shifter protection? Not much affects those guys." He laughed again. "And the kid is right. You know anyone else you can count on like him? He takes any job there is, and he gets it done. At least he did until now."

"Yeah. I know." I sat back. My remaining fries and burger didn't look so appetizing anymore. "Can I get this wrapped to go?"

"Sure. Speaking of jobs, you still do the little ones, or do I have to find me a new witch?"

"I'm not looking for a house on the east side yet. Whatcha got?"

Tino wrapped the burger expertly in aluminum foil and took out a bin for both it and the fries. "Granny Garcia needs some perfume. Hide the depression, bring out the beauty."

"Okay sure." Granny Garcia was never the same woman. Tino put in various orders, specifying if the "perfume" needed special spells for relaxation, herbs to make a woman more beautiful, or whatever. Aromatherapy was generally one of the weakest spells out there, but for some clients, that was as far as they wanted to venture down the magical trail. Perfumes like this were really Matilda's forte, but not every client wanted to walk into a public shop.

"Single dose is all she needs," Tino said. "She makes her living cooking tortillas. Had a tragedy. Needs to surround herself with something cheerful."

This was more than I usually got. Lack of info sometimes meant the client didn't like the perfume, but in this business it was pay first unless the client was longstanding. If the client was willing to provide enough information or money, sometimes I'd throw in a few samples until we got the mix perfect. "I'll bring it by."

"I'll have the cash."

"Thanks."

When I got home with groceries and supplies, the cactus pot still hadn't moved. Lynx either hadn't stopped by or he had ignored the request. Reluctantly I moved a second pot to a different location to indicate that it was important.

In the meantime, there were spells to be spun. Under the circumstances, the lab represented the safest place in the world for me right now.

My hair was the most likely object held captive by the Big Bad Witch. To counter such, I designed glass beads filled with a spell made from holy water and appropriate herbs. Blowing glass beads strung together with a thin filament of silver thread was not easy. The result was a lot like my tortillas. They were bulky and not very round. Still, the elements I needed were trapped in the glass.

The whole mess was easily entrenched in a French braid with extra beads for a necklace, bracelet and ankle bracelet. I didn't think I could stand the beads at night, but at least I wouldn't be completely vulnerable while walking around or attending any more public parties.

I used the remaining herbs in a lotion. It was a desperate attempt because it was very difficult to get enough magic into a lotion to effectively bounce a spell away.

While I was spelling, I got out Lynx's old protection packet. Taking something from the old one and weaving it into a new one would make the new one stronger. I put some of my best work into the new pack. He was a shifter, so I couldn't use silver, but I did mix in threads of yucca fiber, new cotton, and dried corn silk. Inside with the herbs, I nested a tiny blue turquoise carving.

I hesitated then, but given the current dangers, I couldn't afford to leave out protection against witches. It was hard for a witch to protect against her own. I couldn't use an arrowhead because it would interfere with my own magic in setting the protection spells, so I chose a round malachite pebble in the image of the sun to protect him from evil spells.

The gift might help when it came time for me to make my apology. If he let me, I would weave in a snippet of his hair to tie it all together.

Feeling more relaxed, I set it aside and looked at the clock. It was getting late in the day, but I couldn't put off visiting Vi. I gathered up an extra strand of beads and put the jar of lotion in the old ratty backpack I had found in the back of my closet. Harold couldn't wear the beads, not in public, but it wouldn't hurt Vi to wear them. The lotion wasn't likely to do much more than help with dry skin unless I made it a lot stronger.

I put it back on the table and drove over without bothering to call.

Vi answered right away when I knocked.

"He's home safe and sound?" I asked politely of Harold.

"He's home." Vi sounded breathless, like she had been running. She had on white shorts, a white silk tank and thin sandals. Her fingernails would have looked better if she hadn't bitten them to the quick.

"Did your husband mention he lost his checkbook?" As usual, I had to encourage her to let me in. I stepped into the cool tiled entrance, forcing her backwards.

As she backed into the living area, I went into a shortened explanation of what had been about to happen when I took Harold's checkbook.

"Oh my God. I wish you had called. I thought she had taken it! All he remembered was that he talked to her. When we couldn't find his checkbook, I canceled everything!"

"Good."

"Good? But I didn't need to if you rescued it!"

"Did you hear what else I said? He had been *about* to write a check for ten big ones. You would have had to cancel everything anyway. You need to reopen all bank accounts in your name, and not allow Harold to carry anything but some cash."

"I can't do that!"

"Yes, you can. It may be damned inconvenient, and it may not stop her anyway, but there is no point in making it easy. If she goes for his money, at least he won't have checks or credit cards for her to tap. I think it was another attack on his self-esteem to prove she is boss, but she didn't get the money, so she is likely to try again."

Vi put both hands to her head and pulled hard on her hair. Strands came out in her fingers. I noticed for the first time that on the right side of her forehead she had a small bald spot.

I winced.

"She wanted that money to get to me! Harold wouldn't have even remembered writing the check. I'd have made a fool of myself trying to track the money down thinking it was fraud, and all along he would have willingly signed it."

"You could be right. I'm almost certain that the check was to a charity." The plan was sheer genius really, cruel and well thought out. "You would have looked pretty petty trying to get it back."

"I hate her," Vi snarled. "I will kill that woman with my bare hands if I ever see her again."

I knew how she felt, but I was willing to bet that in any kind of fight Vi would lose. "Listen, Vi, you're out of your league here. She probably planned to do this in front of you to make it more personal. What could you have done?"

"I'd have ripped that check up in her face. I don't care if it was for charity!"

I sighed. "Maybe you would have. Maybe not. The point is, she could have done it, but she didn't. You *must* keep Harold from public functions. I don't care if it means his entire career, Vi. I won't do that kind of job again. She's too powerful, and doing the kind of thing I do in a public forum is beyond stupid."

"Who was the charity?" she demanded.

"HF...I think it was HFP Gonzales, something like that. Why?"

"I'm taking them off my list for good." She went over to a cabinet and extracted a phone book. She leafed through it. "H...F...Home for Pets?" She ripped the page out and handed it to me.

The ad looked legitimate, although it appeared to be a veterinarian service rather than a charity. "There's more than one office," I noted. "There are a couple of phone numbers concerning strays. I'm guessing that's the charity part. It could be the right place."

"What does Homes for Pets do for her? I guarantee you she didn't force Harold to write that check out of the goodness of her heart. She's using *me* to pay someone off!"

I had to agree that Sheila didn't seem to be the charitable type. "You could be right."

"As long as she needs money for her projects, Harold and I are in danger." Vi clenched her fists. "Find out who they are. Find out if there is something we can use to get money back from this charity if she steals it again. There has to be a way because she's going to keep coming back for more until we're both dead."

"Okay, okay," I agreed to calm her down. I pulled the extra set of glass beads out of my backpack. "In the meantime, maybe you should have a little bit of protection for yourself." I didn't like the idea of giving her something that was from the same batch as my own protection, but she deserved something. "These beads might block a quickly done spell and cause it to bounce."

Her eyes took in the beads, both the ones in my hair and in my hands. "I don't know which is stupider. Paying you for magic or letting her take the money by writing checks. It's all the same, isn't it?"

I shook my head. "You're a scientist. Not all scientists are the same. I'm quite sure that not all scientists even believe in witches."

"I am a researcher, not a scientist. This was something I didn't understand. All the signs pointed to something--hypnotism, mysticism--something that was not natural. I didn't have to believe in it to start studying it."

"The chemical reactions on the brain aren't magical," I said. "Coercion drugs or chemicals that stimulate passion are all just chemicals."

Her eyes flashed angrily. "But only witches seem to know how to target the brain like Harold is being targeted."

"Scientists too," I said. "Sheila is as much scientist as witch. She mixes potions and tests their effects. If you stop thinking of witches as all the same, it will be easier."

"Whatever. I studied it and needed help. I'm glad I didn't end up with a complete crackpot." She stomped towards the kitchen, her sandals slapping the tiles like a brittle warning of a woman about to crack.

I waited, not certain where she went or why. When she returned, she handed me cash. "Everything else has been canceled. I'm sure your kind are quite used to cash transactions."

She hadn't asked how much the beads cost. Although I had told her I would accept triple for the party, five thousand was still overboard. "The beads don't cost quite this much."

"It would have cost me ten had you not been there." Her voice hiccuped. "I know you're in this for the money. Maybe the next time you're around when Harold is in trouble, you'll rescue him instead of calling me to get him out of trouble. Consider it an advance for the next time." Tears streamed down her face. If she hadn't been so pathetic, I would have been insulted and angry.

"That isn't what happened, and you know it." I took my fee from the money she had handed me and left the rest on the chair. "Keep getting him help, and spend as much time in protected areas as you can. You need to find him another job and get him away from here."

She didn't answer. Turning away, she put her knuckles between her teeth to keep the sobs inside.

I showed myself out since she wasn't pretending to be a capable hostess. Witch magic had harmed her husband. She associated me with that evil even though it wasn't my fault the spells had left scars behind.

There was nothing I could do about that.

Sometimes being a witch was very, very hard.

Chapter 28

I was running low on herbs, I needed to get my wig back, and it would be a good idea to pick up some easier work to pay the bills. To do job number two and most of number three, I had to find Lynx. From the unmoving cactus pots on my porch, it was apparent that he wasn't interested.

I had tracked Lynx in the canyon, but I wasn't sure that it could be repeated because the aura I had used was weak.

Heading to my bedroom, it didn't take long to find the tuning fork I had used to find him. The fork was still in the bottom of the plastic bag Lynx had made out of my rain poncho. The tie to Lynx wasn't strong because it was nothing but sweat and aura.

Even if the fork worked, using it again would probably be unethical. Lynx wasn't in danger--none that wasn't of his own choice.

I shook my head and left the tuning fork in the pile.

My best hope was to track Zandy. I didn't want to do that, but I might be able to get a message to Lynx through him. The only other alternative was to go back to Tino's groupie nightclubs. That wasn't going to happen.

I used the hair Zandy had left behind and linked it to a pager. It would vibrate if I happened near a "scent." The second hair went to a newly carved tuning fork. Once the pager alerted me, I could use the tuning fork to get me closer.

Heading to the plaza, I made the rounds. Sure enough, White Feather had left the signal for a meet.

I smiled. I wouldn't mind seeing him again. Taking his padlock, I replaced it with mine so that the meet would be at San Miguel where I already had an overdue date with a wig. The padlock also included my telephone number this time. We knew too much about one another to keep playing the subterfuge game.

Next stop was the ski slopes high above Santa Fe. I took the Winsor trail at the top and wandered through the forest in search of aspen bark and a few other items. The forest here was not entirely friendly to me; the earth vibes spoke of snow and ice even though it was far from winter. The winds scoured the landscape, a stronger power that often threatened rather than soothed. There were patches where I felt more comfortable, where the magic eased to a softer pace, but like all magic, it drifted and moved, flowing to and from various crannies.

The magic did call to me, and I yearned to able to hike to the meadows for sweet grasses, but there wasn't enough time today.

I drove back down the mountain, feeling better about my accomplishments than I had in days. Fresh mountain air had more magic than any herb packs I could make.

My next stop was out on Old Bishops Road towards Tesuque where I could gather most of the lower elevation herbs that I needed. The trail was south of Tesuque at the very edge of civilization. Houses with tall wooden fences backed to the first part of the trail, closing it in like a tunnel.

Interestingly, as I walked from the dirt road onto the trail, the pager gave a faint buzz. I pulled the tuning fork out of my backpack, but it barely quivered. The signal wasn't strong enough to tell which direction was freshest, but unless Zandy could jump the six-foot high, tightly lashed juniper fences on either side, he had to have gone along the trail recently.

I walked quickly. The fences and high brush not only trapped Zandy's aura, they trapped the smell of burro and horse droppings.

It wasn't hard to believe that Zandy had been out in the mountains; he had probably traveled as a coyote. It was careless of him to take coyote form so close to the city, but carelessness fit his profile.

I hiked past the property fences into the forest. Piñon and juniper studded the hillside. Along the river, there was a short wire fence put up by the forest service to protect the river environment. It may or may not have helped, but it did keep witches from collecting the pure spring water and moss until further up river.

I walked past the occasional dog droppings and the fencing. The faint traces of Zandy disappeared as the area opened up.

I hiked over a mile, taking my time, gathering moss, piñon seeds and juniper berries.

Finding the traces of Zandy made me wonder. Had he been out here because he lived nearby or for some other reason? There were packs of werewolves who hunted out in the mountains for good old running fun, but what if werewolves were out here for other reasons? The body Lynx had told me about wasn't near Tesuque, but who was to say there wasn't another one, newer or older?

Hiking alone wasn't new to me, but worrying about packs of werewolves was. The undergrowth was thick near the water. The hillsides were covered with trees. A nice big ponderosa could hide a threatening stranger, man or wolf. A felled piñon would make the perfect spot to conceal a dead body.

I sniffed lightly and then deeper, but there was nothing other than pine needles and normal decay. My imagination didn't force me to run back, but I did listen carefully. Mexican jays mocked me, dodging close and calling out warnings to their feathered friends.

It was impossible to watch for anyone while walking back through the fenced area. The stream noises covered even my own footsteps. The fences were tight, high and constant.

Against a wild animal, I would lose in any kind of race through the narrow trail. If I had to, I could levitate over the fence. Then, if I didn't kill myself by hitting one of the trees, I could hope there was nothing dangerous waiting on the other side.

Halfway back, the pager buzzed again. I checked the tuning fork, but it was mostly an excuse to look behind me again.

There was no one. The fork vibrated slightly, like the pager. Even those faint traces stopped as soon as the trail widened to the dirt road.

Breathing heavily, I got back in my car. I drove up to the main part of Tesuque, stopping once in a while to try the tuning fork. It was doubtful I was going to find Zandy this way. He had either not come this way recently or he had been in a car, leaving no aura.

I took Tesuque Village Road back to highway eighty-four to head home. I was almost to the turnoff when I spotted a billboard for "Homes for Pets--Adoptions, Services, Care."

"Aha!" Mr. Eyebrow's likeness was right on the front, although someone had trimmed the caterpillars and dyed them black to match his hair for the ad. The sign had "HFP" in the bottom corner. I hadn't planned on doing that particular bit of reconnaissance today, but since I spotted the sign, I followed the directions to a parking lot a quarter of a mile ahead.

May as well make sure the charity was a charity. I'm not sure what else Vi thought I might find. Sheila could still get money any time she wanted as long as Harold had access to any.

The clinic was a typical adobe building with a small penned area in the back. There were no outdoor cages that I could see. The place looked a lot better cared for than, say, a county humane society.

The minute I got out, the pager went off.

Even more interesting, when I reached back inside the car for my backpack, the witching fork nearly jumped out. "Zandy? Here?"

Zandy sure as hell wasn't the charitable type. He must live in the area. This place wasn't very far from the trail where I'd picked up his scent, but a vet's office? "What kind of pet does a werewolf keep?"

I drifted through the lot to the door. Gold letters stared back at me from the glass pane. I stopped with my hand on the door, frozen.

The big embossed letters answered a lot of questions in a hurry. "Arturo Gonzales, DVM," glinted off the window.

I stared at the name. I hadn't made the connection at the party because I had no reason to associate the Spanish and English, although many Hispanics switched their name from English to Spanish depending on who they were talking to. I hadn't thought of Arturo-the-werewolf-pimp in the party setting even when I saw Dr. Arthur Gonzales on the check. If it hadn't been for Zandy's aura when I got out of the car, I might have believed the name was a coincidence.

With a hard swallow, I backed away without going in.

As I got in my car, my heart beat faster than the witching fork had twitched.

Chapter 29

It seemed to take forever to get home and find my phone book. Then, at first, I couldn't find any connection to Homes for Pets and Dr. Gonzales because the doctor's name wasn't listed in any of the "Home for Pets" ads. I finally found it under veterinarians, just as it had been on the door.

"Arturo Gonzales DVM" didn't have a separate ad in the book. He had to be the famous Arturo, the one setting up dates for werewolves. Why else would Zandy's scent have been near there? And what in the world was a vet doing hiring out werewolves? Had he treated a werewolf at one time or another and branched out into the "dating" business? Or was he a werewolf himself?

With his eyebrows, I could believe it, but lots of facial hair wasn't exactly proof. Even if he was a werewolf, why was Sheila getting Harold to give Arturo money?

I checked the internet. The good doctor Gonzales was associated with the HFP charity in several articles. There were four charity locations listed; one on either side of Santa Fe, one in Albuquerque and one in White Rock. Hmm. Another possible tie to Sheila. Were they neighbors?

More searching found a likely address for Dr. Gonzales on Brownell Highland, off Bishop's Lodge. The north Santa Fe location made sense if he worked out of Tesuque frequently. There were multi-million dollar homes on the west side so he could keep his eyes on his rich neighbors in case they were interested in dating werewolves. Not that he could market the service in the open. Maybe he identified rich teenagers, and then had Zandy or some other werewolf approach them.

That still didn't answer the question of who was killing the women. If Arturo was interested in keeping his dating service open, why didn't he keep the berserk werewolf out of the business?

I rubbed my fingers across my silver bracelet, worrying about Lynx. He shouldn't be messing with these people.

Before checking out the other clinic in town, I called Mom. My nerves in the Tesuque canyon didn't seem so out of place when I heard what she had to say.

"Two more," she gasped out as though she had been running from the werewolves herself. "It was a *threesome.*" Dramatic pause.

"Two women?" I guessed cautiously.

"Can you believe it?" She gave a magnificent snort to show her disdain. "What are these girls thinking? Men are animal enough without this other garbage." She ranted and raved for several minutes about the dangers of men.

When she stopped for air, I inserted, "Did the girls go together for protection?"

Another snort. "Anyone willing to gutter with an animal, pah!"

I took that to mean that mom's neighborhood had decided the girls had sunk to such a level that not only were they willing to date werewolves, they also might be interested in a threesome even without a werewolf. "Mom, where--"

"It isn't safe for you to go out at night! You should be in bed where it is safe and warm. If you're worried, you come and stay here. Who are you dating that has you so worried?"

"Dating? No one."

"Oh, you can tell me." My mother giggled. "You know I can check with the neighbors, and if he is a wolf, I will find out." Though her voice was teasing, she wasn't joking. Her collection of neighbors could strip the mystery from a man faster than the FBI. They could find out stories about his ancestry that the guy didn't know himself.

"Don't worry, Mom. I'll bring all my dates home for a check-up."

"When? I can't wait that long. You come for dinner tomorrow night."

"How about next week? Saturday or Sunday?"

"Sunday," she said. "What do you want me to fix?"

That was an easy one, and she already knew the answer. "Tamales. Fresh ones."

She laughed. "I know! I have the eye."

"Yeah, right." I never knew how much vision my mother really had. Guessing what I wanted for dinner wasn't magic. Tamales were my favorite dish, and I was far too lazy to fix them myself.

My mom advised, "You bring a friend if you want. You need more friends."

She was right about that. Even better would be friends I could *find*.

I hung up and decided I wasn't done checking on Arturo. How did a vet fit in with the political schmoozing crowd? Vi might know, but telling her that the "charity" guy might also be pimping for werewolves was probably not a good idea.

My sister was into schmoozing with rich crowds, but I hated to ask her for anything, including information. I had one or two rich old biddy customers who might help. Matilda had even more of that type of customer.

Unfortunately, rich old ladies gossiped heavily and while that was good for getting information, it wasn't so great if word got around that a witch had come visiting with questions. My sister, on the other hand, wouldn't mention my visit to anyone. She might even take pains to hide it.

I grinned. Perfect. I could irritate her and get information about the snob crowd all at the same time.

I grabbed a couple of useful herbs as a peace offering. "Oh, you'll love these." It was all the rage to drink chamomile after a stressful day. She wouldn't accept an actual spell from me. Then again, she probably wouldn't use any herbs that came from me either.

There was no point in calling Kasandra because she would make an excuse to either meet me elsewhere or not meet me at all. She guarded her mansion as though it were one of the million dollar homes rather than a quarter-million dollar home on the edge of a wealthier neighborhood.

On the way there, I went south of town until I found the "clinic" where Arturo supposedly did his charity work. It was on a remote dirt road. I would have missed it except for the "Homes For Pets" sign.

A note tacked to the inside of the glass door announced hours on Thursday from six to ten in the morning and then again from four to six in the evening. According to the small sign, Thursday was the only day to drop off stray animals or get a pet "fixed" for a small fee.

There wasn't a soul in the dirt parking lot nor could I detect any animals. Surprisingly, the pager didn't go off, not even when I walked around to inspect the outdoor pens. The signal was completely absent. "So Zandy doesn't pick up dates here, at least not recently."

Looking at the trash blowing against the fence, I could see where the place wouldn't impress too many females, especially rich spoiled ones.

I wished again that I had something of Lynx's to see if he was hanging out around any of these places, but there was no use wasting time on the thought.

I got back in my car and drove to my sister's place. It was the beginning of rush hour as people tried to get home for the evening. Thankfully, when I left her place, I'd be going against the traffic.

It took me an extra fifteen minutes to get there, but only a scant moment for Kas to answer the bell. I sailed in with, "Darling, whatever have you been up to?"

"What are you doing here?" She peered back outside, checking her circle drive.

"Don't worry, I parked my little car behind the oak tree. It barely shows."

Kas shut the door, eyes very like mine, staring at me critically. I had worn Levi shorts, the real ones with hems and everything. My t-shirt was dark purple and nicely decorated with silver lizards that matched my silver earrings. My outfit was nothing compared to the spiffy pink linen pants, pink blouse and heels she was wearing.

"They'll think the cleaning lady is here," she muttered.

I started out teasing and light, but it backfired because I got angry. "Sally drives a nicer car than mine, Kas. And she's a lot nicer than I am too."

"She probably makes more money than you also. How is Mom?"

I raised my eyebrows. "Fine. I talked to her today. Aren't you keeping up?" I handed her the herbs I brought. "Some soothing chamomile tea. There's also nice purple lavender salts for your bath."

"I know the bath salts from the teas." She took the package and shifted it from one hand to the other without looking back up at me. We both stood there in the tiled entryway listening to the air conditioner come on. After the heat of outside, it felt good.

I sighed. "I came to ask you about a guy I met the other night."

Her eyes went wide.

I waved my hand. "No, I don't mean your personal opinion. I meant you might know him because he is likely to be in your circle, rather than mine."

"Oh." She licked her lips and shifted the herbs again. Hesitantly, she took a step forward and then stopped. "Should I make some of this tea?"

I shrugged, pretty certain my excellent teas and bath salts were going to go to waste. "Do you have a soda? It's kind of hot for tea."

She smiled, letting out a breath of air in a puff. "Yeah. Sure. Or ice water. We just had a new filter installed in the house."

I followed her dutifully to the kitchen. She set the package down carefully on the spotless tiled island. No plastics in my sister's house; she took two crystal goblets from her maple-wood cabinets and filled them with crushed ice. "The filter does the whole house, including the showers and the fridge. The fridge had to have an extra thing inserted on the back, but I tell you it's a world of difference. Gary loves it!"

I forced a smile and took the glass, sipping in the approved manner. "Mm. Good and cold."

"So who is the guy?"

"His name is Arthur Gonzales. Or Arturo. I think he goes by both. He's a veterinarian."

"Arthur...Art...Gonzales...?" She blinked, frowned and finally asked, "Should I know him? Where did you meet him?"

"He's a vet, and I think he sits on a charity board, Homes for Pets. He was at a function I attended for a client the other night. I'm trying to figure out where he fits into the society scene."

"What function?"

"An art party this past Saturday. Some political thing, schmoozing up in the mountains, over by the forest where all the roads are sixty-seven with letters."

She set her glass down hard enough that water sloshed over the side. "Saturday?" she squeaked. "Up in the mountains? You wouldn't be talking about Bethalane Manard would you?"

I thought about it. "Yes, I think that was the name on the invitation."

"Oh Lord. An art party, is that what you called it?" She rolled her eyes and hid behind her glass, sipping her water frantically. Her nails tapped anxiously against the counter top.

"You know her?"

"She's not your client, is she?" Kas almost, but not quite, spit her water out as she asked.

"No."

"Oh." She set her goblet down, more carefully this time. She leaned against the counter, folding her arms across her chest. "She's *only* the artist of the century, Adriel. Not to mention the patron to several other artists around here. How did you get invited to one of her soirees?" She scanned my outfit in dismay.

"Don't worry. I wore a dress."

"I should hope so, even if you didn't get someone to do a one-of-a-kind for you. Bethalane is very avant-garde, you know. She did those sculptures in the airport, the ones of the Indian mothers called "Madonna with Child" only with wolves and cougars in the background."

Not one to pay much attention to art, especially with it around me all the time, I started to say I hadn't heard of her, but the description rang a bell. "Didn't she sell postcards that were basically paintings of her work?"

"And note cards, Christmas cards and photos. A couple of the sculptures were redone into miniature ceramic pueblo settings. I think the Madonna part was downplayed, and it was mostly an Indian village with the wolf next to the beautiful maiden. They are stunning."

"Well, yeah, I guess that was the party."

She stared at me, chewing her lip. "How in the world did you get invited? I'd have killed to go."

"That's why I'm asking you about this guy. I'm hoping you already know some of these people, and maybe they know something about this Arthur Gonzales. I can't figure out what a veterinarian would be doing hanging around at a party like that."

"Did you say he was into a charity?"

I nodded. "Homes for Pets."

"That could be it. Bethalane is into causes, although mostly it's art causes. If the guy has money, she might invite him anyway. Arthur…doesn't ring any bells. If you know his wife's name, I might know her."

"No, only that he might go by Arturo sometimes."

She stared at me blankly. "Well sure, but that only makes sense, right?"

"Yeah." Lots of Hispanics gave their Anglo name when talking to an Anglo. "I don't know if he is married so I can't tell you about his wife. If she was there, I didn't notice."

"Oh." She sipped her water again and looked out the kitchen window. "You know, Marcella might know him."

"Who is Marcella?"

"Marcella Castello. The lady I told you about with the cat."

My forehead wrinkled. I thought hard, but I didn't remember a cat or a lady named Marcella. "Nope, never heard of her."

"Remember I asked if you would adopt a kitten? She is constantly trying to find homes for kittens. She gets them spayed or neutered or whatever and then tries to find them homes."

"Oh. After Christmas when you were trying to get Mom or me to adopt a pet?"

She nodded. "Marcella wanted us to take one." She stuck her tongue out. "Can you imagine the mess? And I host Gary's friends from work all the time too. A cat of all things."

"Doesn't she have dogs looking for homes too?" I teased.

Kas sniffed. "She does, but I don't want one of those either. I cannot imagine."

I couldn't either. Kas didn't have it in her to adopt a pet. "Can I call her? Ask her if this guy is a good vet or a good charity at any rate? Is she the type to have been invited to the party?"

"Absolutely." She rubbed two fingers together. "I thought of her because I am pretty sure she was invited. I don't see her often, but she's into crafts and this and that, so she probably knows Bethalane. *Personally*, I mean." Her eyes goggled with the wonder of it.

"Do you think I can call her?"

"Lemme get her number." She clicked her little heels off to the study. I followed. "You might have to adopt a cat or a dog or some such," she warned.

"Don't worry, I'll make up an excuse. I'll use your name."

Kas looked pained, but in a pleased way. Then she bit her lip. "You, uh…"

"No, I won't announce to her that I am a witch."

Kas's face got red. "I wasn't going to say that."

I took the phone number from her. "Thanks. Let me know if you hear anything about Gonzales, but don't go asking questions. I don't need any stray gossip."

"Sure, sure." She followed me through the house to the front door. Something was different in the living room. I knew she would appreciate it if I noticed. Unfortunately, I couldn't decide if she had added a new Ethan Allen piece to her collection or maybe a new vase on top of the bookcase. I skipped trying to be gracious.

My hand was on the doorknob to leave, when she stopped me. "Adriel?"

"What?" I looked over my shoulder.

"What was she like? Bethalane, I mean? Is she artsy? Or regal?"

I opened my mouth, but no words came out. Without meaning to, I sucked in my lip like she had just done.

She stared at me, and then her eyes closed. Air puffed out of her lungs, collapsing her shoulders in disappointment. "You didn't even meet her, did you?"

Not only hadn't I met her, I hadn't even seen her. Well, I probably had, but I hadn't cared enough to know. "It was a very fancy place. She had a bunch of minstrels, very good ones. Her sound system was integrated through the whole house." I tried to think of other details that would interest my sister. Her eyes had opened hopefully, but I had reached the extent of my knowledge. "The party was very unique. The artwork was fabulous." And I couldn't name a single artist. In fact, I had destroyed the work of at least one artist, but I didn't mention that.

Kas and I stared at each other across the entryway. It was like looking in a mirror, except we were in two different worlds.

Chapter 30

On the way home, I debated checking the nightclubs again for Zandy. It couldn't hurt. Well, it could, and it probably wasn't worth checking until after ten anyway. Even the thought made me yawn. I needed a nap before any nighttime activities.

When I got home, there was a message from White Feather. It was terse. Mom hadn't exaggerated. "Both girls were sixteen," he ground out. "They took a pact of secrecy. Not a single other high school friend knew about the date. They were last seen getting into a car three blocks from the high school. Both were found dismembered in the car the next morning." He hung up.

The next message was from him too. "Oh yeah. We found another body, but your werewolf friend must have changed tastes. It was a guy this time. Or maybe he got in the way by trying to stop a date. Ever think of the people trying to help here?"

"Moonlight madness," I swore. A guy? It was not Lynx. Tino had said the kid had come in. Two days ago, but still. It was not Lynx. Maybe it was Zandy? I had a bad feeling that I had better find Zandy before White Feather did. Of course, even if I found him, I didn't know what to do with him. I wasn't sure I could talk Lynx out of his protection racket, never mind someone as involved as Zandy. That's if Lynx was still alive.

The third call from White Feather was more polite. "Since I'm sure you're familiar with The Owl, perhaps we can meet there for dinner at six tonight instead of midnight at the church?"

"Or not," I grumbled, looking at my watch. I doubted he would still be sitting there since it was now past seven o'clock.

It was too late to call Marcella, too late to meet White Feather for dinner, and too early to go looking for Zandy or Lynx. If White Feather could make it, I assumed we were still on for the church date.

To bide my time, I settled for a relaxing bath with sprinkles of vanilla oil. Vanilla oil was like eating a batch of cookies without having to cook.

By the time I got out, I was half asleep. "Just a little nap," I reminded myself as I fell into bed. "Short enough to give me energy."

I should have set the alarm.

The banging on the door at half past midnight did the trick.

Bouncing out of bed, I grabbed the garlic from the headboard. I reached under my extra pillow for the knife before I remembered I had moved the silver blade under the bed to keep from spearing myself accidentally.

The knock came again. "Vampires don't knock." But it wasn't the code knock that Lynx used either. It sounded as though whoever was out there was hitting my door with a heavy stick.

Maybe I shouldn't open the door. Vampires might take that as an invitation, right?

I eased into the hallway, keeping low, not that I expected the vampire to come flying overhead, not with all the noise at the front door.

Glancing to make sure the back door was still secure, I slipped through the living room to the front door. "Go away," I yelled during a pause.

"Adriel or Merlin or whoever you are, I need some information."

"White Feather?" I peered through a side window. He didn't have a stick. Apparently he had felt a need to get rid of some aggression by pounding on my door with his fist.

"Who the hell else did you stand up for dinner that would bother to trace a phone number to this address?"

"I got in late." I unlocked the bolt. "Besides," I said reasonably as I turned on the light and opened the door, "if a girl doesn't answer whether she is going to dinner or not, it's hardly a standup."

"What about the church?"

"That," I said with a glance at the clock, "I'm guilty of."

I stepped back from the door to let him in. He started to speak. Then he blinked and stared. "You in the middle of a spell or something?"

I matched his gaze and looked down at my chest. Giant bulbs of garlic met my inspection. "Oh. No. I was asleep, and I thought you were the vampire."

It took me a moment to realize that he didn't follow me in because I turned my back to unload the garlic, the knife, two blessed crucifixes, and a bunch of silver strands I had looped around one arm.

"Vampire?" he parroted from the doorway.

"Yeah, had the unfortunate experience of a visit the other night. Turns out he wanted my help finding someone looking for *him*." I turned around to find White Feather staring at my neck.

"A vampire?"

"It was a few days ago."

He looked at me suspiciously. I was not going to bare my neck any further to prove I hadn't been bitten. His next remark showed I was way off-base in reading his thoughts.

"Did you invite one over? Do you think they are sexy?"

"Sexy?"

Apparently White Feather couldn't read my mind either because he grunted in disgust, stepped inside and slammed the door shut. He glared at me the entire time.

"White Feather." I blinked rapidly. "Vampires. Are. *Dead*."

"I know that."

"Dead is not sexy. It isn't *alive*."

He grunted again. "That doesn't seem to keep a lot of people from thinking they're great."

"They're dead!"

"Well," he defended himself, "what about how great it is supposed to be to be bitten by one and how you end up with half their power? ?"

I shook my head. "The bite of a vampire is for one purpose only. It is so the," I gulped, "beast can feed. That is not sexy. Getting bitten doesn't convey half the vampire's power to the recipient of the bite. It kills. Period."

"How do you know?"

"How many half vampires do you know?"

He shrugged.

"That's right. None." I went to the couch and sat down. "I bet you know of a few hundred vampire sightings, a handful of vampire killings and several unsolved cases of bodies left to rot after a vampire fed to his satisfaction." I held up a single finger to emphasize my point. "But I'll bet you don't know of a single person who lives in the light of day, flies around with super strength, lives off *food* and has only half a bite or some such nonsense."

"Because you can't be half-bitten."

"Because half vamps don't exist. Simple." I held my hands wide in an open and shut case.

"Then why the heavy rumors?"

"Who cares?" I shrugged. "You find me a guy living the life on this side with a bunch of extra powers, and I'll take the rumors seriously. Otherwise, it's vampire propaganda. Maybe they start out sucking a little blood to get a line on a feeder, but it's still a drug that kills."

"But if a vampire visited, why didn't it go after you?"

I swallowed hard at the memory. "I was protected. Somewhat anyway. He was here to get information, to make a deal."

White Feather's face paled. He left the realm of rumors in a hurry. "What did he want?"

"He claimed he was trying to figure out who might want vampire blood." I looked away uneasily. "He seemed to have stopped by to make sure it wasn't me."

"Lord," he swore.

"I think I convinced him otherwise. Sent him on his way. I don't do business with vampires."

"What if he wanted to force the issue?" White Feather looked at my neck again. Since I had been planning on getting up after a nap, I had on a regular t-shirt. It allowed him to see enough to tell there weren't any bites.

"I didn't look the vamp in the eyes, and I don't think I told him anything I didn't want to."

White Feather sat down next to me and gripped my hand. I squeezed back.

He licked his lips. "You're sure?"

I rolled my eyes and looked up at the ceiling, baring my neck. When he touched either side, I didn't expect it, nor did I expect the gentleness. For a second or two, I wondered if he was letting his power flow over me.

My skin tingled. He traced my jaw line, searching with his hands, not his power. Gently, his finger trailed down to the collar, lightly tracing underneath, checking the skin above and below. I nearly moaned, and he wasn't even trying for that affect, at least I didn't think so.

I certainly couldn't tell because my eyes were closed. When he touched the side of my neck again, I couldn't help but give him better access, letting my head tilt away from his exploration, exposing even more of my neck. His hands lingered. The feel of his eyes compelled me to open mine.

"I--"

"You look fine." His eyes, the color of wind in the forest, demanded an age-old answer. His hand slid to the back of my neck, and it was only a breath for him to close the distance from his mouth to mine.

His other hand dropped away, brushing one breast accidentally. My nipples hardened. Apparently the rest of me wanted the same careful inspection he had given my neck.

I met his kiss more than halfway, hungry, forgetting everything except the man in front of me. Even when his power touched me, I wouldn't have stopped, but it must have been a message to him, because he pulled away, abruptly.

"God." One hand on my shoulder, he ran the other through his hair. He blinked and shook his head. "I came over here to scare you into telling me everything you know."

"Okay," I whispered.

He looked back at me. "You're irresistible."

I nearly lunged for him. The look on his face matched my own longing. We ended up staring at each other hungrily, neither daring to move.

"I better go." He gulped air.

"Now?"

He chuckled, but it was weak. "I don't think the vampire got you." He stared at my neck and lower. My breasts moved rapidly with my breathing. I stopped breathing, forcing his eyes to mine. He reached out and touched my cheek. "Absolutely stunning."

For a second, I knew he was going to kiss me again, but there it was once more, a rush of his power, hitting me through his fingertips. The feeling it brought was a total rush, and I didn't exactly need any encouragement anyway.

He stood up, agitated. "I better go." At the door, he took a deep breath. "I wish you'd tell me what you know." Looking back, he choked on a laugh. "It's pretty obvious I'm not going to be able to force you into it."

"His name is Zandy," I blurted out. "But that is all I know. He's young, blond, coyote, and I haven't been able to locate him. I know he killed Dolores, but he probably didn't kill any of the others."

He paused, his hand on the doorknob. "How do you know?"

I gave him the highlights of the shirt and walking in on Zandy.

"You get around," he said softly. "You're sure he isn't feeding you a line? Maybe he didn't have time with Dolores to tear her up?"

I shook my head. "He came here pleading for help, asking me to get rid of any evidence against him--as if I could. I don't think he'll turn himself in because not only would he be blamed for the other deaths, he isn't what you'd call an upstanding kind of guy."

White Feather paced back toward me. "There's more than one werewolf."

I wondered how much to tell him about Arturo. Unfortunately, I had no proof that Dr. Gonzales, the veterinarian, was the same "Arturo" that Zandy and Lynx talked about. "How much do you know about the dating scheme?"

"I know about it. I haven't got any idea why anyone would do such a thing, but enough women are more than happy to sign up for a date. Not all of them are getting killed, either. Enough live to tell the tale, and that keeps the flock coming." His eyes glittered with anger and even though he wasn't next to me, I felt his power leaking. It was different now, more dangerous.

I put my hand out to touch it.

The power was gone, instantly.

"Sorry."

"It's okay." I felt drawn to him, but stayed on the couch.

He walked back one step. Then another.

Finally he sat with a big sigh, putting his face in his hands. "I have a little sister. Not little actually. She's almost seventeen."

It took a moment to register, but when it did, I gasped, "She's not!"

He nodded. "Interested in a werewolf? Unfortunately, yes. She isn't like me, and that apparently bothers her. At least one of her friends has gone on one of these dates and come back unscathed."

"You verified it? The friend isn't just bragging?"

"I'm as certain as I can be." His eyes were angry and hurt. "My sister isn't a witch. She sure as hell isn't a shape shifter either, but that world has always been right there, living with her because of me."

"Knowing a witch or a warlock isn't exactly the same thing as going on a date with a werewolf."

"No, it isn't, but she always wanted to be a witch and since she isn't, she's decided this dating scheme is her thing. I keep telling her that she's too young to know what she'll be or do. Why can't she see that?"

"Because she's sixteen?" I had always thought it a curse that Kas didn't like what I had chosen to do with my life. She showed no natural ability in that direction and was glad of it. It never occurred to me that it would be worse when someone wanted to go in that direction and couldn't. "Look, maybe I could train her," I offered. "Your power is different from mine. It's stronger, and it positively breathes the earth." My hands twitched towards him, eager to feel that power again, but he had tamped down to perfect control. "Most of mine is just spells."

He looked at me, incredulous. "Just spells?" His hand reached out to touch my hair. "Haven't you any idea what your own witchery is like?" He breathed deep. "It's like flowers. Like sunshine. It's not mother earth, it's a call to it."

"Me?"

He laughed softly. "Oh yeah."

I had no idea I emitted anything of the sort. I blushed. "I wasn't trying to--I mean, I don't get my spells internally like you did with that wind thing. I'm not elemental like that."

"No?" He took hold of my hand and turned it, his hand flat against mine. "You have something. You have it and training my sister in a couple of spells won't be good enough for her." He sighed and released my fingers.

It took me a few seconds to gather my thoughts. "Have you ever given her the chance to learn?"

"She hung around a couple of witches in junior high. Kept getting involved in one disaster after another. One of the girls ended up with blue hair. Permanently!"

"That sounds like experimentation, not training. I think you're right when you say she can't know yet. It might be worth trying some real training."

"Anything beats dating a werewolf."

"Not all shifters are bad, but right now werewolves aren't safe bets" I said. "But I don't think catching Zandy is going to solve the entire problem. There's something else out there."

His mouth formed a grim line. "Maybe. You can't be certain."

"Look, if I find Zandy, I'll try to get him to at least stop with the dates."

"What are the chances?"

I had to be honest. "Slim. Very slim."

"Thanks for telling me his name. I now have at least one person I know to keep away from my sister. Any other date is pure guesswork."

"You aren't trying to pick your sister's dates?"

"What else can I do? I can't know every werewolf in the county! I can only check backgrounds so quickly."

"White Feather." I shook my head. "She'll sneak out. Then you won't know anything at all."

"But what else can I do?"

I smiled. "Now here's where I really can be of some help. All I need is her name and maybe a picture." If Lynx wanted to provide protection so be it. He could help with this by making sure she *didn't* date a werewolf. I already knew he would take money from both sides assuming I could find him.

"Why do you need a picture?" White Feather asked suspiciously.

My smile got bigger. The more I thought about it, the more I liked the irony. "It's not for a spell. It's someone in the underground who might be willing to watch out for her. I'm fairly certain he would be willing to tell me if a date got set up." I raised a hand. "For a fee that's probably equal to what protection is going for, but I think it might be worth the investment."

He thought about it. "I'm not sure--oh hell. Her name is Tara."

"Good." I stood. "Bring me a picture in case she doesn't use her real name."

"You sound like you know a little too much about this subterfuge dating." He stood up and took out his wallet. He handed me an obvious school shot, but she was every bit as pretty as White Feather was handsome.

"Wow," I said. "Let's hope we can find her talent soon and get her focused on that."

"Should I leave you money now, or later?"

"Later. I'm not sure what he'll charge yet. I'm guessing somewhere in the neighborhood of three or four hundred."

White Feather didn't flinch. "Let me know." He put his wallet away. "And thanks, Adriel."

"We haven't won the race yet," I warned him.

"Yeah. But it's nice to have someone else out there with a baton." He reached out and touched my hair, just barely.

"Oh. Well." I tried to shrug, to be casual, but his eyes were such a perfect mix of light and air, green and blue, and oh, so close.

Shaking his head, he stepped away. "I better go." He strode to the door, looked back as though he might say more, but then stepped through and shut it behind him.

I stood there for several moments after he left. When I finally moved, I locked the door and headed to my workroom. It wasn't until I set down the picture of his sister next to my computer that I remembered the wig. "Moonlight madness! I forgot to ask him for the key to the church."

My heart skipped a beat. I wasn't sure if it was fear over the wig or because my heart knew I'd have to set up another meeting with White Feather in order to get it back.

Chapter 31

Considering the interruption in my sleep, it was no surprise that I didn't wake up until five minutes to eight. Around a large yawn, I mumbled, "Early bird gets the worm." Turning away from the giant red numbers on my clock, I said, "Who wants a worm anyway?"

I dozed for another half hour, but the chores awaiting me were like a snooze alarm inside my head. After showering, I made myself a fully-caffeinated cup of tea without a single useful herb.

At nine, I called Marcella.

"I'm Kasandra's sister," I introduced myself. "I was at Bethalane's party the other night, and I met Dr. Arthur Gonzales. He was raising money for the Homes for Pets, and my sister mentioned that you might be able to tell me more about Dr. Gonzales and his charity." The phone crackled. I realized with dismay that her cell phone connection wasn't good.

"Dr. Gonzales? Wonderful veterinarian. And the charity is wonderful, of course! I help run it. You won't find a better cause, my dear."

"Oh, for some reason I thought Dr. Gonzales ran it," I said.

"No, no. He loans us interns to help with the spaying and neutering." She rattled off an address in White Rock. I caught the first three numbers, but missed the rest. "I'd love to have you stop by for a chat. I'll be there all day working with a falconer. Dr. Gonzales won't be in White Rock today, but I'm sure I can answer any questions you have. If you can't make it today, call me, let's see."

I heard what sounded like running water for several seconds. "Marcella?" No answer.

The phone cackled again, then went back to engine noise. Finally, I heard her voice. "Maybe you'd like to volunteer a few times before you decide what kind of pet is best? I always advise that," she said with a laugh. "Are you free Friday? We can do lunch."

Next Friday might as well be a light year away. By that time Lynx and Zandy would probably both be in jail if one of them wasn't already dead. I refused to think about that possibility. "You're at the White Rock facility today?"

"Yes, I could meet you there. You sound like a girl who could use a big, strong dog for protection. It should be a fairly quiet day except for the falconer. What are you looking for?"

I grabbed the phone book and flipped pages. Instead of answering her question, I asked, "Does Dr. Gonzales work with falcons?" Finding the Homes for Pets address in White Rock, I jotted it down.

"No, no, I work with them to rehabilitate them into the wild. Nothing to do with Dr. Gonzales. Seth isn't a veterinarian, but he knows his birds."

"I see. What exactly does Dr. Gonzales do for the charity?"

"Oh, he's very generous, and once you get a pet, I highly recommend his services. He allows us to use his old clinic out on the south end of Santa Fe, and the one up here in White Rock for pet adoptions."

"But he's part of your charity, right? I mean, he helps with the fund raising and sits on the board?"

"Heavens no, but whenever he has an intern in training, he makes sure they do a stint to help handle the spays and neuters. And of course, he was going to sell the clinic on the south side, but he kept it and lets us use it rent free so we have a center when we need it."

"Oh, of course." So why had Harold written him a check for ten big ones?

"I'll pencil you in for lunch on Friday, shall I?"

I let her set the date, but I needed to check out the "charity" office in White Rock anyway. If I caught Marcella there, I'd try to get what I needed and cancel Friday's lunch.

After thanking her, I hung up.

I double-checked the address she had rattled off. It didn't match the one in the phone book, but she had been driving. Maybe she got it wrong.

As I packed Zandy's pager, I considered that Sheila could have created a pager exactly like it for tracking me. There I would be in White Rock. She could drive by and happen upon me like a mouse sampling cheese in a trap.

I packed a lot of protective spells and several gallons of water in the trunk. Sheila wouldn't know I was there. She wouldn't even be looking for me.

Just before I got in the car, I went into the bedroom. The rain poncho pile was still waiting to be cleaned up. The tuning fork with essence-of-Lynx was lying on top.

Before I could change my mind, I grabbed it and stuffed it in my backpack, way at the bottom.

It was a precaution only. But what if he was another unfound, dead body? Or what if he was already the male, dead body that had been found? I refused to think about it, but I had to find him.

* * *

Driving north through the mountains was usually a good thing, but my thoughts were anxious, leading me in circles. What did Arthur need with ten grand? Why was Sheila getting people to write checks? And how in the world was Arthur getting away with a scheme for renting out werewolves who killed? And why did Lynx have to be involved anyway?

Wind blew across the desert stretches in big gusts, shoving my car here and there as if warning me away. If Lynx wasn't such a good source of income leads for me, I would leave him to his latest schemes.

Well, probably not.

Everything in White Rock was within a few blocks of State Road Four because the Rio Grande Canyon stopped development almost before it could start. I found the clinic on my first try. Like the other Home For Pets center the building appeared to be a house converted to a veterinary clinic. Instead of a fenced area in back, there was an old corral.

Unfortunately, the clinic was closed. As I walked up to the door, Zandy's pager buzzed.

Like the clinic in Santa Fe, the pet adoptions were posted for only one day a week, all day Wednesday. On Saturday, according to the sign, Dr. Gonzales, provided vet services.

I had assumed since Marcella was coming up here, the place would be open, but now I understood the different address. If I had to guess, she was coming up here to meet with her falcon buddy today, and then staying to do her charity thing tomorrow.

I sighed. With the place closed, I couldn't expect to figure out whether Zandy had been inside. Just like in Tesuque, all I had was a bit of Zandy's aura around the building.

Unlike Tesuque, the building was quiet with no one to see me snooping. If Lynx had ever been inside with Zandy, his aura might be strong enough for me to pick it up, especially if it had been recent.

I wasn't sure what that would tell me, other than he had been here, but I wanted to know one way or the other. I got back in the car, drove a couple of blocks away, parked and walked back. Lucky for me, the porch was conveniently landscaped with a row of hawthorn bushes that blocked most of the view from the road.

The back door would be a safer entry, but there wasn't much traffic to worry about anyway. I sat behind the hawthorns and pulled an illusion pack from my backpack in case I needed it later. If someone spotted me before I got inside, I'd tell them I was leaving a note. I took out a piece of paper, wrote a note of thanks about my non-existent dog and folded it.

It took a few minutes to devise a spell using a magnet, some mint oil and my Swiss Army knife. The front entry lock was a single deadbolt, a remnant of the house owners. The lock was a piece of cake for my spell.

I slid inside and relocked the door. The only evidence of my tampering with the deadbolt was the lingering scent of mint oil.

The entry room still looked like a living room, although the carpeting had been pulled out, leaving concrete floors. I could feel the pager on my hip vibrating. "Okay, you've been here for sure." But why?

As I pulled out the fork linked to Lynx, I heard squeaking.

I froze.

There it was again, along with a snuffling noise. Then, to my relief, I heard a small bark.

With a gulp of air, I realized there were animals here. Of course.

Hopefully the noise didn't mean there were humans.

I edged forward carefully and peeked around a corner into a hallway. Two of the doors along the hallway had been removed entirely. The first contained several cages with cats and kittens. The next one contained two small cages with puppies.

The third door was closed, but the "bathroom" sign held true when I opened it to check.

I went in, closed the door and pulled out both forks. Zandy's quivered steadily. Lynx's fork wasn't as clear, but it definitely twitched.

"Okay, you're dealing with Arturo more than you admitted, aren't you kid?"

I slipped back out. On the other side of the living room, I found the kitchen. It looked as though it had been converted into an operating room. There was a door that led to a closet containing rows and rows of supplies. Another door led outside to the back. Cages were out there too, next to the corral.

To the side of the kitchen, there was another door, but it was locked. It didn't say bathroom.

More supplies?

It was even easier to activate the unlock spell because I had just done it.

"Voila," I mouthed, just before the sound from within hit my brain.

Squeaking. Lots and lots of squeaking.

My hand stopped in the act of reaching for the light. Little red eyes reflected from the light spilling into the room from the kitchen. Swallowing hard, I hit the switch.

There were cages and cages of them, probably fifty rats. They were all healthy, normal looking rats.

I let out the breath I had been holding. Arturo Gonzales wasn't getting money from Sheila for charity. He was Sheila's supply chain for rats. She must have decided to make Harold pay for them, keeping her name out of the entire transaction.

Because of the mind-numbing disgust, it took several seconds for the scrape of a key at the front door to penetrate. The first sound to actually register in my brain was a heavy object hitting concrete followed by the slap of flip-flops across the living room.

Sheila!

My options were limited. There was the supply closet or the rats.

No way. I yanked the door to the rat room closed and hit the back door so quickly, I didn't even waste time with the illusion spell. There was no need for the unlock spell because there was only a twist doorknob lock.

Once outside, I dodged behind the cages, but there was a large dog housed in one of them. It started barking.

Illusion spell it was, not that it fooled the dog.

Zandy's pager still vibrated steadily against my hip even though I was outside.

I slithered behind the row of cages and then hopped the corral fence. I tucked myself behind a tree.

The dog calmed down slightly. I was damned lucky I hadn't walked outside into a chained link fence where dogs ran free. I stared back at the house. Nothing but windows looked at me.

I held my breath and watched.

My arm itched. I looked down. There was sunshine on my arms. I held a hand out. Warm. Not freezing. I felt no urge to run back and commit suicide by giving myself over to the witch.

Slowly I let out the air inside my lungs. Not Sheila?

Someone had to come and feed the dogs and...other animals. It probably wasn't Sheila.

Still crouched, I kept a close eye on the house while taking out the witching forks. Zandy's twitched, pointing to a walking trail straight off the corral. The signal wasn't strong, but I followed the trail anyway to get away from the clinic and whoever was inside.

The wind started to gust again, picking at me. Some witches heard voices in the breeze, some could even bend it to their will, but all I heard was the whispers of footsteps behind me. When I turned to check there was nothing there but the wind. The gusts tossed pebbles and dust at me as it rushed through the trees. With nary a sigh, it stopped as though it saw something to devour. With a twitch of its tail it decided where to go next.

I stayed low until I was well away from the clinic. After some distance, I angled across the weeds to Highway Four where I had parked. Off to my left, I saw a hawk almost level with me flying over Pajarito Canyon.

Belatedly I remembered Marcella and her falcon friend. Marcella worked with Arturo. It would be very easy to keep an eye on things if you had a falcon that could fly overhead.

The canyon was on my left. The bird circled, riding the winds.

I felt trapped. I would have ignored the twitching of the fork in my hand except it was too strong. To my surprise it was Lynx's fork signaling. The twitch was so intense, it yanked itself free of my fingers, falling to the ground, humming.

I stared at it, following the line of sight to a dark mass under a bush.

"Lynx?" I peered closer. Maybe the fork had lost its signal. There was nobody there, just a dark mass of weeds or maybe a bunch of matted hair… like a…wig.

I gulped. A gust of wind suddenly teased the black lump, and I had a vision of a face beneath it. *"Lynx?"*

I raced over and crawled underneath the bush. Lynx didn't wear a wig! Sure, he never combed his hair and…I stared toward the highway, towards the Home For Pets, and looked nervously over my shoulder.

The falcon was gone.

I put the fork near the wig. It sang happily.

The dirt was scuffed. There were possible signs of a struggle, but then again, a dirt devil might have passed. I searched for broken branches, clothing or some other sign.

Nothing but desert scrub and open sky.

I looked at the wig again. "Oh Lynx, you are in big, big trouble, aren't you?"

My heart in my throat, I yanked a strand of the wig free and tied it onto the fork. The link to Lynx would now be stronger than before, but outdoors, the signal wasn't going to last, especially in the wind. I crawled under the tree and looked on every side. The only thing I could find was a broken branch. There was no blood.

Had he touched the tree? Struggled against it?

Stowing the rest of the wig in my pack, I swept a large path. I circled the undergrowth, ignoring any tugs that led back towards the clinic. Near the canyon the fork was dead, giving me nothing when I walked near the edge.

I made the highway, breathing way too hard for the pace I was keeping. Looking at the fence across the highway, I tried the other side of the road, but there was nothing until I crossed back over and hit a spot where a trail ended on a turnout.

"Lynx, tell me you didn't get into a car," I moaned. What had he been doing out here at the clinic in the first place? Had he seen the rats and panicked when he realized that Arturo was involved with Sheila?

Zandy had been here too, and there was no telling what Zandy did for Arturo.

I tried the witching forks again, heading southwest, sweeping back and forth across the highway. Had they gone back to Santa Fe?

Once in a vehicle, I didn't stand a chance of tracking them.

In despair, I headed back to my car.

It was in sight when the wind grabbed at Zandy's fork.

Wishful thinking?

No, Lynx's fork twitched too. Maybe. It was so slight, aiming…back across the highway towards private, fenced land. I stared at the barbed wire and the no trespassing sign.

"Oh no, bad idea." The land was none other than the Los Alamos high security area. My arm dropped. Lynx had no reason to go in there. Neither did Zandy. "Oh no."

My throat was parched. The pinched skin around my eyes stung from the wind and dust.

I crossed and hiked off the road to the barbed wire fence. There it was, strands of coyote hair caught on the fence.

My car wasn't that far. I'd need more supplies. More importantly, I'd need a way inside if I was going to follow the possible trail.

I took the hair and marked the spot before jogging back to my car.

There was only one person I knew who might be able to get a pass into Los Alamos land. It was a long shot because a local policeman wasn't likely to hold much sway.

It didn't matter. White Feather was my only option. Even if he couldn't get me into Los Alamos land, as a cop, surely he could at least put out a bulletin to help find the kid.

I had no choice but to make the long, hour plus drive back to Santa Fe. I needed supplies, White Feather's number off my answering machine, spells and a miracle.

Chapter 32

Even if I had been hiking in the dead of winter, the dry air would have left a fine layer of salty sweat across my skin. Because it was summer, it was rather more than a fine layer and combined with the dust, my face was a chalky powdered mask.

While dialing White Feather's number, I wiped the worst of the mess off my face, drank some water and gathered myself.

He answered on the sixth ring.

"I need help finding a kid. The one I told you about who I thought could help your sister. He's disappeared."

"Have you filed a missing person report?"

"No. You see, he is homeless. I don't even know his real name, assuming he was born in a hospital where normal paperwork was filed. He's lived on the street as long as I've known him."

"You're trying to find a homeless kid?"

"It's a long story, White Feather, but he has been bragging about getting into the protection business. I told him any shifter messing with that business was going to end up dead. I thought I might be able to help keep him out of trouble if I could talk him into giving me the names of women who wanted protection, including your sister if she got involved."

White Feather growled, "Shifter? He's a werewolf? You were going to have a werewolf protect my sister?"

"No. He's not a--" I caught myself. Actually I had no proof. I was ninety-nine percent sure Lynx wasn't a werewolf. He was a shifter but... well damn. I guess it was possible.

"This is going to be complicated, isn't it?" he asked.

"I don't think he is a werewolf," I said. "I know he isn't the one who killed Dolores Garcia. Can you help me or not? I've got to find him. He's in trouble."

"You mentioned that." He sighed. "I'll be over in twenty." He hung up.

I headed to my workroom to gather spells. My backpack wasn't big enough because I wanted every ingredient I had.

On my fifth trip to the car to load things, White Feather drove up.

He got out, stared me up and down and asked, "Are you certain you want to put out a bulletin for a homeless kid who could be hiding in a gutter somewhere? "

"I think he's been taken inside Los Alamos somewhere. I need someone official, a cop, the FBI, whatever it takes, to get in there and look."

His face turned red. There was a long silence, and then he grunted.

"Well? Don't you believe me?"

"This charade." He waved his hand. "I'm not exactly a cop."

My heart sank. "What do you mean, not exactly?"

"My brother is the cop. I'm freelance. I'm a scientist, not a detective."

The blood drained from my face. "Scientist? Do you work at Los Alamos?"

"I have before. As a contractor." He held up his hand. "Look, I got into an argument with my brother a couple of years ago about police work. About how you have to be in the subculture or have ties to it in order to get information. It's the same as science. You have to dig deep, interact with the particles you want to change and know enough about the environment to recognize when you're changing it."

"What does all this have to do with you posing as a cop?" My voice rose dangerously.

He smiled. "I never said I was a cop."

"Are you White Feather or not?"

"Of course. But White Feather isn't a cop. My brother Gordon is the cop. I offered to get information once. And then," he shrugged, "I kept providing it."

I touched the silver at my wrist, hoping for calm. "Can you help me or not?"

Instead of answering he said, "You never told me whether you are Merlin or not."

"Of course I am!"

He smiled, satisfied. "At the party the other night I suspected you, but the magic you were using wasn't yours. Then the other night, your aura was so strong, I couldn't believe you were only an apprentice. I was almost positive you were Merlin, but your disguise when we met in church was so good, I couldn't see how you could have been posing as Merlin."

"And I never suspected you could easily give Merlin a run for her money in the magical department. But I did think you were a cop." The worry escalated again.

He put a hand on my shoulder. "Where in Los Alamos?"

"I don't know." I ran down a quick description of my activity with the witching fork and where the trail ended. "I found his wig." My voice caught. "He's in trouble."

"We'll get in." He looked at his watch. "I'll meet you back here at three in the morning. That will put us in good shape to cross the fence before daybreak. We can take a look around, see if there is any sign of him or trouble. It will be a lot easier to do that than get Gordon involved officially."

I had no choice but to trust him. "White Feather--" I didn't know what to say. "I think this might be dangerous."

"We're dealing with a shifter. Of course it's going to be dangerous." He turned and walked back to his car. "Three o'clock."

I was still nodding even as dust billowed up from his tires as he drove away.

* * *

The workroom was my only comfort. I spent the evening starting spells, leaving them half finished, and trying to guess what I would need. I unpacked the trunk several times, repacked it, and then went grocery shopping. Every single grocery item I'd ever used went in the cart. It still wasn't late enough so I went back through the store and added sandwiches, Gatorade, sausage, jerky and potato chips. Buying the chips made my eyes sting. The kid loved potato chips.

Back at home, I unloaded everything, but it was only eleven. Desperate to find some kind of balance, I prepared the spell for Tino's client.

A hint of anise star and a brush of fennel were the base. The smells might remind his client of slaving over a hot stove or soothe her with happy memories. I added a touch of vanilla to help her thoughts linger on sweetness. I withheld flowers; no rose nostalgia, no smells that might remind her of a decaying funeral wreath.

Tino hadn't indicated a special, high tipping client, so she got a sea-green bottle with a transparent stopper. The antique atomizers with auras of past perfumes and lingering essences were more expensive. Magic built up over years was rare and valuable.

Sometime between one and two, I fell into a doze on the couch, but I was up and waiting when White Feather knocked.

"Do you have an extra set of car keys?" he asked, first thing.

"Yes, hang on." I grabbed them out of the kitchen drawer. "Why?"

"Never hurts to have an extra set, and I assumed from the packing you were doing, you planned on taking your car rather than mine." He took the key and put it in his pocket. "Did you leave any room for my pack?"

Since he only had a daypack across his shoulder, I rolled my eyes. "Plenty of room in the backseat."

We trooped out to my car, stashed his pack and were on our way.

As I guided the car through the quiet streets of Santa Fe, the eeriness of the three o'clock hour settled around us. The very earth was quiescent, including most animals and insects. The early hunting was over, the morning hunting yet to begin.

Once on the highway to White Rock, with the silence and peace around us, I filled White Feather in. "I'm not sure what happened to Lynx, but I know he was with Zandy. He wouldn't willingly leave his wig behind. I've known him for three years already and have never seen him without it. I didn't even know he *wore* a wig."

"You're sure it's his?"

I nodded. "The fork had enough of his essence. I'm not sure what he was doing up there with Zandy, but I think they were working for Arturo." I was driving so I couldn't look over at his face. "I'm not positive, but I think Arturo--Dr. Gonzales, is the person who has been setting up the werewolf dates."

His head whipped around. "How do you know?"

I told him about Vi and Harold. "Sheila, the witch at the party with the nasty spells, was getting Harold to write a check to the guy. I didn't realize who Arthur Gonzales was--or who he might be until I saw his name on the vet's office. Lynx has mentioned an Arturo as the one setting up dates. He's got to be the same guy."

"Why was Harold writing a check?"

I told White Feather about the rats.

"That's a lot of money for rats," he said.

I shrugged. "It might not only be for rats. Who knows, maybe the two of them are doing the dating business together, and she owed him money for something. All I know for certain is that Zandy and Lynx are working for Arturo--and he has to be the same person as Dr. Gonzales because there is no other reason for their auras to be around his clinics."

"My brother isn't going to be able to do much based on similar names."

It was a slim link, and I knew it. Arturo could be a cover name and have nothing to do with Arthur Gonzales, the vet. But he was guilty of supplying Sheila with rats, and she was guilty of any number of ills. The cops might not be able to tie the pieces together, but there was enough evidence for me even if I didn't understand every crime the two had planned.

It wasn't until we were almost to White Rock that White Feather said, "Might be easy to meet young women who are interested in animals if you run a vet clinic."

I hadn't thought of that. "I guess. Does your sister have a pet?"

He glared in my direction. After a few minutes he said, "Drive through White Rock."

I followed his directions, going slowly. We ended up further than I would have liked from Zandy's last signal, but not very far off Highway Four. "What if someone sees the car?"

"I'm going to take care of that."

He didn't explain, so I got out and loaded my pack across my shoulders. He took the extra key and put it inside a case with a magnet. He attached the case under the passenger door. "The car won't be left here for long."

The next question was obvious, but since getting back home wasn't the immediate problem, I moved on. "How are we going to get in there?"

"Over the fence."

"Illusion?"

He smiled. "There are acres and acres of land. It's dark out. Trust me when I tell you they can't watch every inch, every second."

Getting into Los Alamos land was vastly different from when Lynx and I did the break-in at Sheila's house. White Feather simply picked a place where trees and scrub oak blocked the view of the highway. Night goggles worried my brain, but White Feather didn't appear to share my concern.

We climbed through. I didn't have to fly. There were no sirens or dogs. Nothing but a cricket broke the silence. The smell of sleeping juniper forest surrounded us. There wasn't a single car this early in the morning.

"There are other fences inside this one," he told me. "We'll parallel this one until we get back to the last signal you felt."

We walked quickly, keeping trees between us and the highway as much as possible. There was no aura in the slightly shifting breeze, and none when we got back to where I had last felt a humming.

"There's a lot of territory to cover." The weight of the task ate at my stomach. I tried telling myself that Lynx was fine. Anyone could have climbed the fence like we did. Maybe Lynx had escaped with Zandy into this area.

My stomach argued with my logic, pointing out that maybe Zandy had carried Lynx across, disposed of the body and walked back out.

White Feather kept a more level head, worrying about facts. "If your friend crossed, he is on foot. He will either have crossed back out and gotten in a car, or he's still in here. I don't suppose you can tell if he was traveling as a werewolf or not?"

"He isn't a werewolf," I said reflexively.

"If he changed into anything, that might tell us how fast he is traveling."

"Good point. He could go a lot faster if he changed. But no, I don't know that. His aura is exactly the same whether he's a kid or not."

"Okay." Even though I had the tuning fork, White Feather led the way for several paces. I stayed behind him. We hiked across rocks, around trees and up a slight incline. The desert terrain crunched beneath our shoes. In the early morning dark, I tripped more than once, but kept my feet.

When we were five hundred yards or more from the road, White Feather stopped. "Let me borrow the witching fork."

I handed it to him.

He stood silent, his hand on the fork, the other hand flat out, slightly away from his side. The light breeze swirled gently towards him. It wasn't any different than before. It could have simply been the force of nature. Even the eddies around my ankle could have been the cool morning air drifting.

I had never met a warlock before, not one like him. Warlock magic was a subtle fate magic, associated with earth powers. I wasn't at all practiced, but I had dabbled. It was hard not to because that type of magic was all around. Ordinary folks with not a lot of experience could do warlock magic at times. That day all the traffic lights were green? Probably brought on with warlock magic--a good mood in tune with the earth, a magic that swirled for an instant and suddenly fate went your way.

Of course, most people were usually so out of tune with anything magical, they couldn't get a green light to save their life, and if one happened, an ambulance would come through from the other direction blocking the intersection anyway.

But with White Feather, he was all air-born magic, all perfectly tuned. I could feel the smooth breeze, there and then gone. Had I not been standing next to him, had I not already known what he was, I may have sensed the power, but it would have been like the elusive smell of a spice I couldn't quite name. I might have appreciated the moment, but not thought too much about it.

"Let's see if the wind can find something for us," he said.

When he handed me back the fork, we walked again. The fork didn't quiver, nor did it pull, but I had a sense it was sending a gentle breeze out ahead to look for the scent.

The night sky gradually lost some of its black. A quail warned of our approach, which was good because when the flock moved, I didn't panic.

We zigzagged back and forth, going steadily deeper into Los Alamos land, down one rugged incline and scrambling up another.

For a while, we shared nothing but the puffing of our breath.

When we headed downhill into a rough valley, White Feather said, "About a week ago, I caught Tara reading an email from a woman claiming there was nothing better than a werewolf in bed. The lady claimed she was going to take the next step and become one."

I hid my surprise behind a non-committal, "Uh--hmm."

"Tara said she might as well become a werewolf or date one. She didn't have anything to lose, nothing to train."

"Pretty big leap of logic there."

He grunted. "I thought so."

"Did you try to talk to her?"

He shook his head. "Not this time. We've been through it all before. It always comes back to her thinking I can't understand because it was obvious from about age two that I had talent worth training. My grandfather took both my brother and me under his tutelage."

"What about your sister?"

"My grandfather didn't bother with her. It had more to do with her being a girl than anything."

"Being female isn't much of an excuse for not training her." I tried to keep the insult out of my voice.

"I agree, but what was Tara going to do? Request the class in high school? I didn't even notice she was paying attention to any of the stuff I did with grandfather. He never invited her along. He spent a lot more time with me because I was interested. My brother didn't care as much. He certainly didn't end up suicidal over not mastering particular spells."

"But your sister must have been trying. Or wanting to try. Even without much natural talent--" I looked over at him. "And buddy, you have that in spades. Not just anyone can tap into earth elements on a whim. Your sister may never learn that."

"I know."

I swung the witching fork around a bit, but it remained quiet. "Of course, she could be talented. If she hasn't actually tried to train, there's no way of knowing."

"That's exactly what I told her."

"So why aren't you training her?"

He looked over at me and blinked. "Me?"

"Sure you. Who else is going to do it? Your grandfather didn't."

"But...it's different with her."

I rolled my eyes. "You mean because you are a guy, and she is a girl, you assumed you couldn't teach her a spell or two?"

"Well, no." He looked confused and a little sheepish. "It's that if she has talent, I don't think it is the same as mine. I don't do much mixing of spells. I tend to trigger spells by setting a string of events and then let nature take over."

I knew exactly what he meant because I had felt his aura a few times. He was wind with a subtle mixing of earth as the wind went by. Still, it wasn't that different. "Chemical spells can go in some pretty nasty directions unless the chain reactions are set properly. It takes mastery and vision to figure out where to set things in motion, whether you're setting off a chemical reaction or an event."

He scratched his ear, readjusted his pack and then his cap. "I suppose."

It probably wasn't easy to train a person. I hadn't tried, other than to show Kas a few simple spells. She was about as interested in training with me as she was in owning a pet spider. She viewed all magic as black magic, rather than breaking it into its scientific parts. I had often told her that while I did a lot of magic, I never had to dabble with black magic. It was more work to do magic by science, but it was a heck of a lot safer.

White Feather stopped suddenly, his head tilted to listen.

I tried to breathe quieter, not knowing why he stopped. It wasn't until I relaxed my grip on the witching fork that I could feel the humming, just the tiniest bit.

Chapter 33

We stood next to an outcrop of rock, breathing hard. It was barely light out with clouds obscuring all but the reddish glow of the sunrise. White Feather knelt down.

'I joined him. "You feel a link?"

He sat and straightened his lower back. "I don't know. What's the stick say?"

"It's humming. No direction."

"That's pretty much what I'm getting from the wind too."

I leaned back against the rock, glad to take a break. A short ledge above my head would have protected us had it been raining. In the lower corner, I spotted telltale blackening that meant it had been used by Indians long ago.

I held the fork away from my body, slowly moving it from right to left. The humming never changed. "We could be out here for years." I set the fork down, took my backpack off and reached inside for my water bottle.

The witching fork turned very slowly and pointed at the rock.

I stared at it. Witching fork spells did not move on their own unless the signal was very strong. Then again, this one had been enhanced by a wind spell. Maybe it had the wind at its back. I picked it up and rested it on my palm, the fork away from the rock.

It spun again.

The ledge wasn't that deep. After scooting several feet, I finally stopped and looked behind me. The wall curved around, smooth as could be. I went back for my pack and my flashlight.

Sitting, with the fork on my hand, I turned in a circle. It pointed straight at the rock wall every time.

Lynx was behind the rock? Was he buried? Dead?

"Caves twist around," White Feather said softly. He moved to crouch next to me, his strong shoulders pushing against mine when he leaned further in. He turned on his flashlight. The light bounced off the rock around us.

When he pointed the light straight up, it was lost in blackness. The crevice that led upwards wasn't more than a rounded hollow, but the two of us could probably squeeze into it.

"It looks like there might be a cave back in here," he said.

I strapped my backpack on again. My hands were sweating even though the morning air was cool. "I don't like caves."

"Me either."

We moved together, climbing up by using the sides of the wall. After a short distance, it leveled and opened up enough for us to stand.

Our flashlights showed mostly smooth walls carved from water. Rocks were strewn across the floor, no doubt having fallen.

White Feather sighed. "It would help if we had better equipment."

"It would help if Lynx hadn't gotten himself lost in the first place." Darkness didn't bother me, but being enclosed in anything tomblike did. "Let's check it out. If the willow doesn't give any further indication soon, maybe it's because he's waiting around the outside bend of this mountain."

"Uh-huh." White Feather rummaged in his sack. He pulled out a pencil and marked the entrance. I yanked out a piece of my long hair and secured it under a rock.

White Feather held up his pencil and pointed to my hair. "That will help you, but it won't do me a bit of good."

"You could wrap a strand of my hair around the willow branch. Here." I trusted him to keep my hair safe. Before I could yank another strand free, he reached out and grabbed my wrist.

"Not necessary." He plucked a stray black length from the side of my backpack and held it under the light. "Let's not get separated."

He stuck the strand of my hair deep inside his jeans pocket anyway, just in case.

Even though we were through the rock barrier, the willow fork took a while to respond better. While the direction remained adamant, the vibrating was minimal. We weren't that close or there was a lot more rock between us and Lynx.

After the first few hundred yards, there wasn't much of a path. More reassuring, there wasn't leftover animal bones from whatever had inhabited the space from time to time.

The space widened and then shrank. Once I thought I heard water, but White Feather said, "Wind. This must open into other places."

We kept walking, leaving clear marks near any side tunnels. There was a spot where someone had cleared debris and a tunnel with dynamite marks.

The humming didn't get stronger, but it began to pulse as though it was breathing.

The wind spell maybe? I had never seen a witching fork breathe other than perhaps as an indication that the signal was fading and then getting stronger. "He might be moving," I whispered.

White Feather grunted, and we picked up the pace.

The light from our flashlights was hollow, hypnotizing. It was hard to look too far away from the spheres of light.

White Feather put his hand out, stopping me. He held his light above his head, away from our bodies. I turned mine off and followed his light.

Two wires, like silver snakes, climbed the rock wall. Neither had an insulating cover. A third wire was covered in typical black plastic.

White Feather knelt down and found the wires crossing near our feet. "I don't know why some of this wiring is exposed, but it looks like it probably carries a current."

"I think it's silver." I knelt next to him. "It would stop some things that regular wire wouldn't."

"Ah, I didn't notice that." He took a knife from his pocket and cut the wires, moving the length aside.

"What if you just notified someone we're down here?"

"Let's get moving."

"Maybe you'd better leave any more wires that we find," I suggested, my worry growing. "What if whatever was kept from crossing this wire was better off that way?"

He grunted.

We used his light, shining it ahead. Where there were larger piles of debris, White Feather climbed, checked and then waved me forward. We reached a branch in the tunnel.

"What does the fork say?" he asked.

It still breathed in and out like a bad radio signal. "Hang on. Let me try Zandy's." I leaned over and set Lynx's fork down. As my grip relaxed, the fork swiveled, making it obvious we needed to go left. I looked up at White Feather with a shrug and pulled Zandy's fork out of my backpack anyway.

Even without White Feather's spell on it, the fork spun left, mimicking Lynx's fork. Instead of pulsing, it hummed steadily. "This signal is very strong. We've got to be close."

"Okay, let's go."

We moved forward again, almost jogging. With both forks in my hands, I couldn't have used my flashlight if I wanted to.

Lynx's fork didn't give me any richer a warning, but as we rounded the next corner, I almost lost Zandy's fork when the signal jumped a notch. I reached up to tap White Feather's shoulder to let him know and nearly choked. A tiny red light flashed on the side of the rock right in front of White Feather's head.

"Ssstt." I grabbed White Feather.

At my warning, he turned the flashlight off, but it was too late. As soon as the light was off, I saw another red beam on the rock wall near the floor. His leg had already broken the beam.

"Mayan sacrifices," I cursed.

White Feather turned his light back on. He grabbed my hand and helped me as I leaned over to step across the beam at the bottom and avoid the one at the top.

My heart beating like mad, we rounded the next corner.

The first person I saw was not Lynx.

I halted and stared. If it hadn't been for the fork in my hand, I wouldn't have recognized Zandy. He was bruised and dirty, with large welts across his chest and thighs. "Where is Lynx?" I reached to substitute Zandy's fork for my flashlight.

Zandy's eyes were no less wild than the first time I had seen him. He bared his teeth, but the snarl sounded more like a sneeze. His eyes alerted me to the camera lens. White Feather saw the frightened look at the same time. Without hesitation, he moved to the lens and smashed it.

"We've got to move," White Feather said. "That beam will have alerted someone. The cameras likely sent pictures."

Ninety degrees from the tunnel where we had entered, there was another opening big enough to walk through standing upright. White Feather shone his light down its length, but the beam was swallowed.

"Is Lynx in there?" I pointed down the tunnel.

"You can't leave me here." Zandy's eyes flicked to the corridor leading out.

"Fine." The collar he wore around his neck made me think of the wires White Feather had cut. I bet those wires weren't to keep us out. They were to keep Zandy, and probably Lynx, in. "The tunnel is clear. We cut the wires. You should be able to make it through."

"Can you take it off?" He raised his hands to show burned palms. "There's an electrical shield out there, man. It'll kill me."

Not trusting him, I said, "As soon as you tell me how to find Lynx."

Zandy shook his head. "Your buddy didn't make it." He swallowed hard, rubbing hard at his neck. There must have been silver in the collar because his skin was red from more than chaffing.

"Where is he?" I snapped.

"He didn't cooperate." Zandy pointed to a jagged hole off the side of one rock wall. A misshapen boulder almost blocked it from view.

I glanced at White Feather, but we had no choice. It was now or never. I crawled to the hole and shone my light in. Several small rocks lined the opening. The space wasn't big enough for a person. I couldn't breathe properly, even thinking about it. I set Lynx's fork across my palm. It fell off my hand, pointing at the opening.

I picked it up and said, "I'll check."

On my hands and knees, I moved forward faster than my brain could command me to stop.

The space was too small for White Feather. It was really too small for me. I couldn't tell if it was getting smaller, because that part of my mind refused to work properly. Everything in me told me that the rocks were closing in.

So long as I fit through the hole, I kept moving.

"Lynx?" My teeth were clenched so hard his name was more of a gasp. Would the walls crumble? Would the entrance be closed when I backed out? I couldn't turn around; I'd have to slither backwards.

I thought I heard a groan. "Lynx?"

Swallow. Breathe. In and out.

I concentrated on White Feather's voice. He was interrogating Zandy.

"Not my fault, man. The werewolf she was keeping got away. She said she needed another one but after I got Lynx here, she wouldn't let me go either."

I couldn't hear White Feather's response, but Zandy was louder.

"No way, man. That other werewolf is the one that's been doing the killing, not me! She thought she had control of it, loaning it out to Arturo, but the thing didn't do what she wanted."

The cavity didn't get much bigger, but I could smell something rotting. It stunk more of bodily functions than a dead body.

A final squeeze forward left me flattened. A boulder jutted from the ground, cutting my guts in half. The front of me was inside a small hole, the back of me wanted to wiggle out to freedom.

"Lynx?" I could see a naked, dirty foot. He had moved rocks around when he buried himself.

"I'm going to pull on your foot," I said. The flashlight was in my way. The shadows, when I set it to my right, made it look as though the rocks had caved in on Lynx. "We're going to get you out of here."

I moved a rock carefully. The ground was nothing but loose dirt. I was too big for the space and far too panicky.

My hands shook. I couldn't get a hold of a second rock. I was going to crush the kid if I didn't get it together. The thought of being smashed caused a hiccup to come from my throat. Small moans punctuated my breathing. I clutched the light for support.

"Adriel?" White Feather yelled from somewhere behind me. "Don't keep going if you haven't found anything. We've got to get out of here."

I took a deep breath. A small amount of haze cleared from my eyes. White Feather was saying something about coming back with help.

"It will be too late," I whispered. Maybe it already was. Lynx could be dead. I hadn't even checked to see if he was breathing. My shirt was stuck on a rock. When I started wiggling backwards, it tore.

I reached forward again, shining the light. The foot moved. "Lynx." I shut my eyes. "Talk to me, buddy." *Because if you don't, I'm going to crawl back out of here screaming like a lunatic, and we'll never get you out.*

I pushed forward enough to slide another rock. Dark brown eyes, round ones that I recognized, peered back at me. He didn't speak, but now I had a face, I had another person. He was something besides crushing rocks.

White Feather cursed from the entrance.

"I'm coming out!" My voice was barely a squeak. Lynx went from pain to fear. He hadn't understood my words because the echo didn't sound like me.

He whimpered and tried to crawl away.

There was nowhere to go. "This way out," I enunciated slowly. "This way out." I moved a rock, then another. Purposely or not, Lynx had used this area as a latrine.

By the time I'd cleared enough rocks to see him better, I guessed it wasn't on purpose. He had been badly beaten. "What isn't broken? I'm going to have to pull you out."

He might have looked down. I felt up his ankle. When I pulled, gently as possible, his eyes rolled back into his head.

I kept right on pulling, doing my best to protect his head, but in the end, I dragged him out, painfully backwards.

White Feather grabbed my feet. Panic roared in my ears, one part of my brain shouting "hands" and the other "rockslide." I lay there panting, while he pulled and tugged. I fought the pull until he realized what was happening.

"It's okay, Adriel! You're almost out. Let me help."

He dragged me out. I was shaking so badly, I couldn't hold onto Lynx's ankles. I pointed back in.

"What is it?" He wiped at my face, at tears I hadn't realized were there.

"Get...Lynx." My teeth chattered. I wrapped my arms around my knees and tried to hold myself still. Clenching my jaw, I muttered the ingredients to the first spell I had ever learned. From there, I thought through to the second one, then the third. I muttered until I thought my teeth would break.

When White Feather grunted, I forced my head off my knees and took in the mess that was Lynx.

Without his wig, he looked closer to fifteen. His eyes were still too big on a small face, but without hair falling all over the place, his head wasn't as lost, wasn't as much teddy bear. Stubble from an almost shaved head stood straight up. I could finally guess that he was Hispanic. He was still small and with his eyes closed, he looked almost innocent.

"Let's go," White Feather commanded.

"Wait. The collars." My hands were shaking so badly I wouldn't have been able to complete the unlock spell except that I'd had so much practice lately.

The second I finished the spell, White Feather shifted Lynx to a better carrying position. He moved back the way we had come in. When Zandy's collar fell away, he took off down the tunnel, pushing around White Feather.

I couldn't tell if the warning prickle at the back of my neck was someone tracing the spell I had just used or nerves. I moved faster, but the silver at my neck didn't subside. As I ran out behind White Feather, there was a rumbling growl from the tunnel we hadn't explored.   I didn't look back, I just ran faster.

Even though I had been sweating and was now half-jogging, I felt a sudden chill. There was no way to know if it was the cool air of the cave or Sheila trying to reach me through solid rock with a spell. There were enough tunnels and air currents through here that it was possible a spell could find its way to me--or not.

I ran.

Lynx woke once and whimpered, but he didn't protest.   He probably smelled fresh air and decided it was a good thing.

Zandy tracked all the way out without any help.

When we squeezed out the entrance, White Feather punched numbers into his cell phone. He waited for an answer and punched in more numbers. "We're going to take a slightly different route back and end up closer to where the last signal was.   I had Gordon move the car while we were tracking. He left me a message to tell me where he left it."

I took White Feather's pack, grateful to feel the warm sun.   I clutched my silver as we jogged. The beads in my hair felt loose.   When I reached up to touch them, I found nothing but bits of crumbling dust. I swallowed hard.

The beads had shattered.

Instead of feeling good about the fact that the beads had helped against a vicious spell, I felt worse. *The spell had destroyed the protection through layers and layers of rock.*

Sheila couldn't know yet whether her spell had succeeded or failed, but there was no doubt in my mind she would work on a new one anyway. That was bad news for all of us.

White Feather carried Lynx ahead of me.   I feared for him. For them both.

Zandy sniffed out our old trail, and he stuck to that until White Feather barked, "east here."

He fell behind then, following.   I didn't turn around to make sure he stayed with us.

Chapter 34

To get out, we had to climb over the fences in broad daylight. The best we could do was make sure there were no cars coming.

I was disoriented, because we went out a different spot than we had gone in, but the car was waiting where White Feather expected it.

Breathing hard, White Feather deposited Lynx gently in the back seat.

"You're in back with him," he told Zandy.

"Man, I won't be able to move! There ain't room with him all over the seat."

I would have happily sat in the back with Lynx, but White Feather didn't want Zandy up front, so that was the way it was going to be.

Zandy stood, trying to decide whether to get in the car or not. I went to the trunk and retrieved a blanket, food and water.

Lynx was still out cold. He needed a lot more medical attention than spells, but there was no way he could go to a hospital. He was under-aged, had no guardian that I knew of and no record of his birth. Someone would probably arrest White Feather or me on battery charges.

"My house," I whispered.

White Feather nodded grimly.

It was the safest place I knew and full of chemicals we could use in place of a good doctor. I also needed to be where I could block spells of any kind.

I climbed in the front seat. Zandy got in back and closed his eyes. Within minutes, he was either sleeping or pretending well.

The ride back to Santa Fe seemed hours longer than the trip to White Rock.

Lynx never moved, not even to groan in pain.

When we finally arrived at my house, White Feather carried Lynx from the car. I carried in the extra food. Zandy wasted no time following us inside and making himself at home in my kitchen. Apparently he hadn't eaten much during captivity.

"Where should I put Lynx?" White Feather asked.

"Put him in the spare bedroom. He'll probably rob me blind when I'm asleep," I pretended to grumble.

"Is he dangerous?" White Feather halted in the act of opening the door I indicated.

"Not to me." Lynx wasn't, but Zandy was. Now that the lanky teenager was free, he exuded an adrenalin confidence, one that completely ignored that his rescue had come from outside hands rather than his own wits.

White Feather followed my glare as I tracked Zandy around the kitchen. "I'll be right back." He disappeared into the guest room with Lynx.

"Where can we drop you off?" I asked.

Zandy stopped in the act of stuffing a last piece of rolled lunch meat into his mouth. "Me?"

He blinked rapidly, and I had to acknowledge that despite his energetic eating, he was dead on his feet. "Let me get you a t-shirt." I went into my bedroom and got the largest shirt I owned. Though I didn't think much of the guy, he probably should see a doctor. The wounds crisscrossing his back and sides needed attention. Grumbling under my breath I went into my bathroom and found some peroxide.

I took them both back out. White Feather was standing over Zandy, waiting.

"You should probably clean your wounds," I said.

He grabbed the shirt. "I get it," he growled. "The kid can stay here, but I'm nothin' but a garbage bag!"

"Did you kill her or not?" White Feather asked, in what must have been a repeat of the question.

"He did," I said quietly. "But you can track him down later. Tonight he gets the peroxide, and we take him wherever he asks." I wanted him out of my house. Lynx I could tolerate, but not a half-adult who had accidentally killed an overzealous client.

"Let him disappear? That doesn't make a lot of sense. We have him here now, and you're telling me you saw him kill her!"

"I didn't say I saw it. I said he's the one. He knows it, and so do I. You could take him down to the station right now, and the first place they are going to send him is a doctor anyway."

"I'm not letting him walk out of here."

Zandy finally figured out he wasn't off scott-free. "I deserve a break, man. I didn't kill her, not exactly. She did it to herself!" He spread his hands, his eyes darting between White Feather and me.

I frowned. "Don't act like a complete idiot. She didn't strangle herself."

"She attacked me with the silver!" He backed away. His eyes telegraphed his move to the door.

I reached out and grabbed White Feather, but he tore his arm away effortlessly. I tripped him or he would have had Zandy without a problem.

From the carpet, he swore. "What the hell did you do that for?"

I put my arms around myself. "I wanted him gone."

"My brother could have been here in five minutes!"

The shivers didn't stop. I rubbed my arms and sat down. "I wanted him gone."

White Feather opened his mouth, but then snapped it shut. Neither of us moved. Finally he asked, "Do you have any coffee?"

I nodded. "Yeah."

When I didn't make a move to make any, he stomped into the kitchen and banged away. When I felt I could, I got up and followed him. My hands were still shaking, but I managed some juice. "I guess Lynx could probably use some food." I stared dumbly at the glass of juice. "Or water or something." My brain started thinking of herbs that would help.

"He has a lot of bruises, and I think his arm is broken." White Feather watched the coffee drizzle into the carafe instead of looking at me.

"You do realize he can't waltz into a doctor's office like a normal kid with problems?"

"I don't suppose so. But if he's hurt badly, he needs a doctor to check him over."

I shook my head. "He doesn't have insurance. I'm not depositing him in the emergency room. He'd escape the minute he was able." I rummaged through bags until I found the Gatorade. "I'm gonna put this in his room."

Before taking the Gatorade in, I went to my lab and cut a short length of walnut from my store of various woods. I gathered some herbs and went to the bedroom.

Quietly, I opened the door. He would know it was me. His brain could distinguish smells whether asleep or unconscious. In the half dark, I called out, "I brought you some Gatorade. If you wake up and want food, I'll leave a couple of sandwiches in the fridge." I was unbelievably tired and didn't know how I was going to find energy to make sandwiches. "I have chips," I said, but my voice hitched.

I set the Gatorade carefully by the bed. "I'm going to put some herbs around your arm and splint it to keep it steady. Here's an extra package of herbs too. If you think you can get in the bath without drowning, they will help."

I couldn't see much in the dim light, but his arm was swollen to the touch. "I gotta get some water."

White Feather must have known what I was doing, because he was suddenly there. "Nuked some water." He held a steaming bowl.

Together we swabbed some of the dirt away and set his arm.

"That stick is hard. I hope he doesn't roll over on it," White Feather said.

"He isn't going to roll on that arm. Not for a long time." I dribbled Gatorade down Lynx's throat. He didn't choke, but he didn't open his eyes either.

White Feather took the messy bowl of water back to the kitchen.

I whispered to Lynx, "You can stay as long as you like."

"Let him rest," White Feather said from the door. He came in and touched my arm, drawing me back out.

"You look like maybe you should eat something yourself," he suggested.

I didn't remember him putting his arm around me, but I found myself leaning against him. When we got to the kitchen, we stood there for a minute, watching the coffee pot. "I should have told him I'd make some pasta. I think Zandy ate all the lunch meat."

White Feather laughed. "I imagine he'll find the pasta if you leave it instead."

The thought of food cheered me a little. I put a pot of water on to boil. When I turned around, White Feather was taking milk from the fridge.

He grinned. "Maybe we should've stopped and gotten takeout." He glanced down at his dirty clothes. "Can they refuse to serve you at the takeout window?"

"Probably." My clothes were worse than his.

We made the pasta and ate in exhausted silence. He didn't suggest leaving, so I got blankets out. "The guest room is full. The other room is a study," I said by way of reference to my lab.

He took the blankets. "This will work. Sit with me a while."

"Okay." I looked down the hall. "Do you think he's thirsty?"

He took my hand, and we checked on Lynx. I spent another five minutes dribbling Gatorade down his throat.

When I was done, we sat on the couch. He took his shoes off and settled against the arm. I leaned against him.

In no time, I was fast asleep.

Chapter 35

Morning was less awkward than I would have expected. Lynx had always been good at making an entrance. For a possible cat, he didn't sneak very well either.

He stumbled into the kitchen, nearly knocked over a chair and announced, "I have to go back. She has my blood."

He promptly collapsed. White Feather jumped up and headed toward him, leaving me to fall bonelessly across the couch. "Oh my God." He had to be wrong. He had to be.

"Give me a hand, would you?" White Feather said. He got an arm under Lynx, but couldn't lift the kid without mashing his broken arm.

I stood up. If Sheila had Lynx's blood, getting him back into bed wasn't going to help matters much. I moved forward anyway.

White Feather half supported Lynx on the side of his healthier arm. I helped lift so that White Feather could carry him back in the bedroom.

While he got Lynx settled, I made a healthy herbal tea and sweetened it with mashed frozen strawberries. Lynx could use the vitamin C in a big way.

I took it into the bedroom. Lynx's eyes were wide open. He made a funny noise in the back of his throat. "She has my blood."

"Sheila?"

"She's working with Arturo."

He had just confirmed my worst fears. I handed him the cup of tea. "Drink it all."

He looked like he might bat it away.

"First thing is to get your strength up," I told him. "The rest we'll take care of later."

"I have to get it back!"

"I know." I glanced nervously at White Feather. Now that the emergency was over, he looked like an owl that had been rudely awakened during a daylight nap.

"He needs a doctor," was his only comment.

"How is your arm?" I asked Lynx

Lynx gulped his tea without answering.

"I'm going to get you some food." I pointed to the Gatorade. "Drink a bunch of that."

White Feather followed me back to the kitchen. "His arm needs to be set."

I took out eggs and cheese. "I don't know. I've heard that if he can change back and forth, he can heal it."

"Rumor. It might not be set perfectly, and if he changes, wouldn't it then be stuck wrong?"

"Or maybe it would straighten out." I cracked the eggs into a skillet. "I mean, if there are changes, the bone has to change."

We stared at each other, wondering. When the eggs sizzled, I added slices of cheese. I handed White Feather a plate with some of the eggs. The rest I took into Lynx.

He was starved, but around mouthfuls he declared, "I've got to go back."

"Yeah, Sheila still has something of mine too."   There was an exclamation from the doorway.   I didn't want to face White Feather, so I watched Lynx.

Lynx said, "Bastard, Arturo. I started to wonder, you know? I wasn't working for him. No way. But I offered my protection services. So did Zandy, but then he'll do anything, always branching out. Offered me in on a deal, supposed to be easy stuff. Deliveries."

"Deliveries?"

He paused in his eating. "He brings animals that he gets from Arturo up to the clinic in White Rock. The witch, she picks what she wants. Cats, dogs, anything he captures. Rats. Remember them?"

I nearly gagged. "Not only rats?"

Lynx shook his head. "She sews them together. Spells them, whatever. Mixes them up, tries to do something to them." He shook his head with incomprehension. "It's like she thinks she can make a shape shifter by taking parts from one and adding it to another."

"That doesn't make sense, Lynx. Everyone knows that shape shifters come from whatever bit them. Or infected them. Is she trying to--" My mind boggled. "Is Sheila looking for a cure?"

Lynx gave me a look of total disgust. "*Cure?*"

"Okay, okay." I held up my hands so he wouldn't smack me. The pounding of my heart was obviously getting too much blood into my head. "The fact that she is a scientist confused me for a moment."

"She ain't trying to create a shifter, because she collects those too." His hands fisted. "Zandy set me up. He hired me. Because I was the next delivery."

"Oh...no."

"Only this time, she took Zandy too. He thought he was so smart, but I almost got away. I saw those rats, I knew something was up."

"You made a run for it."

He nodded. "But it didn't work out. Zandy's a shifter too."

It probably wasn't often that Lynx couldn't outrun something. "Why does she want shifters?"

"Zandy said she needed us because the shifter she had escaped, but that ain't true. Well, maybe one of them escaped, but who you think did this to me?" He looked down at the bruises. They were already healing, but he was covered with purple, green and yellow bumps.

"A shifter did this to you?"

"Maybe it wasn't a shifter, maybe she created it, I don't know." He looked up, his eyes haunted. "It was a thing. It wasn't human, and it wasn't any animal I ever seen."

White Feather drew in a sharp breath. "She is running experiments on shifters."

Lynx shoveled more food before answering. "I think she's trying to make a shifter that can shift into more than one thing, but I dunno. The thing I saw…whatever it is…it shifts, but it's never human."

"Are you," I choked. "Are you okay, Lynx?"

His eyes cut to mine and for the first time, there was humor. "You worried what I might do?"

I nodded, completely serious.

That earned a smirk, but then he shrugged. "She wanted me to change. Made Zandy change. Zandy said he'd help her. He gave her blood, took some kind of shot." Lynx wiped his mouth with the back of his hand. It was shaking. "I gotta take a shower. Water helps, right?"

"Some." Now wasn't the time for false hope. "There's herbs by the tub. It's a start."

I helped him up. "Did she give you any shots?" I asked fearfully.

He shook his head. "No way. I wouldn't even eat. I made my own grave, and she was gonna have to dig me out if she wanted my body."

We made sure he got to the bathroom without collapsing.

Back in the kitchen, I fixed more eggs and cheese.

"What does she have of yours?" White Feather finally asked.

"I don't know." Haltingly, I gave him highlights of the break-in and why.

"We can't leave the situation like it is," White Feather said when I was finished.

"I know." I finished picking at breakfast and rinsed the plates in the sink. "I didn't know she had shot Zandy full of something either. You were right, we should have kept him here."

"We'll get him." White Feather sounded a lot more sure of it than I felt.

"Before or after he does damage?" My voice was raw. Everything felt raw.

"I guess that all depends on what she gave him." He squeezed my shoulder. "I think it's time I gave Gordon another call. He can start looking in certain places."

I nodded. While White Feather made phone calls maybe I could figure out a way to protect myself against Sheila. Then again, probably not. I was way outside my league. The things she dabbled in wouldn't even cross my mind.

Still, a witch had to try.

Chapter 36

It made the most sense to go in broad daylight when Sheila was at work, break in and get what we were after. I was certain I could get Vi, via Harold, to call me when Sheila arrived for work at Los Alamos.

Between my spell making and Gordon's latest information, that plan ran way late.

The spell to protect myself was pretty simple; double silver crosses that worked a lot like a circuit breaker. They were connected with silver wire and spelled with my hair, skin and blood because I didn't know what Sheila had of me. In theory, if Sheila hit me with anything, the first cross would absorb the spell and then break the circuit between the crosses. The bad spell should remain trapped in the silver. Hopefully, this design would work better than the glass. Under pressure all the beads had shattered, probably from a single spell. With the circuit breaker design, I should, theoretically, be able to stop more than one spell.

Once my protection was finished, I struggled to make a spell to protect Lynx. He was a shifter. He couldn't wear silver. I knocked at the guest room door and tossed him the protection packet I had made for him days ago. It wasn't going to be anywhere near enough.

"You don't have any problems with silk, right?"

He peered blearily at me. "No." The one eye he had bothered to open, closed. I chewed my lip anxiously. Silk was a good block for dormant or inactive spells, but it wasn't much use against active ones.

"Will silk protect you from silver?"

Both eyes flew opened. "What?"

"I'm concocting a spell to protect you from Sheila."

"She has my blood. Ain't nothing that works against that." His eyes flicked to the packet that had landed on the bed. Disdainfully, he ignored it and looked toward the window.

"Not entirely. But it wouldn't hurt to have something stronger to deflect spells she might throw at you."

It went downhill from there. I tried the silk, but it wasn't enough protection against the silver. He screamed outright.

"I'm sorry, sorry!" I was near tears myself.

White Feather came running. I explained what I was trying to do. "Leather," he suggested.

"Hmm." I went back to my workroom. White Feather followed.

He had other things on his mind besides concoctions. "I talked to Gordon. The DNA finally came back. Looks like you were right about Zandy. The DNA traces on the wolf that killed Dolores didn't match the other kills."

"I told you that." I had thread in my mouth so it probably wasn't very clear. Would a leather pouch be better or a flat piece glued to silver?

"The good news is that now Gordon knows for sure to look for more than one killer."

I pointed to the willow stick that contained Zandy's hair. "I could have used Zandy's tuning fork to prove to Gordon that Zandy was only connected to Dolores. Zandy's aura wouldn't have been anywhere near those other bodies assuming he was innocent. It would only show up on Dolores."

"Auras?" He stared at the stick. "You could tell me if the werewolf was the same in all the other cases?"

"I could tell you if the auras were the same around all the bodies. But doesn't the DNA already tell you that?"

He nodded. "It does, but could we get more out of the aura?"

I thought about it. "I don't know. It isn't as though I could tell you who it is unless I already had something from the wolf. Then it's a lot like DNA; I could match it to the auras left on the victims."

"But maybe you could find something we missed. On the man who was killed, there was no DNA other than his own, nothing to send to the labs. Everything they sent matched up with himself."

"That's odd."

"The body was torn apart, like the others, but there was no evidence of a sexual crime and no other DNA anywhere."

I hunted through my cabinets for leather lacing. "I could tell you pretty quickly if there was another aura around the guy, but auras are a lot like DNA. They can be cleaned up also."

White Feather wasn't one to give up easily. "Understood, but it's worth a try. Whoever cleaned up the DNA might not have known to clean up the auras. I'll get some samples." He disappeared out the door, leaving me to my spells.

I shrugged and turned back to my Lynx problem. "Kid, there has got to be a way."

Probably an hour before White Feather returned, I hit on the answer. I prepared a spell much like my own. The only trouble was that Lynx didn't want to donate any blood.

"You walk in there trying to take what is yours unprotected, she will end up owning you," I told him.

"I'll die first," he snarled.

"It won't be your choice. You know that."

"There's plenty of other werewolves she can have! Why she gonna bother again with me? Shit, Zandy, he took that shot, she told him she was going to let him go, live his normal life. All he had to do was come back for appointments."

"Pretty easy to make him do it too," I said.

There was a lot of silence on my part and hard breathing on his. He wouldn't look at me, he just clenched his fists over and over. When I got up to leave, I saw claws.

"How much?" he asked.

"A drop on the silver."

His eyes got wide. "Silver?"

"Here's the idea." I explained how the blood spell would hit the silver and then break the circuits. I explained how he was going to wear it wrapped in leather. Then came the hard part. I looked away from his wide, desperate eyes. "You're going to take the silver out of the pouch and hold it in your hand." He started to shake his head, but I kept talking. "The silver and the pain should be enough to help you resist for long enough that the spell gets trapped in the silver. You drop it back in the leather."

"This sounds like a one-time deal."

"She probably won't have too many spells sitting around. She's going to try to call you back, and you have to be ready. Once you break the first one, she's only going to set a stronger spell, but the idea is that we get the blood back before she has time to work the next spell."

"She might run out of blood."

"She probably won't," I said.

A long, pointed fingernail slid from his forefinger. He pricked his own hand. Off-guard, I almost didn't get the silver beads underneath the blood in time.

"I'll be back." I went to the lab and finished the spell. Lynx had beads instead of a cross and several more in a row than I had made for myself. Sheila would have more than one spell ready. Hopefully, the first bead would stop some. Anything that got through would get stopped at another bead and so on.

I took the spell back to Lynx. We used leather to secure it around his upper arm, one of his least injured spots, although he was healing fast. At some point he must have changed, because his broken arm didn't look broken anymore.

"When?" he whispered.

"I thought we'd go today, but I had to do the spells. Tomorrow, I guess, while she's at work."

He glared. "Night is better."

"She'll be there at night, Lynx. We don't want her there."

"I'm going to kill her."

"One thing at a time," I said.

It was like making spells. We had time for anger, but not for mistakes.

Chapter 37

I was back in the lab cursing myself for not thinking of gold sooner when White Feather came back. The reason I hadn't thought of gold for Lynx was pretty simple. Usually if my clients wanted it, they had to pay for it. Lynx wasn't the sort of client who had gold, and I wasn't the sort of witch who had much of it either.

After knocking politely on the open door to the lab, White Feather said, "I've got some tissue sample slides, and a couple of clothing items."

I squinted over at him. Lynx must have let him in the front door. "Okay, come on in." I was almost finished melting the only gold chain I owned. It contained enough gold to make two small balls. I hooked a silver filament between them. "Sheila's blood spells will probably blow through this like a screen door," I mumbled.

White Feather shuffled his feet. It distracted me, but I wanted to finish so I ignored him. I needed more blood from Lynx. "Hang on a second."

Thankfully, Lynx cooperated a lot quicker this time.

Coming back to the lab, I checked the filament and pronounced it done. Turning to White Feather I asked, "What have you got?"

"Can I set these here?"

I moved a few things from my worktable. He set down a large load of plastic bags, lining them up neatly. They were all labeled.

"Wouldn't this go badly if a jury knew these came here?" I asked.

"They're all extra samples. You'll notice I only brought fragments of the clothing, not the entire garment. In two of the cases, there were no clothes."

I went to my store of willow. "Let's see what I can do."

There was no point in using much of the wood. With everything right in front of me, I didn't need full forks. Size and flexibility were important, but if the spell worked we could get fancier later if necessary.

"Why didn't you try this with your own abilities?" I asked while I whittled.

"I never thought of it. Sensing magic is pretty easy for me, but I've never tried to separate auras." He shrugged. "There are auras around these items, but I'd have to study the problem for a while before I could do what your spell does."

"What about when you used that spell to help me track Lynx?"

"All I did yesterday was tack the wind onto your spell. The focus was already there. So was the magic from the willow."

"Oh."   I showed him the strands of Zandy's hair that were tied to the fork. "Following an actual signal takes some natural ability. I know witches who can make the forks, but couldn't find their own socks with it. I've also sold a fork or two to normals who can use them without any training. This is a spell you can teach your sister. It's very basic and almost anyone with even the slightest talent should be able to make it work.   Same for witching for water or other elements."

When everything was set, I loaded the first fork by touching the tissue sample. I set it aside and loaded the next one.

On the second fork, as soon as I linked it to tissue, it tugged. I let it spin freely. It aimed between two of the clothing bags. "These belong together."

He nodded. "Two of the girls went on their date together. There was a lot of shared body fluids and everything else at that scene. What else does it tell you?"

I shrugged and continued working. "Not much."

The third fork pinged strongly back to the originating tissue. I set it aside.

The forth one spun all over the place, falling off my open palm.   It landed pointing at the table, but all the objects were on the table. "Hmm."

"Contaminated?" He frowned over the bags, studying the codes.

I moved the objects further apart, and then picked up the fork.   It oscillated frantically between two of the loaded forks and the other objects on the table. "This isn't Zandy's sample, is it?"

He checked. "No."

I went and retrieved Zandy's fork. It found Dolores' tissue sample and a DNA sample, but ignored everything else. "Let's separate these more."

We got better organized.   The fourth fork went most strongly for the tissue it came from, but it also pinged every other fork and item except that of Dolores and the DNA I assumed must belong to Zandy. "Who is this?" I demanded.

"It's the guy--the one who had no other DNA on him." He grabbed the fork. "Let me try that."

The fork swung around and with White Feather's adrenalin behind it, it landed on the floor. The thing looked like it might hop its way over to the original tissue. He picked it up again. "How do I control this thing?"

"Hold onto it. Don't put your magic anywhere; it doesn't need it."

He got pretty much the same results only the fork kept falling off his hand. "What does it mean?"

"The guy was somehow linked to the samples of the other five women," I said. "Did the DNA show that?"

"There was no foreign DNA on him. They found nothing at all."

"Yeah, I know, but did they find his DNA," I pointed at the slide, "on any of them?"

White Feather stared at me. "I don't think anyone looked. Each of these was handled weeks apart. Samples were sent in. The investigators were looking for foreign DNA. There was no sexual crime against the guy and no foreign matter."

"So no one took his DNA and compared it to the foreign DNA on the other victims?"

"We thought he was a victim!"

"What if he is the werewolf? That would explain the link to the women."

White Feather stared back at the fork. "You might be on to something there."

"He was tied to them somehow, no matter how far apart the murders."

We stared at the samples for a bit and moved forks around. The results were the same every time.

"None of this explains how this guy died," I mused. "Was his body found like the others?"

White Feather nodded. "Torn apart. There was a lot less blood. The investigators figured he had been bled out elsewhere. The other victims were torn apart too, but there was blood everywhere and no missing body parts."

"I bet if you run the foreign DNA from the other crimes scenes, it will match with this guy."

"Okay. Any other ideas?"

"If I had more time, I could use one of these forks to find places the victims had been--or in the case of the foreign DNA, we might find traces of where its owner had been. Those places might provide a clue as to who the guy was." I explained how I had used a pager to track Zandy. "It was arbitrary though. I had to hope that I went places Zandy went, otherwise the pager wouldn't go off."

White Feather nodded. "And if this guy was the attacker, he isn't going to be attacking anymore."

"We can hope."

White Feather went back to the kitchen to make his phone call. I took my gold and gave it to Lynx. He was a lot happier with it than the silver.

Chapter 38

The rumor about vampires flying was true. They flew a hell of a lot better than I did from what I saw, and I doubted the guy had magnets in his shoes.

It was four in the morning, but since we were in White Rock, I wasn't the least bit sleepy. Lynx and I were still arguing about how to break-in. He wanted to go in right away, dead of night and all that.

"It makes more sense to wait until morning and make sure she leaves for work," I pointed out for the millionth time as we stumbled through the weeds and grass towards Sheila's side fence.

"You don't know nothing 'bout break-ins. Proved that the last time." His jaw was tight, and he kept reaching up to touch the gold talisman.

Sheila's fence was a row of spears in the darkness. I didn't want to cross that line, ever.

"If the safe is in her bedroom--" White Feather started.

Lynx interrupted. "She works in the labs at night from about two on. There was only one night she came down before midnight and that night she worked all night."

"Three days isn't enough to guarantee a pattern, especially now that you and Zandy have escaped," I hissed. "What if she has your blood down in the lab? We help ourselves to coffee while we wait for her to leave?"

"I'll go. I'll check. I'll come back."

"Right." Sheila had his blood. He could come back having been told to kill us, and we wouldn't know the difference until it was too late. My stomach knotted harder.

The vampire saved me the trouble of further arguing. One minute we were contemplating the fence, the next he floated over it. Unlike our black jeans and long-sleeved t-shirts, his outfit was a loose flowing cotton that resembled a ninja outfit without the hood.

I sucked in a choking breath and detected the slight smell of decay. Instead of a sense of alien power, I felt a distinct tugging as though he were reaching for my very essence or maybe…my very soul.

The vamp landed gracefully, hands held out in the universal, "nothing to hide." He said, "You need a distraction so that you can get in undetected."

What I needed was a new job. A new life. "Go away!" I hadn't found time to make a vampire stake, but I clutched my silver for all I was worth.

His head turned to me, and I saw fangs. "You aren't very good at networking, are you?"

"What do you want?" White Feather sounded calm, but I could feel the edges of his power, not really radiating, but building inside of him, ready.

"Blood?" I guessed.

Lynx made a gurgling sound in the back of his throat.

The vampire was polite if nothing else. "I owe you a favor. Perhaps now would be a good time to pay the bill."

"You owe me nothing. I think I was clear about that."

"And I am clear about paying debts. You led us to she-who-hunted us, and although she captured the tiniest amount of blood from our weakest, your information," he tilted his head and laughed softly, "saved my life."

"Sheila was the witch hunting you? Then why do you still have word out at the pubs for the best witch?"

The vamp smiled, no fangs. "Why would I look at pubs for a witch?"

"But--"

He silenced me by baring his fangs. "Sheila was the one at the bars looking for the best witch, fool. She also had the call out for the best werewolf and the oldest vamp!"

"But doesn't she consider herself to be the best witch?"

"Of course. But she wasn't going to run experiments on herself, now was she?"

My face drained. "Oh."

Lynx gave me a look of disgust. "Can we get moving here?"

As soon as I found my heart and got it beating, sure. I edged away from the vamp. "You owe me nothing. Sounds like she got her vampire blood anyway."

"He has been eliminated. She will not call him. We will see to it that she can't call any of those connected to him either. In the meantime, we are watching. There will be a break in her defenses, there always is."

"You can't go inside her house? No invite," I guessed.

Lynx said, "The cave ain't her home, but she caged us there. It's connected to her basement. You watching the cave?"

The vamp's head swiveled so fast it made my neck ache. "What cave?"

Lynx described the area where he had been held. "The cave has a direct tunnel into her lab. I don't know if the tunnels fall under your rules."

The vampire tilted his head away from us as though listening, but there was no sound that I could hear. "This cave is a natural one?"

I nodded. "There were a few places that had been opened up with dynamite."

"Did she ever live there?"

I almost laughed. "Not likely."

"She never went in there," Lynx said. "The creature she kept there dragged us back into her lab whenever she wanted."

"Where is this cave?" the vamp demanded.

White Feather described the way we got in, but it wasn't much to go on.

"Our kind can go through the cave, at least to a point," the vamp said. "We'll distract her from there and give you time to get into her home."

"That might work," White Feather said.

"Only if the samples are in her safe," Lynx said. "If they ain't, they're in the lab, and I'll have to go there next."

"First things first," the vampire said smoothly. "I need one of you to help me find the cave."

I sucked in a breath, but didn't volunteer. White Feather didn't show even that much reaction.

Lynx surprised us both when he said, "I'll go."

"Are you kidding?" I burst out.

"There's a good chance my stuff is in the lab," he said. "I wait until she's gone, go in through the tunnel, get it, then I'm out. If it's upstairs, you get it and you're gone."

"Uh, Lynx, there's a couple of problems with that." I took a deep breath. "We need *you* to get into the safe. And you probably need *me* to find your blood if she hasn't already spelled it into an amulet." I pointed to my backpack where I had placed his witching fork.

"No." Lynx shook his head. "You don't need me. I'm gonna give you the combination to the safe."

"You still remember it?"

"It saves time when I have to go back. You'd be surprised, but there's lots of jobs that turn into two or three, same safe. I give you the combinations to the safe and to the door that looks like a wine fridge in the kitchen. Then I go with the vamp. I can travel faster than you two anyway. We give you the distraction, you get the bounty and you get out."

Lynx was talking too fast; his mind probably working faster. He wanted in there, and I didn't think he was going to calmly wait for Sheila to leave. "The vamp can't help you in the lab. And that trinket I gave you isn't going to save your hide past the first attempt she makes to control you."

His eyes glittered up at me, glowing yellow. "She ain't never even gonna know I'm there." He jutted his chin at the vampire, who remained motionless, waiting for us to figure out a plan. "You ready, bloodsucker?"

The vamp smiled, showing his shiny fangs. "The outside cameras suffered an accident every time she replaced them with the exception of one on the other side of the house. We left that alone so she could see certain images we chose to send her." He waved a palm at Lynx. "I'm ready when you are, fur ball."

Lynx said, "Easy in, easy out for you two. Three numbers for the safe upstairs. The one in the kitchen has a trick to it so pay attention." He gave me the numbers. The spinning of the dials was not standard. "She put more work into the one in the kitchen, but I guess we know why." He finished his instructions and turned to go.

"Lynx--" He didn't stop. "Be careful!" I yelled in a whisper.

I never saw the vampire leave. All I heard was, "We get you in, the debt will be paid."

Whatever.

Chapter 39

We gave Lynx and the vamp almost an hour to get into place. We were cutting everything close, but the sun was threatening to rise, and the longer we waited the worse I felt.

Going inside Sheila's house made my skin crawl. Like Lynx, I clutched my protective talisman, and probably unlike him, I prayed.

I was worried about my wayward friend. What did Lynx have planned? The kid would die before he left this place without his blood. He probably wouldn't have left the first time had we not carried him out. I didn't want to have to do it again because I suspected he'd be dead if it came to that.

White Feather had apparently picked a lock or two in his time, because he got the back door opened without my help. I stood off to the side while he worked his mundane magic.

When White Feather pushed the door open, it didn't squeak. If there was an alarm, we couldn't hear it. He closed the door softly behind me.

As we had agreed, he put his hand on my shoulder, and I led the way, using my memory as a guide. My hands out in front, I slid my feet forward, moving slowly, silently towards the stairway. I could feel the antique buffet in the dark. I kept my distance and didn't even dare look at it for fear of what I might see in the shadows.

Sheila had no nightlights, and her living room blinds were all the way down. When I looked up the stairs, nothing but darkness waited. If I didn't stare directly, I could make out the shape of steps.

White Feather's hand on my shoulder was heavy instead of reassuring. I couldn't hear him breathing and while that was good, it was scary.

The top of the stairs was a bit lighter, but not much. I edged towards the bedroom.

The door was closed. My heart jumped. Had it been opened when she wasn't home? I was positive that it had. Did this mean she was inside sleeping? Or waiting for us with a weapon?

White Feather must have known it was the right room when I stopped. He slid next to me and elbowed me aside. I didn't like him going first. We hadn't agreed to this. In fact, we hadn't even discussed it other than to decide I would lead the way after getting inside the house.

What was I going to do, yell at him?

We both wore suede gloves lined with silk. He eased the door open. No squeaking. I wondered if my doors at home were so quiet. I resolved that

I would put spells on all of them, something to tell me when my haven had been breached.

We had better hope that Sheila didn't have any notification spells.

Light from the windows outlined a large lump behind the bed curtains. I wanted to cry. The only thing that kept me from running was fear. She was here. In the room. With me.

White Feather reached back and grabbed my hand. He squeezed my fingers. I remembered to breathe. The whoosh of air into my lungs sounded loud to me, but White Feather didn't react. Neither did the figure in the bed.

At least Lynx was safer than we were. The kid might find his blood and be free. If he didn't, we stood only a small chance of getting it out of the safe without getting caught.

It took another heartbeat or two for me to realize that White Feather was waiting. He held a hand out to the right, but the closet with the safe was on the left. I squeezed his hand and gently tugged the other way. He slid quietly that direction.

His hand pressed mine, and then pulled down. I nodded. There wasn't enough light for him to see me. I moved his hand to my face and nodded again. I would stay put, shout a warning, distract her, kill her, whatever it took if she woke up.

White Feather moved my hand to his lips for an instant before letting it go. He drifted through the dark to the closet. I kept my eyes on the form in the bed, slowly reaching to my ankle for my Leatherman knife. The blade was super sharp, dipped in silver and etched with a twenty-four karat spell.

I very quietly opened the blade and held it ready.

My attention was split between White Feather at the closet door and the bed. Since I expected Sheila might sit up, jump out of bed or even throw something, I almost missed her slide out of the *bottom* of the bed. Maybe she moved a pillow behind her so that the top of the bed still looked like a person sleeping, or maybe I wasn't paying enough attention. All of a sudden Sheila was slithering along the floor behind White Feather, about to take him down by his ankles.

I screamed.

It wasn't until I jumped on her back that I realized she was a snake. Literally.

Slick scales defied my grip and the creature undulated, tossing me right back across the room. My knife was somewhere embedded in the snake. The knife might work its magic, but knifing the back of a snake wasn't a very effective killing method.

"White Feather!" By the time I yelled, he certainly knew he wasn't safe. I yanked a chemical light stick from the side of my backpack and broke the element. In the high greenish glow, I could see White Feather pinned against the wall near the closet. The snake was six or seven feet long and at least as big around as a person's body.

I searched along the side of my backpack again. "One, two, and over one," I counted. I yanked the spell free from the pack, stumbled to my feet and launched myself across the room.

The head moved incredibly fast and was almost on top of White Feather until he raised his hands. I felt the punch of wind crash into the head, deflecting it.

I jumped on the snake, my legs around the neck. The jaws snapped. The tongue flicked towards White Feather. When the wind came again, I was ready.

The snake jaws opened wide. I tossed my packet into fleshy snake lips.

There was a second spell exactly like it attached to the other side of my pack, but before I could get it, the creature flopped over backwards, smashing me underneath. There was a sickening crunch. I thought maybe it was my back breaking. All the air was gone from my lungs. My pack was under me. I couldn't reach anything, although I tried to move my hands.

Third spell along the edge? Which hand was I moving?

I was disoriented. I hadn't said the words to activate the first spell. "Misbegotten," I mumbled. "Gutter." Nothing happened. Had I grabbed the wrong one?

No, because the spell would have gone off under me, even were it attached to my backpack. "Misbegotten gutter," I screamed, realizing the spell was shielded by layers of snake.

There was a thunk above me. The tail, as fat as the rest of the snake, lashed sideways. My legs were temporarily freed. I saw the spark of the spell and then a fireball as it ignited, coming out the snake's mouth.

I rolled. "Get back," I tried to shout. There still wasn't enough air in my lungs to create more than a squeak.

White Feather or the snake grunted. I looked at the snake. The back half still undulated back and forth, but the side of its head was on fire. My knife wobbled from one side of its scales. "White Feather?" Tears from the smoke of my exploding spell blurred my vision.

Another grunt, but from the opposite side of the room. "What the hell was that?"

I coughed before answering. "Firebomb. A really big firecracker."

"Next time warn me before you set it off, okay?"

"Sorry." I scooted further away from the snake, staring at it. "Is she a shifter?" I couldn't believe it. "A snake?"

"Hardly." White Feather got up, wincing. "I think it's a simulacrum."

"It's a little substantial for that, don't you think?" I still struggled to get enough air.

White Feather eased over and retrieved a large blade from the floor. He reached up and stabbed the snake's smoldering eye. Keeping watch over its head, he pulled my knife out from the back of the creature and handed it to me.

"Gross." I wiped the goop on the floor and turned away, breathing shallowly. White Feather put his knife through the other eye, making sure the brain was dead. I assumed the other two or three noises were him severing the spine.

I kept breathing, hoping he didn't need me. "I think it's a guard--a familiar. She must leave it here so that...so that she knows what is going on in her absence," I ended in a whisper filled with dread.

"Whatever it is, it's dead. Let's get what we need and get out." His own breathing was harsh and uneven.

"It's not hard to tie a notification to a living object." I stared back at the snake. "It's dead. She'll know it."

We both looked at the yawning doorway. We hadn't heard anyone approaching, but we'd been rather distracted.

"She would know the minute this thing moved to attack, wouldn't she?" White Feather asked.

I shrugged, knife in a defensive position as I righted my pack across my shoulders and checked the location of my remaining spells with my free hand. "It depends on how much control she had over the creature and how she set the spell. I'd have to do a lot more studying on the subject before I could answer that."

"I'm not up on the subject myself." We stared at the doorway, not moving.

"She's not coming, is she?" I whispered.

"She could be waiting for us downstairs."

I listened with every ounce of my being. "She could be otherwise occupied."

White Feather let out a hiss. "Do you think Lynx is keeping her distracted?"

"Knowing Lynx, he's trying to kill her. My only concern is that she won't be distracted by that for long." It would be child's play to work through my puny spells and control Lynx. "We can get the stuff later. We better find Lynx."

I moved toward the door. White Feather didn't like me going first. He moved ahead of me, or at least his aura did. It blew out the door and down the stairs, searching for danger. Now that Sheila knew we were here, there was no point in not using magic. His was a neat trick, one I'd like to mimic in a spell when I had the time.

White Feather didn't find enough of a threat to stop us, so I crept down the stairs with him glued to my side. The light from the bedroom made going down easier, but our shadows were in front of us. I wasn't certain, but I thought chasing our own shadows was a bad omen.

Chapter 40

The door through the kitchen was easy enough since Lynx had given us the combination, and Sheila hadn't changed it. I expected to go down the stairs slowly, listening for danger, but once the door was open, the noise from below was loud and violent. No one was going to hear us coming.

We took the stairs two at a time.

The vault door going into the lab was already open. The place was in chaos. Cages were on the floor, rats squeaked, and from the scurrying across the floor, some had obviously escaped.

The opposite side of the room was where the real danger waited.

I thought it was a shifter, but it was hard to tell. Some shifters were more animal, some more human. When shifted, there were a few who didn't even remember their human side. I didn't know if the awareness was a choice or if certain shifters didn't have room to be aware of both. Face it, some humans were less human than others, whether or not they could shift.

Lynx was in a battle for his life against the bear-like creature. It stood upright, but that was its only human feature. What fur it had was in mangy patches; blotches of skin ranged from a rash-like pink to dark, mottled black. One arm ended in a stump, the other had long claws, but they stuck out sideways from the end. Where eyes should have been there was nothing but shaggy fur overhanging an odd shaped, bear-like snout. Teeth that would have done a boar proud gnashed and splattered saliva with each heaving grunt.

Lynx crawled backwards, enticing the monster to follow him through a door and into a tunnel. The tunnel had to lead to the caves where Lynx and the vampire had gone--and probably should have stayed. The kid was injured again, burned from the looks of the black across his lower jaw. If his tattered shirt was any indication, the gold amulet had exploded off entirely when Sheila reached for him with her amulet magic.

Our entry into the lab probably saved Lynx's life. Sheila was at the far end, working over a pot of chemicals. She stopped to shriek when she saw us.

"Aaaaaaiiiiii!" A glob of black goo dripped from her wooden spoon. It started smoking, eating through the tabletop. The rest of the glob was on its way to us.

I ducked. Sounds like her feral yell usually meant a spell was about to activate.

The glob missed, but she reached inside her shirt. How many amulets could she wear and control at once? Aside from Harold, I knew she had something of mine and something that belong to Lynx, but surely--

I screamed. The amulet she pulled out contained whatever I had left behind in her house. She held it high, reveling in her power and my pain. Cold ice raced across my skin, piercing me like jagged needles.

As suddenly as the pain started, it stopped. The silver circuit I had created snapped, just as I had designed it.

I flopped to the floor anyway. Let her think she had me cowed for the moment. "Stop her," I cried out, crawling away as though in pain. Hopefully White Feather caught the wink and even if he didn't see it, surely my obvious words would keep him focused.

Wind breezed across the distance. I rolled under a bench, praying the rats wouldn't come after me.

Sheila deflected the wind easily enough. She had felt it before, and she was ready. She shoved it into the creature attacking Lynx.

"Ahhhhhh," it sighed, almost a purr.

I smelled the backlash and gagged.

Every witch who works with spells knows something about earth elements. I knew the power that lay in the belly of the earth, waiting. Every time I used a spell, I touched it, but the idea was to encapsulate the power, to make sure that a tiny bit stayed within the lodestone, within the silver, within the bits of plant and trees.

Whatever Sheila was using was like earth power, but she twisted it. Worse, she made no attempt to contain it. Instead of matching like elements, she threw bits of earth randomly. Some of the power deflected White Feather's wind, the rest landed like pieces of hot ash.

The creature howled again, forcing my attention back to it. Lynx inched backwards using his arms. He reached for the doorway. A white hand hovered, ready to pull him, but he wasn't quite far enough. The beast leaned down, grabbing at Lynx with its teeth even though some pointed out, and too many pointed straight up. The fur across its forehead shifted. Hollow, furred sockets contained no eyes. Instead, it made shuffling, moaning sounds as though sniffing.

Lynx had three feet to go. He clawed another few inches forward.

White Feather ran towards the back of the beast, but Sheila threw something at him. His body arced sideways, hitting the wall so hard, he may have broken bones.

"Bring him to me!" Sheila shrieked, rubbing one of the amulets. "Bring my baby home!"

The creature bobbed up and down eagerly, its whole body quivering with delight at the command. It swung an arm down to Lynx, battering him. The stump on the end could not grab him, but once the misshapen bear felt

Lynx's leg, it fell upon him, banging with the stubbed arm, snapping with its teeth. One of its legs ended in a hoof that kept sliding uselessly across the concrete.

Lynx yelled and pulled hard towards the tunnel. "Now, man, now!"

He wasn't far enough. His back stiffened suddenly, and he screamed.

I picked up an empty cage and threw it at Sheila.

She turned to me with a smile. It only took her a moment to grab a different amulet.

Rolling under the bench, I went for the beast on hands and knees. Lynx had changed directions. He was now almost hugging the beast, trying to crawl back to Sheila. "Nahhh."

Sheila's spell hit me again, but this time, instead of playing dead, I rose to my feet with a shriek. With everything I had, I ran straight into the back of the monster and shoved it towards the tunnel where the vampire waited.

A single claw went over the line into the tunnel. A white hand reached out, but stopped cold, as if it hit a wall. Like a child teasing, it touched the claw, but couldn't grab it.

The circuit on my last silver popped. The spell came at me full force, and I gasped, squirming away from the grotesquely furry creature. Tears blurred my vision. My body shook. Turquoise burned hot, then cold. "Stooop!" I clutched at the first spell I found.

I threw it. I didn't know what words to yell because I didn't know which spell I had grabbed.

Lynx yelled, "Go, go, get back!" He still crawled towards Sheila.

I shoved my legs against gnawing teeth. "Die," I screamed.

"You'll die," Sheila replied with a happy cackle.

The wind was only a brush, a gentle caress, but it blocked her magic a bit. Needing more, I breathed it in, drawing it and holding it.

With sudden control of my feet, I pushed again and this time, the vamp had more than a claw. The vamp yanked the giant monster inside the tunnel.

There was a second of deadly silence.

My eyes found Sheila. She was frozen, her lips opened in a soundless wail, but I don't think she was feeling pain. It was the sudden snapping of her link to the monster that left her momentarily stunned.

White Feather was as focused as I, only he moved stealthily towards her, while I could barely move.

Lynx curled into a ball, shivering.

Sheila sucked in air and turned to her pot. Grabbing a rat, she sliced it open. Blood poured over the cauldron. The next thing that went in looked like a cat, one that already had strangely long claws.

Chemicals smoldered. She mumbled words, arcane and powerful.

The pot burbled. It tried to crawl away. No, it was a creature, crawling out.

I felt her call to the earth, a resounding flash of power from under the floor.

"No!" I bellowed uselessly.

The power hit the rat-like creature coming out of the pot. It absorbed the power, blowing itself full, like a balloon. One eye popped out, the other found its focus on me.

Calling the elements directly was dangerous, foolhardy. Like a heartbeat, I knew they were there, but I respectfully tiptoed around them, taking only what the earth might consider pretty baubles. I never took more than bits and pieces of rocks or plants that mother earth didn't need.

Sheila's magic was outright theft.

"How do we kill it?" White Feather yelled, weaving back and forth trying to distract the new beast.

"Kill it?" It wasn't alive, not technically. It might have a heart--or two or four. From the looks of the thing, the animal had died in the chemicals, and she had somehow animated the various parts. "I don't think it's alive."

"Too bad, we've got to kill it anyway!" he snarled savagely.

The creature came towards me, its pointy rat nose twitching. The thing was almost as large as a full-grown German Shepard with talons that belonged on an eagle. It was a mindless mass of energy, no more than a bundle of molecules torn into rogue compounds, an unstable mess. Dangerous sparks, like electrical shocks gone haywire, snapped from its body as it tried to eat up more energy.

"I don't think we can kill it," I said again, barely audible. I scooted backwards.

From the floor, Lynx threw a glass vial towards the creature. When it hit, the glass instantly shattered, the lethal shards coming back at us. I ducked.

White Feather rolled behind a cabinet. "Can we burn it?"

I had no idea. Nothing in my spells could break apart the thing she had created and put them back where they belonged. Burning would only add heat to the reaction, possibly making it...hungrier. It could not be sated. "It has to go back."

My mind ran through a few explosion spells, including the two or three on my pack. "Back to source, reassemble...how much power to tear it to pieces? Maybe we could drown it."

White Feather tipped a table sideways in front of the creature, but it didn't matter. The rat-thing pulled itself up and oozed over. A back foot reached out, and the thing stood on two hind legs, using a long naked tail for balance.

"Water?" White Feather repeated hopefully. He rolled near a sink, turning the faucet on full blast. Climbing to his feet, he shoved nearby paraphernalia into the drain.

Lynx threw more vials at the creature, slowing it down. I looked at Sheila because I couldn't figure out why she wasn't attacking. She had gone completely still, holding onto the side of the pot with one hand and an amulet with the other. Her eyes stared straight ahead, ignoring us.

She was somewhere else. She was pulling the energy that controlled this thing.

There were many types of earth magic. The red earth of the cliffs had a different voice than the sandy desert soil that blew in the wind. One type was quick and shifted with the whims of a breeze. The other was old, like a deep artery, feeding many channels. The magic danced across all of it, but it wasn't all the same.

We needed the old magic, the one with bare threads in the air.

"I can hear it," I said.

"So can I," White Feather yelled back, leaping closer to me and further from the rat. "What about it?"

Was the earth called to this thing or repelled by its existence? "Could you enhance the call? What would happen if you pushed even more power into it?"

"Are you crazy?"

"Can you deflect it? Or push it back where it came from?"

White Feather tried. I could feel his power, a breeze from the tunnels, from the cave, from the earth. It swirled around us like a net, blocking some of the raw power in the room. I pulled the magic to me, almost giddy with relief.

Grabbing Lynx, I dragged him by the arms into the water that spilled out of the sink. It wasn't much because the drain wasn't completely plugged, but it was better than nothing.

Rats squealed, squeaked, and protested. The cacophony was almost too much to bear. Standing in the water, I reached for White Feather. He swung a cage on top of the rat creature that was almost upon us.

I was afraid the only way to kill it was to kill Sheila.

The vampire must have agreed with that thought. Like death itself, he appeared in the tunnel doorway.

"Welcome," Sheila crowed. "Come inside, little pet, come into your new home."

I choked.

Sheila cackled madly. "You drank the blood of my creature, and I control its blood! Now I own you!"

I noticed two things at once. Although Sheila's attention was not on the rat creature, it still came at us, dodging White Feather's attempts to pummel it with the metal leg from a table. Secondly, I noticed the vampire's smile. I had seen this guy smile more than once; fangs, and no fangs. This was the first time I had ever seen the smile light his eyes.

"Thank you for the welcome, witch."

I never saw him move, but he was across the threshold and next to Sheila in the blink of an eye. As quickly as he arrived, he was thrust backwards, hitting the wall hard enough to dent it. The vampire snarled, fangs dripping.

Sheila hadn't invited the dead to her table without preparations. She reached up again, maybe to grab an amulet or a spell.

I didn't wait. I activated the first spell I came across by pulling a string that would allow the chemicals to mix and threw the packet right at her. "Catch, witch!"

My spell, probably a deflection or illusion spell, did absolutely nothing against whatever she worked, but my yell gave everyone a half a second when she looked at the object flying her way.

She returned almost immediately to her focus. The unholy earth fire that she had called to animate the rat was nothing compared to what she unleashed now. The floor under her cracked, and her arms went up as though propelled. Her feet came off the ground.

The force of her calling blew a hole through the side of the room, but the vamp was no longer standing there.

In a blink, the vampire was again next to Sheila. She snarled, but couldn't redirect her unleashed power without blowing herself to smithereens.

"Did you actually believe I would eat any creature of yours?" the vampire hissed. His hands wrapped around her neck.

"Wait," I cried. "She has to send this power back!"

I heard the snap of her neck. Sheila's head lolled to the side.

We were doomed. The raw energy that Sheila had unleashed had nowhere to go. Like a tornado, it howled, ripping through the stone, forming another tunnel before bounding back into the room.

The rat creature didn't stop coming for us either. I was pretty sure Sheila was dead, and if she wasn't, the vampire was going to fix that soon enough. The problem was the energy. It swirled, feeding the rat creature and devouring anything in its path.

"Goodbye," I said.

White Feather heard me. He turned, but I waved him off and raised my arms, mimicking Sheila. He probably knew a lot more about channeling than I did. He probably knew it was too dangerous to mess with, but we needed a way for the power that thrumbed through the room to flow back to the earth.

I didn't have a lightning rod, but I knew how they worked. It was foolhardy, dangerous, and I would burn.

Power was not something I knew how to actively call, but I understood how to link things. I was of the earth. My silver was of the earth. The air, the breeze from White Feather, was from the earth.

There was no time to understand how Sheila had done it.

I could only link what I knew. My hair stood on end as if wind were blowing up through my body. I pulled my turquoise necklace free and held it high. The silver chain blew straight up.

Lightning rod.

I focused on every earth element on my person, calling earth to earth. The blue stone was from the earth, but it shattered under the huge energy force that came at me. I let the energy flow through me, but I could not control it. It was its own law and once unleashed, I was merely a wire for the electricity.

I screamed. Even that primal sound was taken from me as the earth rushed into my lungs. My feet were on fire. My hair stood straight out, but then the heat curled it, singeing.

It hurt. I think I had done the spell backwards.

Earth magic arced across the ceiling and linked with the tornado, gathering dust, glass, tabletops, and broken, hopeless pieces of animals. It circled, looking for a drain. The only way back out was the channel I had formed.

I couldn't move, couldn't even breathe. I hadn't intended for Lynx or White Feather to be hurt, but once called, the earth had its own purpose, mindlessly swirling. Sooner or later, the laws of nature prevailed, and the earth was going home even if it swallowed everything else with it.

"You're *crazy!*" White Feather yelled.

"You just figurin' that out, buddy?" Lynx bellowed. His claws were out, literally, digging into whatever he could find. As the center of the storm, I was not being torn apart, merely used, but Lynx and White Feather would be sucked into the maelstrom and would die.

White Feather took a wicked blow from a tabletop. The force of it threw him into Lynx. He grabbed and held onto him.

I couldn't move. I wanted to help, but I was rooted to the spot.

With a strange feeling of inevitability, I watched them tussle for control. I turned my head away, beseeching the earth not to tear them to shreds. When my head turned, I realized that while my feet were rooted, the rest of me was not.

My entire body appeared to be reaching for the energy as though to draw it in.

"Get away," Lynx yelled.

But White Feather shook his head, never taking his eyes off of me. As the center, where I stood was the calmest. He grabbed Lynx and hauled him closer.

"Adriel?" White Feather screamed into the noise. "Can you turn this off?"

Things were going black. Was the storm causing clouds or too much dust?

"Adriel?"

I heard my name again, but from far away. When had I last drawn a breath of air?

"--turning blue."

Lynx was a cat. He changed in front of me, maybe to have more strength, maybe to help heal his injuries. He was too small to be a Lynx. The kid was a bobcat, not a Lynx. Maybe he had chosen his name because he wished he were the bigger cousin. He changed again, reverting to human.

"Why are her feet glowing?" White Feather asked.

"She stores stuff there," Lynx howled back.

I giggled. How had Lynx guessed?

It didn't matter now. I would ride the storm into the heavens, flying, really, truly flying. Everything would look better from the sky, lighter, freer. The black that crowded me now would disappear--

Whomp!

I spun dizzily, swirling wildly. The roar wasn't gone from my ears. I still couldn't see, couldn't breathe. The cold wet of water soaked my back.

I wasn't flying higher, I was flat on my back. Someone sat on my lungs.

"There's no air to push out," Lynx said.

The weight went away. I had an urge to cough, but I couldn't. "Swoooooo!" I tried to tell them I was dying. Could they see me if I waved goodbye?

Instead of a sky filled with stars, there were only two bluish green ones.

"Adriel? Take a breath again."

Again?

He was so close I could feel his breath on my face. He was so... earthbound. His hand grabbed mine. Where my fingertips touched his, they tingled. He squeezed. "Breathe, Adriel."

I forgot how.

He kissed me. I sucked in a breath, and he helped, his lips touching my face gently, my cheeks, my eyes, my lips. I must have been breathing, but I wasn't sure. His air was my air, a scent that wasn't the lab. It wasn't the earth either, it was pure White Feather.

"Don't you two think we should get the hell outta here?" a crabby voice asked.

I blinked. White Feather's face got further from mine. Everything went blurry. "I'll carry her."

"Whatever, let's blow this place!"

White Feather set me on my feet. They were cold where previously they had been so very hot. I looked down. My shoes were gone. "What--" I croaked.

White Feather pointed. A mass of smoking leather lumped over melted rubber. "The power seemed to be worst at your feet so I took your shoes off and knocked you away from the wind. The power sucked back through your shoes."

The sneakers still had a strange glow. "Magnets," I said. "Earth back to earth through earth."

White Feather gripped me tighter.

I looked around the room. Where the rat creature had been there was nothing but a burned blotch. It, along with several other spots in the lab, was still smoking. Where Sheila had been standing, there was now a strange burnt shadow dusting the floor in the hazy outline of skeleton. The power she had called had burned right through her body. "The amulets?"

"Couldn't find them," Lynx complained. He kicked his feet around scraps of tables and a few pieces of metal that used to be cages. "Nothing left over there but dust."

Indeed, the pot Sheila had been using, the chemicals, and the entire table were piles of ash. Whatever she had had of mine was gone for good. Thank God.

"What happened to the vamp?" I asked.

White Feather's shirt was half torn off. When he shrugged, a piece of sleeve floated to the floor. We all looked around, but there was no sign of him. "I don't think vampires need to breathe. Maybe he fought his way through the edge of the storm down one of the tunnels. We were close enough to you that we managed to keep breathing."

"I was trying to ground her power," I explained.

"You did that. After you called a bunch of power of your own."

I shook my head. "I don't even know how to link to the earth like you do to the wind."

He slanted his eyes at me. "Right." He used one hand to wipe at the dirt and sweat smeared across his forehead and used the other to tug me toward the stairs. Lynx hightailed it across the debris, scampering ahead of us.

When we reached the kitchen, Lynx headed for the back door. I stopped him. "We still need to empty the safe upstairs. We were interrupted before and didn't check it."

He looked back, his sudden eagerness held in check. "Good idea." He changed direction.

White Feather and I followed. By the time we got up to the bedroom, Lynx had the safe wide open.

"I guess we probably can't get paid for this, huh?" Lynx flashed me a big smile.

"You thinking about holding these items hostage?" My disapproval was obvious.

The smile disappeared. "Anything else, yeah. This shit." He shook his head.

"You take the papers. I'll get the box." My shirt had some good tatters again. I ripped a strip off. Like before, the amulets were lined up across the velvet, only this time, there was an extra one thrown carelessly to the side.

I frowned. When we were here last, I had taken one from the middle. There had been seven, now there were eight total. "Harold maybe?" It would do the man a lot of good to destroy the object of his captivity.

Using the edge of my shirt, I took the whole box without touching any of them. "Let's get this stuff burning."

Lynx found a cigarette lighter in a kitchen drawer on our way out.

We burned the papers first. When they were gone, I looked at the box of amulets. "One of these might belong to Harold." I looked at White Feather. "He deserves to be the one to destroy it, to know it's gone."

Lynx snarled, "Burn them all, and then he'll know."

I swallowed. It would be easier. And faster. I pushed the box toward the fire with a stick. "It would help him heal," I said, stopping before the box actually reached the flames.

Lynx frowned mightily.

I looked from him to White Feather and then used the stick to push the box away from the fire.

White Feather walked to the side of the house and turned on the hose. He doused the fire.

Using sticks, we cobbled the box over to the car. I forced each of the amulets into a water container in the trunk. The water would hold the evil at bay. Hopefully.

Being a witch wasn't easy. Being a responsible one was even harder.

I felt pretty bad about it until White Feather reached out and grabbed my hand.

Together, we got in the car. On the way home, he didn't let go of my hand. I had a feeling he would be helping me with the amulets until we were both satisfied that their aura was dead and gone.

Chapter 41

I was half asleep and aching all over when we got back to my house. White Feather and Lynx didn't look much better than I felt. Unfortunately, the items in the trunk of my car were like a disease. As long as the evil cache existed, it was hurting someone. We couldn't leave the amulets in existence any longer.

While Lynx raided the fridge, I limped to my bedroom for some moccasin slippers. No way were my burned feet getting squeezed into shoes.

On the way back to the living room I stopped in the lab to make sure that I still had a strand of Harold's hair. Thankfully, it hadn't disappeared from the silk-lined box where I had stored the papers with his signature.

White Feather joined me and handed me some Gatorade. "Can we do this testing outside?"

I took a much needed drink and then shook my head. "We can't test for his aura while they are all sitting in water." I handed a silk wrap to White Feather. "We may as well bring them in the lab." Every pore in my body protested. "Let's find his if it's there. We can save it for him and destroy the rest."

While White Feather retrieved the jug, I pushed the DNA samples aside and stacked the willow from that experiment off to one side. From my untouched stash of willow, I cut another fork.

Lynx came in and took my stool, keeping his distance. While I set the willow fork with Harold's hair, White Feather used tongs wrapped in the silk to fish out the amulets.

One by one, he laid them on the workbench.

I was lucky I was facing him when the fifth amulet came out. It was the greenish stone, the one I assumed was Harold's, but it wasn't the fork in my hand that twitched.

The forks on the table fell over with a clatter as one of them swiveled around to point at the dangling amulet that White Feather had yet to lower to the table.

I stared. "Did you see that?"

White Feather stood frozen in place. Lynx scooted the stool backward, while I stepped forward. "Which one was it?" I scanned the pile of willow forks, but while the samples were coded and marked, the forks weren't. I wasn't positive which one had moved. Even if I had been, I no longer knew which fork belonged to which sample.

White Feather set the amulet down. "Should I get the rest out?"

I nodded. "I'll make more forks."

We started fresh in order to be sure. We laid out the DNA samples, redid fresh forks for each, and traced the aura.

"It's the guy," I said. "The one whose aura is on each of the female victims."

"Sheila was controlling him," White Feather said.

Lynx spat, "Experiments."

I turned to him. "She wanted to use you to replace a shifter she lost, right?"

He showed teeth, and they didn't look like human ones. "That's what Zandy said. Take a few injections, and we could go."

"And come back now and then for an appointment. She used the amulet to make certain that the wolf came back."

"Until it didn't anymore," White Feather said. "Who killed it? There was no foreign DNA. The body was torn to pieces."

"Maybe he did himself," Lynx said sourly. "Maybe he didn't want to answer the call no more."

"Maybe Sheila did it." I shuddered. "On purpose or by accident. The way she spelled things, she might have pushed too much too fast and the guy exploded." I thought of the shifter in her lab and the rat creature. The bear creature had been missing a hand. The rat creature lost its eye even as it was forming. The creatures weren't normal--or healthy.

"One too many shots." Lynx made a cutting motion across his own neck.

White Feather and I exchanged glances. "I hope Gordon finds Zandy soon," I said on a hard swallow. "What if whatever she gave Zandy makes him kill?"

"This guy was under her control longer," White Feather said. "More experiments."

I grimaced. "Yeah." I moved away from the workbench. I stared at the mess for a long while before I finally got up enough nerve to test the rest of the amulets for traces of Harold.

We didn't find his. I didn't know whether to be relieved or dismayed. "Maybe Sheila only put amulets in the safe after the subjects were dead." I had another evil thought. I took Lynx's fork from my backpack and tested it. His sigh of relief matched mine when it didn't react to any of the amulets. I then tested the things for my own aura, although I think I would have known. It appeared she had only made one amulet for each of us and those had both been destroyed in her lab.

Sheila had never had a piece of White Feather, but we tested that too, just to be certain.

When we were done Lynx hissed, "Burn'em."

I agreed. "But not in here. I don't want smoke or any other trace of this crap in my lab."

White Feather put all the amulets back in the original box. I wrapped the willow sticks we had used, all the silk that had come in contact with the amulets and Harold's hair.

We took everything out back. I hated to contaminate my yard, but the soil could be moved and spread elsewhere.

Lynx produced the cigarette lighter. Using wood pieces from the lab, we started a fire.

I set the box on the flames. Because it was very old, it had been oiled well. It ignited easily. "It needs to be hotter."

White Feather nodded. "Dropping it in a volcano would be good."

"I've heard amulets can withstand that kind of sudden heat. It has to be controlled. Like over a flame until they burst. Hot enough to shatter glass."

We stared in dismay because the amulets, while blackening nicely, weren't likely to burst because of a few burning chunks of wood.

Lynx solved the problem nicely. From behind us, he darted forward. *Bam*! The rock he threw hit and bounced. "It counts if you break'em with a rock, right?" He stepped on the rock with his foot, mashing it into the glass.

I stumbled backwards and slapped at a piece of ash that had spattered onto my shirt. "Geez, Lynx, some warning, would you?"

"You witches take too long. You start thinking spells, how to heat a fire, all that crap." He waved his hand. "If they ain't busted up enough, I can drop it on there again."

White Feather rolled the rock away with his foot.

I peered into the smoke and flames. "You cracked the glass on at least three of them."

White Feather picked up the rock and dropped it again. We used a stick to push the fire back together. "More wood," I suggested.

Lynx complied. The fire went from fizzling to burning nicely.

We did the rock routine six or seven times, pounding the metal parts flat and destroying the glass, letting whatever was inside burn. I threw in some sage to help purify the mess. The glass and metal were melting, but not as much as I would have liked.

"Hang on. I have a portable torch." I went back into the lab to get it.

When I brought it back out, White Feather asked, "What do you use that for?"

"Sometimes I need to take it with me to mold glass."

He looked at me funny, but the torch worked nicely.

We kept at it until the entire pile was melted, mixed, purified and generally destroyed. When we were done, it was impossible to separate any pieces from sand. We doused everything with water. Lots and lots of holy water.

When I reached for White Feather's hand, he met me halfway. Two good people could undo a lot of bad that existed in the world. It didn't hurt to have the occasional shape shifter and vampire on our side either.

Chapter 42

Time was full of magic, although I had never met a witch who could control it. On its own, with no help from mortals, it came in and soothed. Like a river grinding down rock, it wore away the jagged edges of trauma and left a smoother surface. Time swirled around emotions, remixing them. It wound through chaos and left pieces small enough to be re-arranged and handled.

Over three days, I slept a lot, ate my mother's tamales and worried a lot. White Feather promised to take care of our auras at Sheila's place. Lynx promised to burn the place down. I wasn't entirely certain about the compromise, but White Feather swore that after the vamp made Sheila's tunnels and labs his new home, auras were not a problem.

Lynx seemed satisfied that nothing was left living that should have been dead. That totally creeped me out.

White Feather also assured me that Gordon was building a case against Arturo. It wasn't the murder case I would have preferred, but proof of him siphoning off charity money for his own use would still land him in jail. Proving he was running a werewolf pimp operation would have been a lot more difficult.

We still had one important project that I had to take care of even though Sheila was gone. Thankfully, White Feather went with me. We went in the dead of night, of course. Unlike the last time I had visited, San Miguel gave off a peaceful essence. This time I could feel it without trying. White Feather wasn't so sanguine, and even with the peaceful vibes, he was nervous.

I was so excited about getting my wig back that I couldn't contain a whispered "Yes!" when he used a key to unlock the church.

"Shh."

On the way through the gift shop, he absconded with the chair behind the cash register counter. He carried it through to the church and placed it below the loft. "This should get us high enough. You ready?"

"No." The chair looked spindly and unsteady.

"Come here." He grabbed me close, moving his hands down my body to my waist, threatening to graze a few parts in between--a tease. He lifted me onto the chair. "Sit on my shoulders," he commanded. There were candles still burning even though it was almost midnight. His eyes glinted, but I couldn't tell if it was the light or because he was laughing.

I put a leg on his shoulder, but lost my balance. We both nearly toppled over. "Eeek! This is never going to work."

"Sure it will. Climb up. Steady."

I nearly smashed his head when he stepped onto the chair. He had to climb up first on his knees and then to a standing position. "Okay, now you're going to have to stand on my shoulders. Use my hand to help you balance."

"You're tickling my feet," I protested.

"I'm not touching your feet."

But my feet were touching him. And anytime I touched him, there were shivers of him. I wasn't sure if it was because he was a warlock or if my feet were still ultra sensitive after the incident at Sheila's.

"Hurry up," he hissed. "We only have four or five hours to get this done!" He held my ankle, while I tried to get enough balance to get the other foot onto his shoulder.

"Here I go," I said, forcing my knees straight in a single move. My fingers caught the ledge.

For several seconds, we both stood there and breathed. I almost stopped feeling like I was about to topple off his shoulders.

The chair creaked a warning.

"Hurry up," White Feather added his own counsel.

I made sure the railing wouldn't give way, dug my fingers around the beam and heaved myself up. My feet grappled for a spot.

Once I had one, I was up and over with no injuries.

It was dark in the loft of San Miguel.

"Do you have a flashlight?" I felt my way around the floor.

"In the car. Don't tell me you want me to go running back and forth."

What I wanted was for him to have brought the flashlight inside or for me to have thought of it before I got up in the loft, but I didn't say so.

I stretched across the floor with my feet against the rail and my hands above my head. I rolled across the loft. Twice. I did it from the other end too before peering over the rail. "It isn't here."

It took a moment for him to answer. "At least we can be certain that Sheila doesn't have it."

Small consolation. "What if there's someone else who does?"

"Can I help you find something?" A soft voice from the front of the chapel interrupted us. A scrape of matches was followed by the flicker of a large candle.

I would be hidden if I ducked down, but White Feather had hardly been standing down there on a chair talking to himself. "I lost my wig." It was the only thing I could think of to say. I was so desperate, I didn't even care who had found us.

"Ah." Feet shuffled. The light disappeared, and there was the soft click of a door.

With a gulp, I climbed the railing. "White Feather?"

He reached for my ankles, easing me down. I didn't try for his shoulders and in any case, he wouldn't have let me.

I slid down the length of him, my toes barely touching the edge of the chair. "Okay?" he whispered.

"Who was that?"

It wasn't White Feather who answered. "I'm Brother Scott. I believe this is what you are looking for?"

I nearly leapt off the chair.

White Feather eased me to the floor.

After scant hesitation, I met Brother Scott halfway. He didn't try to keep the wig from me.

I held it to my face and breathed in. Mine. It was definitely mine, blood and all. "Thank you. Thank you for keeping it safe."

"This obviously isn't your first trip to the loft. Do the two of you make it a habit of meeting up there?" There may have been some disapproval in his voice.

White Feather spread his hands. "Not me, sir. I'm just helping a lady in distress."

"I was by myself," I agreed.

Brother Scott tilted his head, the candle still held high. "I see."

It was clear that he didn't. "I was hiding in the church because I wanted to leave a message after closing. Only I hit my head and injured myself so I didn't immediately realize I'd left the wig. I needed it back."

He waited. I looked down at the floor.

Brother Scott sighed. "I suppose it is a long story."

I squirmed, nodding frantically. "It's a very long story. We needed a safe place to meet." I stopped. "Not for *that* reason."

"It's a very long story," White Feather inserted. "She was worried about the wig because a rogue witch was after her."

I winced.

Brother Scott blinked. "I see."

I was fairly certain that he did not. He smiled anyway. "I trust you will not need to worry about the witch anymore."

We both nodded.

Brother Scott lowered the candle. "I trust you will put the chair back and can show yourselves out?"

We nodded again, enthusiastically.

"Peace be with you then." He sounded vaguely regretful. When he said those words, my feet, bare of shoes, felt a beat of energy through the church's wooden floors. It was like water running through me, clear, fresh and wonderful.

White Feather replaced the chair where we had found it. He grabbed my hand, and we scampered back outside into the night.

I couldn't help but giggle as we raced across the church courtyard.

He squeezed my fingers. "Shh. He could have called the police."

"Thanks for helping me."

His laugh started small, but it got deeper. He put his hand around my waist and pulled me around, sweeping my feet off the cobblestones. When he put me back down, he leaned close and kissed me in the moonlight.

It was pure magic.

About the Author

Maria Schneider has published many other novels and short stories:

Under Witch Moon is followed by *Under Witch Aura, Under Witch Curse* and *Ghost Shadow.* A spinoff series is in the works too; check out the short story *Witch Way.*

The Sedona O'Hala series (*Executive Lunch, Executive Retention, Executive Sick Days, Executive Dirt*) is a series of contemporary cozy mysteries: Sedona must solve a few crimes while fighting her way up the corporate ladder; mostly she dangles from her fingertips, just trying to survive.

Catch an Honest Thief is an adventurous caper across the New Mexico desert; Alexia is in search of treasure, survival and maybe love.

The *Dragons of Wendal* series is a fantasy romance.

Maria's website: BearMountainBooks.com